BLIND MAN OF BRIDGEBURG

Neil D. Burton

CACTUS RAIN
PUBLISHING

Arizona USA

BLIND MAN OF BRIDGEBURG

Published by Cactus Rain Publishing, LLC
San Tan Valley, Arizona, USA
www.CactusRainPublishing.com

ISBN: 978-1-947646-12-4

Front Cover Design by Debra L. Burton
Certified Proofreader Anita Beery

Published February 1, 2024
Published in the United States of America

DEDICATION

To my wife and best friend Debra. For all her dedication and
love in helping to bring this story to life;
and for saving mine in the process
and giving me a new LIFE.

Debra. I could write a chapter on how much you mean to me,
another on what you do for me,
and still, one on your talents...

BLIND MAN OF BRIDGEBURG

Neil D. Burton

CHAPTER 1

When I retired, I realized I had been working for a corporation who paid me to squander my life away. Other than a paycheck, what had I given myself? The overdue divorce was a good thing, and the rest was time. Time to think about all the things I could have had or could have been. But if I was honest with myself, the truth was I had no ambition. It may have been drained out of me by my dad, to him I had no guts. If he couldn't think of a negative, he would take another shot of rye and tell me to piss off. So what does a kid do with that?

With so much alone time I began to feel depressed, and after awhile the feeling was replaced with anger. What angered me the most was not being able to make sense of what was happening to the world I grew up in. I guess working all those years and putting in extra shifts not only put a strain on my health, but also kept me in the dark.

It didn't seem to matter what I watched, listened to, or read, I was being bombarded with lies. I had a front-row seat to a three-ring circus of greed, narcissism, and stupidity. It wasn't my world anymore and I had to break ties or go mad along with it, so I cut the cord and cancelled my cable TV, my cell phone, and told my newspaper boy we were finished. That was a hard one. I liked that kid, my neighbor's boy. I guess in a way I became a hermit. The only two people I would see were the mailman and at the time, my old friend Jim.

I knew to survive I had to get out of the city and clear my head. Find a quiet and peaceful place in the country, a sanctuary. Who would have thought stopping in an obscure little town for breakfast, called Willow's End, was exactly what I was looking for. More miraculous was finding Grace, the love of my life. I reached out and seized the opportunity like a kid reaching for a double scoop of chocolate ice cream on a hot day in July, and when I did, the world made sense again, at least the one I was in.

With Grace and the community, we were able to rid ourselves of the United World Corporation.

—

For the life of me, I don't know why I do this to myself. I would have thought I'd have more self-control, but here I am two years later, immersed in all the media manure I can shovel. It does become an obsession with climate change, medical and health disasters, the *Punch and Judy* show of political puppets, all the way down to decent, law-abiding citizens, through no fault of their own living in tents.

The Stanley Kramer film *almost* had it right when they titled it, *It's a Mad, Mad, Mad, Mad World.* If it were made today, they could save their breath and just say—*Insanity.*

I turn off the TV, wipe out those thoughts, and wait for Grace to walk through the door with our late dinner of pizza from Rebecca's. This is to be a quiet, romantic evening.

—

"I'm here," she says with a smile she has been lighting up my life with since the first time we met at Rebecca's.

"I brought an extra large, just in case we want some tomorrow. You like it cold, too, don't you, Paul?" she says.

"Absolutely."

From here on, the rest of the night may go down in history—just saying.

CHAPTER 2

The pounding on the front door sheers through our solitude like the first bolt of lightning ushering in a storm.

"Who could that be at this time of the night?" asks Grace, sitting up from my cozy wrapped arms.

As I head for the door, my first thought is this better justify spoiling the rest of our evening.

Next are rapid-fire visions of the previous year's horrific events. I'm already at the door, so it's too late to go back to the bedroom to grab the revolver. In one motion I grip the lock with my left hand and the doorknob with my right and my left foot firmly on the floor, inches from the door.

I crack open the door and find myself staring at two bulb-like eyes. A familiar voice blows in with the cold air.

"Paul?"

It's Charlie. I open the door to see his face in a knot of intense fear. His breathing is labored.

"Charlie, are you all right?" I whisper, in hope of saving our sensual evening.

He struggles to slow his breathing then blurts out—

"Nope."

Like squeezing that last drop of toothpaste from the tube I wait for the rest of it. He finally surrenders two words that send a chill up my spine.

"They're back."

"What?" I already know who, the question is why.

"What's going on? Who is it, Paul?" asks Grace.

"It's Charlie."

Our romantic evening just did a nosedive.

"Come in, Charlie. Looks like you could use a drink."
I place him in the chair across from the couch.
Grace takes one look at Charlie's face and mirrors his.
"Charlie, you look terrible. Are you all right? What's wrong?"
"I might have bad news, Grace."
"You might?" I ask.
With Charlie and his emotions, I make it a fifty-fifty split as to the severity of what he is about to tell me.
"The agents, I think they're back."
He *thinks* they're back? Okay, sixty-forty.
"What?" says Grace. "Why would they come back? Haven't they done enough, lost enough! And look at the friends we've lost!"
I quickly move in on Grace and gently put my arm around her waist to diffuse the acceleration that typically follows.
"Easy, Grace, let's hear what Charlie has to say. Care for some prosecco, Charlie?"
You would think I offered him motor oil.
"Never mind."
I reach up into the kitchen cupboard for a bottle of scotch. Grace calls it the *emergency bottle*. I call it, *any excuse will do*.
"I suggest you pour one for yourself," adds Charlie.
No suggestion necessary. I grab three glasses.
"Well, if it's going to be that bad," says Grace, "you might as well cork the wine and pour me one, too."
Some things are so predictable or inevitable. If this turns out as bad as Charlie makes it out to be, experience tells me this will be the first round of many—and *that* will start to look very familiar.
"So where did you get this information?" I ask.
The glass quivers in Charlie's hand as he draws it to his lips and takes a sip.
"It was early this morning. I had just opened the Emporium and was behind the counter adding a few bucks to the float when this fella comes in. At first I didn't think much about him. He was dressed in ordinary clothes, you know, jeans, plaid shirt: your typical cottager. But as soon as he opened his mouth and asked the first question, I knew he was trouble."

I can feel my right hand begin to clench and the hairs on the back of my neck spike.

"What did he ask you?"

He takes another sip, and if there is one thing Charlie can do is stretch that rubber band of tension to a human hair.

"He asked if I knew *you.*"

"Me?"

"Yep, 'Paul Fenton,' he said. I told him I never heard the name before. 'Are you sure?' he said. 'He lives in Willow's End.' Well, I said, I know a lot of people, how long has he lived there? 'I guess about a year,' he says. Well then, I wouldn't know him. I don't get to Willow's End too often. Then he said something that made me reach under the counter for my shotgun."

Our eyes widen as we lean forward.

"He said, 'I heard you make some pretty good coffee here. I thought I might try a cup.'"

"Oh my god!" says Grace. She downs her drink. "He knows about the Supremes!"

I hold her hand while maneuvering her back to the couch, but not sure if it's to comfort her or me.

"So what did you say?"

"I told him it weren't no different than any other coffee, and that I just opened and haven't had a chance to make any yet. Then he said, 'I guess if I went to Willow's End I might find a pretty good cup at Rebecca's.' I'm sure you would, I said. Then he turned around and headed out the door."

"Did you see what he was driving?"

"By the time I got around the counter and made it to the door he was gone."

"What could they possibly want now?" asks Grace.

"Wasn't Percy, Dr. John, Carl, and Alex enough? And who knows how much of Ben's death may have been caused from the stress of it all." She holds out her glass.

Yes, this is all coming back to me now. I pour her another.

"That's true, Grace, but let's not jump too far ahead of ourselves. He wasn't dressed like an agent, but he could have been an agent for another organization."

Charlie scratches the whiskers on the side of his cheek.

"What are you gettin' at, Paul? The guy comes in off the beaten track and asks about you, my coffee, and Rebecca's. Come on, who else could it be?"

I empty my glass. "What if he was from the FBI or the CIA?"

"Why would *they* be here asking questions?" says Grace.

"How about the murder of Wagner, Rigby, and the two agents? No, make it three. I forgot the one Ben had confessed to killing in his will. What if the UWC didn't want to deal with us anymore and handed the problem to ... let's say, the FBI."

"Well, they can investigate all they want, but they'll come up empty," says Charlie. "Ben made sure of it, and I upped it a notch with the concrete pad and shed over top of those bastards."

"And there wasn't anything left from the car explosion with Rigby to connect you either, Paul," says Grace.

"You're probably right, and perhaps we can ignore the part about the coffee. He may have just asked someone where he could get a good cup of coffee and he was sent to Charlie's. But the one part that's troublesome was when he asked about me."

In the back of my mind I'm thinking we aren't good enough, smart enough to fool these people. Killing and war games is their life's work. I can recall many episodes of *Columbo* and *Perry Mason* where the murderer made one tiny slipup, and I don't want it to be us.

"I guess the only thing we can do is to wait and see if this guy shows up at Rebecca's."

"Or shows up on your doorstep," says Charlie.

"Now that makes me nervous," says Grace.

Thanks, Charlie.

"I know from those real-life crime shows they can get you to admit to anything, whether you're guilty or not."

"Good point, Grace."

"Don't forget, it's TV," says Charlie. "I think a lot of those characters weren't too bright to begin with."

"What did he look like?" asks Grace.

"Is there anything about him we could notice immediately?"

Charlie scratches his chin whiskers. "Like I said, he just looked like he fit right in with the landscape. Let me think. He was tall, taller than me, dark hair—"

"How old would you say he was?" I ask.

"It's funny, the older I get the less I seem to be able to tell someone's age, but I'll say about forty. Oh, he had a bit of a scar just above his left eyebrow, how's that?"

"Good enough."

—

It's been close to three weeks and not a sign of the mystery man, and I'm not sure if it's a good thing or not. The fall weather is in full swing and some of the maples have shed their colors.

Raking the leaves from the flower bed in front of Rebecca's, I can't help but reflect back to the terrifying winter of threats, murder, and the damned business of having me plan every move we made. Just tending to Rebecca's and Grace is all I want to focus on.

Even if the guy never shows, Charlie planted a seed that will have me looking over my shoulder for months, maybe years, because you just don't know. Like a cold case, when the murderer has been living a quiet life in the Ozarks for forty years, and some smart-ass newcomer decides he wants to re-open the case and bingo, he gets his man. I don't need some smart-ass after me.

"Paul!" hollers Grace from the veranda.

"We're running low on the Shiraz and the delivery won't come in for two days! Could you pick up a case at the liquor store for me, please?"

"I'll get right on it!"

Even when she gives out orders she sounds so sweet.

—

The liquor store is unusually busy.

"Morning, Paul," says Bill, from the other side of the counter.

"It's a bit early for you to be shopping for yourself. You must be a little shy at the bar. What do you need, a case?"

"A case of Shiraz will do nicely, Bill."

Bill turns to a stock boy. "Could you get a case of Shiraz for Mr. Fenton, please?" Then back to me. "It'll just take a minute."

"It's busy in here for this time of the morning."

"As soon as people start to see those leaves drop they rush right in to stock up in case we have an early storm."

"I sure get that."

Through the corner of my eye, I detect a tall customer step up to the counter with a bottle.

"Will that be all, sir?" asks Bill.

"Yes, thank you," he says in a soft and polite tone.

I glance at the man and see he's Black, not that it matters to me one way or the other, but what did get my attention was his size—the height Charlie described. He turns to leave and there it is! The small scar above his left eyebrow. I noticed he's wearing a plaid shirt and jeans. I turn away, but his face lingers in my mind. I turn back to watch him leave. By the time I get my case of wine and head out the door, he's gone. So, what am I supposed to make of it? It couldn't be the guy Charlie interacted with for one obvious reason, and plus the fact Charlie wouldn't have excluded that vital piece of information. I let it slide and chalk it up to coincidence. If I don't, it will fester like a small sliver you ignored on the sole of your foot until one day you look down and see a red line creeping its way up your leg. Then again, I don't want it to drive me into the state I was in last year, where I would dissect a fart if it drifted my way.

—

My workdays have slowed to a crawl. The only thing left to be done as far as gardening goes is to wrap some shrubs to protect them from the harsh winter that could hit us in a few weeks or sooner. The only way to drive a bitter-cold thought away is to replace it with warm nights snuggled up by the fireplace with Grace. The fireplace—the colder it gets, the hungrier it gets.

"Grace, I'll go back out and grab a couple of logs."

"Good. It's chilly in here and I don't even have my coat off yet. While you take care of the wood, I'll heat the oven for this lasagna. I'm sure it's only lukewarm after our walk home."

"Owning your own restaurant sure has its benefits. It makes dinner a lot easier when you can have someone else prepare it for you."

"You must mean me," says Grace. "I was overwhelmed last year when we had to deal with one tragedy after another and I had to contend with cooking for everyone who came through the door."

I move in behind her and wrap my arms around her.

"You were heroic. You deserve the Betty Crocker medal of honor."

"I think it should be Davy Crockett. I don't know how I survived it all." She turns to me, "But I did, didn't I?"

"You sure did." I kiss her on the nose.

She puts her arms around me and hugs me tight.

"I guess I should get the wood now."

"I actually feel quite warm now," she says with a smile.

"Hang on to that feeling, we may need it during the night."

"Don't count on it. If there's one thing I know about you and pasta, you'll be out as soon as your head hits the pillow."

She has a point. Those carbs make me comatose at a moment's notice.

"I guess it's too late to change to salad."

—

Saturday morning and Grace is in the kitchen with wonderful breakfast smells of bacon, eggs, home fries, toast, and, of course, the ever-present cup of coffee. I decide to flip on the news and realize I've gone back to one of my bad habits of actually giving a damn about the rest of the world. I know it has to do with the past year's events and how the world I despise has seeped back into my reality with a vengeance.

"Our top story this morning comes from the President, who has been implementing his election promises and signing new bills that will halt or alter past legislation. The Democrats are furious about—"

"The faces may change, but the story is always the same."

"What's that, sweetheart?" asks Grace.

"This new President. I knew he was going to be trouble."

As they cut to a clip of the President speaking, I realize he doesn't sound like a politician. He talks like a businessman and, to be honest, more like a con man—a corporate crony for the one-percenters, trying to sell us a bill of goods.

"The President also mentioned the fact that people are embracing the digital age at such a rate of speed eBooks and audio books are making our libraries obsolete. Physical books will be phased out in libraries and replaced with computers."

"Grace! This is it! Say goodbye to Dewey."

Grace joins me in the living room. "Dewey?"

"They're getting rid of books in libraries! This is exactly what they said they were going to do in Alex's book."

"But why would the President do such a thing?"

"It's not him. He's another tool in the UWC's arsenal. Remember what Hitler did during the war? He destroyed all the books he called subversive."

"But there are all kinds of different types of books in the library, like fiction, non-fiction, educational, art, and books for children."

"Books are the last tangible access to knowledge."

"But you *can* look everything up on a computer in seconds. Isn't it better, faster? And we'll still have eBooks to read."

"Grace, you're not seeing the big picture. This is the big sleep. People are becoming more self-educated. Through research on their computers they diagnose their own health issues and heal themselves. Fix all sorts of problems on their own, and most of all discover the truth about our democracy. And believe me, they do not want the country to know any of it—the dumbing down of society, Grace. Half of them are already onboard after voting for that puppet. The only information we will get is what they want us to know. That's why Alex's book is so important; it blows the whistle on their agenda."

I'm beginning to scare myself all over again. I sound far-right coming from the left.

"What about the news, the media?"

"Grace, please."

Grace turns silent. Her eyes shift as she bites her lower lip. Inside that pretty little head, her mind is in overdrive, and she is one joint short of paranoia.

She finally draws in a long breath, then slowly opens the valve.

"Speaking of Alex's book, wasn't Adam supposed to get it published? If he had followed through on it, things could be a little different now, couldn't they?"

"I haven't heard a word from him." I grab my cell phone. "I'll give him a call right now."

After a couple of rings I hear a message then hang up.

"He wasn't there?"

"More than that, Grace, the number's no longer in service."

"Do you think he moved?"

"And not say a word to us? Not likely. Unless—" Right away I think the worst.

"I'll drive out there to see what I can find out."

"Would you like some company?"

"It will probably be boring and uneventful."

"That's what they said when I moved here."

—

There's nothing like a drive in the country, even when you live here. You just can't beat the fresh air and the scent of the pine trees. A far cry from the toxic smell you get from those two-pack pine tree cutouts at the gas station.

We pull up to Adam's house and spot a new car in the drive. It could belong to Adam since his car and Alex's were totaled by Rigby. I ask Grace to stay in the car until I know what the situation is.

I ring the doorbell and immediately hear a small dog bark. Adam didn't have a dog, but that could have changed. A moment later the door opens to a young woman with a small child in her arms. Things couldn't have changed that fast.

"Yes?" she says, in a tone directed at a furnace salesman.

"Sorry to bother you. Does Adam still live here?"

"Not exactly, are you a friend of his?"

"Yes, I am."

"We rented the house from him about three months ago."

"Do you know where he is? It's very important I get hold of him."

"No, I don't. Perhaps you could check at the post office. He might have left a forwarding address?"

"Thanks, I'll do that. Sorry to have bothered you."

I head back to the car, and I'm still puzzled that he would leave and not tell us.

"So, what's going on?"

"He rented the place out about three months ago."

"So where is he?"

"She didn't know. We'll try the post office to see if he left a forwarding address."

—

The post office had no change of address and no outstanding mail for him.

"I don't understand it," says Grace. "Are you thinking what I'm thinking?"

"It does have the familiar odor of the UWC."

"I wonder if it has to do with the guy Charlie talked to about you and the coffee."

"It wouldn't surprise me. Let's go back to Adam's house. I want to make sure it was Adam who rented it to her."

—

I pull up to the house to see the woman at the top of the driveway with her little one in a stroller. I step out of the car. She turns to see me and walks the stroller down the driveway.

"No luck at the post office?" she asks.

"No. I was wondering if you could give me a description of the man you rented from."

"I thought you said he was a friend of yours."

"He is, but I just want to make sure it was him you rented the house from."

"I'm not in any trouble, am I? I'm very happy here and I've already moved twice in the last three years."

"No, no. This is personal. Could you describe him?"

"Well, he was a tall, handsome Black man and extremely polite."

I don't even ask about the scar.

"Okay, thanks."

As I walk back to the car I hear her ask, "Is that right then? Is he your friend?"

I wave my arm behind me and say thank you. As soon as I get into the car an anxious Grace is all over me.

"Well, was it Adam?"

I wonder if my concern bleeds into my face.

"Paul, are you all right? You look like you're ready to pass out."

There's my answer.

"It was the guy Charlie encountered. The same one I saw at the liquor store."

"Are you sure?"

"I'm sure."

"That means they *are* after us again."

"If the guy was an agent and he rented Adam's house—"

I pull away from the house.

"No! You don't think— but why go after Adam?"

"For the same reason we are, to see if he is trying to publish the book."

"Oh my god!" says Grace.

I have to nip her anxiety in the bud before she loses it and takes me with her.

"He's a pretty smart kid. Knowing they would be after him, my guess is he took off right after Alex's funeral with everything he had pertaining to the book."

"But how was this guy able to rent out Adam's house?"

"Grace, you're asking a good question. I can't answer it."

"Alex told us they would do whatever it takes to get the book published."

She's on a roll now. "Paul, I'm scared. What if they got to Adam, too, and just like Charlie's encounter, they pushed him for answers about you?"

Sometimes I hate when Grace thinks out loud.

Pushed seems light, torture seems more likely. That's where Grace and I differ. I keep the heavy thoughts to myself.

—

I notice how the darkness settles in earlier each day, and once again, like a bad penny, I recall the confused, slow-moving chaos at this time last year.

"Paul?" says Grace, as I open the front door. "What about the agent?"

She's relentless. Please Grace, don't get me going. "I don't know. I would think if he wanted me he would have tried by now."

Not that I'm not happy he hasn't. Wait a minute—

"Grace, he doesn't know what I look like or he would have acknowledged me at the liquor store."

"Hmm—weren't you wearing your garden clothes?"

"Yeah, why?"

"And your hat and sunglasses?"

"That's right; I could have slipped under his radar."

"Exactly, so there is still the chance he knows what you look like, but not in that outfit."

Thanks again, Grace. I feel so much better.

"I guess we're back to securing the house and dusting the spider webs off the motion lights."

"That's probably a habit we should have stayed with anyway."

"Which brings me to another habit we've been neglecting lately." I head into the kitchen.

"Locking the patio door?" asks Grace.

"No, uncorking the wine."

CHAPTER 3

Business at Rebecca's has slowed to its expected autumn crawl except for the weekend lovers who come up to see the colorful foliage and possibly occasional extramarital activity.

I've never had an eye for art. I did think Steve Martin had lost his mind when he started to buy some weird landscapes from some renegade bunch of dead artists up in Canada, until I came up here and discovered the beauty in what they saw in their country and the brilliance in how they projected it onto canvas. You can throw out the statement about not teaching an old dog new tricks—is it maturity, or just life from a different perspective? Perhaps it's one and the same.

Since my garden workload at Rebecca's is down to a trickle, I decide to cut my day short. I tell Grace that I'll head for home and make that stew I had promised her. I have to admit I do try to cut corners when I can. I had asked her about pork and beans on a couple of occasions, but she always insists it should only be consumed by lumberjacks in the middle of a forest.

It's only three o'clock, but my shadow has been growing each day as I walk back to the house. The walk is therapeutic, as long as my thoughts are ambiguous—the moment I feel the dark side rearing its head as I do, then I have to be a goalie and block the shot before it hits the net.

I unlock the door, and before I start this fine dinner of beef stew, an ice-cold beer out on the patio is needed. With my hand on the patio door I gaze outside, and there in one of the Adirondacks is—the BLACK AGENT!

The beer leaves my hand, drops to the floor and spins around, spraying foam in every direction. Thank God he's facing away from the house. What should I do? Go out and confront him? What if he confronts me with a Q3? I'll grab Ben's old shotgun. I sure am thankful Charlie gave it to me.

The gun is tight in my grip and pointing down at my side, and I decide to go out the front door and sneak around the side to the back. Just before I turn the corner I raise the gun to eye level and make my move.

He's gone!

A hand drops on my shoulder along with a voice. "Mr. Fenton?"

He's got me! I'm a dead man! I lower the shotgun and slowly turn around. There he stands. He doesn't have a gun pointed at me, but with his size he doesn't need one. He stares down at me with piercing pitch eyes, like a black panther poised on a tree limb. I can't move or even blurt out, *yes, that's me.* I must look like a figure from Madame Tussauds.

"Aren't you Paul Fenton?"

Like someone squeezing my testicles I manage to peep out a yes that sounds more like Mickey Mouse.

"I'm Tor."

"Thor? Where's your hammer?" Shit. Don't be a smart-ass.

He chuckles, "No. Not Thor, Tor. It's Nigerian. It means *King.* It's actually pronounced *Toor,* but people liked to drop the second 'o,' so it seems to have stuck. I'm a friend of Adam."

"Adam?"

"He sent me here to find you and to let you know he's safe and well."

"Thank God for that. I thought you were—"

"An agent? I thought you might think that. So I decided to hang out in the open on your patio to show that I wasn't a threat."

He looks at the shotgun and smiles. "But I guess I wasn't convincing enough."

He extends his long reach. I raise my hand to meet his, and it surrounds mine like a pitcher's mitt holding a golf ball.

"Boy, we sure could have used you last year."

"Adam told me all about it and the tragic end of Alex. He was a good man, and a brave one."

"Yeah," as I remember his sad demise.

"I'm sorry."

"Me too. Would you care for a drink?"

"Lead me to it."

"Tell you what, you get back to the Adirondack and I'll bring it out. What's your preference?"

"I enjoy a cold beer, but I must confess I'm partial to the hard stuff. On the rocks, if you're so inclined?"

"Tor, I think this is the beginning of a beautiful friendship."

I have the glassware, a bottle of scotch and a bucket of ice.

We sip through the late afternoon with discussions around the United World Corporation and his relationship with Adam. I get the impression they are close—not like Ben and I were, what we had was very special. Funny Tor didn't come up in any of my conversations with Adam. *Don't start, why would it? Just because someone has a friend doesn't mean you have to know about it.* That's true.

"So how long have you known Adam?" I asked.

"I get the impression you aren't quite sure of me yet," Tor said, followed by a wink.

"Well, I—"

"That's all right, I understand. A few years back when I was getting my feet wet in the real estate market he put up a handmade For Sale sign on his lawn, and I was curious as to why he wasn't going through an agent. I decided to talk to him, and in my honest assessment of his situation I convinced him that keeping the house would be to his best interest. He appreciated my honesty, and since then on we have become great friends. From time to time he would give me a few leads with some of them paying off. I would say he has indirectly helped me to grow my business into what it is today."

"Sounds like the perfect friendship."

"It is, but at times I feel it has been somewhat one-sided."

"How do you mean?"

"This business with the UWC and Alex's book, I had no way of helping him except to keep him out of harm's way by providing him with a safe place to live, a place hidden from the UWC and their agents."

"That's very commendable and brave of you."

"It's something you do for close friends."

He continues to tell me Adam hasn't given up on publishing Alex's book, but was so traumatized by his murder and the possible threat of the UWC raining down on him, he's very cautious about disclosing anything about the book or his location.

"If you don't mind me asking, where is he now?"

"He's about an hour from here at a small secluded cottage I own. I think the tranquility and solitude serve him well. He knew at some point you would be concerned about him, so he asked me to find you and let you know he was all right."

"I was very concerned, but knowing you're his friend sure takes a load off. The questions you asked Charlie put us on edge. We were sure you were an agent."

"I understand. Even though Adam told me about Charlie, I was still apprehensive. It just seemed like anyone could be an agent around here."

"Agent!" yells Grace from the patio doors.

"No, Grace!" Too late, as she rushes back inside.

I turn to Tor, "Sorry about that."

Seconds later Grace reappears with her shaking gun pointing at Tor.

"Grace. It's all right," I say in a calm voice to ease her anxiety. "He's not an agent. He's a friend of Adam."

"Adam? Well that's a relief."

"That's what *I* said."

She lowers the gun.

Tor leaves the comfort of the Adirondack and walks over to greet her.

"I'm Tor. Nice to meet you, Grace," he says as she reaches for his hand and is cupped by both of his.

"Adam told me you were an attractive woman, but I think it was an understatement."

Her face glows pink as her eyes follow his height up to his warm smile.

"Thank you, Tor."

Do I like that? Is it a compliment for me, too? Or is it a subtle—*Stop it! You're reading into the dark side. You went through this with Rigby.*

"Will you be staying for dinner?" she asks.

"Dinner—the stew." I leap out of my seat.

Grace giggles. "I thought you might forget, so I brought home a huge shepherd's pie."

"Sounds delicious, Grace," says Tor as he glances at his watch. "But I'm afraid I'll have to pass. I have to see someone in an hour."

"Oh, that's a shame," says Grace.

"Perhaps some other time, if the invitation still stands?"

"Anytime," says Grace, with a smile.

"I'll just have to make sure Paul isn't the cook that day."

"Where's your car?" I ask.

"I left it in town. I booked into Rebecca's for a few days to have some business meetings."

Business meetings; what kind of business? This could be a red flag. *Are you kidding? He's been telling you all about his close relationship with Adam. Why are you so suspicious?*

"Well, you won't find a better place to be. The rooms are cozy, the beds are more than comfortable, and the dining menu is superb."

"Sounds like you might have a small stake in the place, Paul."

"Actually, I have a huge stake, and she's right beside you."

"Good business partners are hard to find," he says.

"Business partners are the least of what we share."

There, that covers it. I smile at Grace and she smiles back.

"Nice to have met you, Grace. Perhaps I'll see you at Rebecca's."

I have to jump in. "I'd like to meet up with Adam. Is there a chance you could pass on the directions to your cottage?"

"Sure thing. I'll give them to Grace when I see her at Rebecca's."

"I'll be there too."

"Of course, what am I thinking?"

Yes, what were you thinking? —*easy, tiger.*

I didn't get the full value of his size until he began to walk along the dirt road and passed under the oak tree. Ben's old truck would touch the lower branches, but Tor had to push them aside to clear his head.

19

I feel Grace's arm around my waist.
"That's quite a turn," she says.
"Turn?"
"You thought he was an agent. It turns out he's a nice man."
"Well, he does enjoy his scotch."

—

Every day I keep a subtle eye on the *very nice man* anyway. He dresses in a suit for lunch along with three other men. No dark suits, but sometimes briefcases, sometimes folders. On occasion there are moments of laughter in their conversations, but mostly of a serious nature. I'll ask Grace to take their orders to see if she could overhear anything suspicious, but as before with Rigby, I don't want her to start to choose sides because she thinks he is a very nice man.

On the fifth day, my day off, I decide it's time for some lunch, and after a look into the fridge, I'm better off at Rebecca's. More variety and I don't have to make it. Also, where are those directions he promised me?

—

I make myself comfortable in the almost deserted dining room. Grace comes with a disappointed look on her face.
"Everything all right Grace?"
"He's gone, Paul."
"Who's gone?"
"Tor, he booked out of his room early this morning."
"Did he give you the directions to the cottage?"
"I didn't even see him."
"Well that was inconsiderate—or deliberate."
"He seems to be a busy man. I'm sure it was an oversight," she says. "He'll be back."

Grace always goes for innocent until proven guilty, and she's right; but there are those rare occasions when they can blow up in one's face, like being set up with the bomb at the fake restaurant last year.

Tor had plenty of opportunities to give me the address. He saw me or Grace at some point every day. If he doesn't show up in town again, I may never know if Adam is alive or dead. Which brings me full circle, is Tor an agent of the UWC?

On that thought a waitress walks up and hands me a business card.

"This was left at the front desk for you, Mr. Fenton."

Assuming it was left by some salesman trying to sell us a new product, I ignore it and place it on the table.

I sip some water and inadvertently place the glass down over the business card. After a quick look at the Day's Specials, I order and take another sip of water. I peer through the bottom of the glass and see the business card stuck to it and notice the name, Tor. I pull the card off and see Tor is a land developer. He builds cottage communities. I turn the card over to see a handwritten note—

Here is the address to the cottage.
528 Sandy Beach Road, Elmwood
Regards, Tor

"Well, look at that. I can breathe again."

Sometimes keeping your thoughts to yourself is a good thing. Grace would have had me eating a buffet of crow along with the egg on my face.

I show Grace the card and she responds with, "I told you he was a nice man."

"I never doubted you for a moment."

"I'll join you for lunch," she says.

"Is it because you were right and want to stick it to me?"

"No, it's because you look so adorable when I am right."

We finish off breakfast with a second cup of coffee.

"I'll do a little bookkeeping and then head to the basement to check our inventory. And what will *you* be up to on this fine sunny day?"

"I thought of going out to see Adam, and since Charlie's is on the way, I'll drop in for minute."

"Does that include an Emporium Supreme?"

"Now Grace, I said drop in, not drop out."

She smiles. "I also know the power of the flower."

"Perhaps just a small one for medicinal."

—

I pull up to the Emporium, and for a moment I sit there with thoughts of Ben. This is the first time I've come here by myself. Damn, I miss that old bugger so much.

It doesn't matter how much Charlie sells of these antiques during the summer, the place still looks like a bomb hit it.

Charlie is in his usual place at the counter polishing an old door knocker.

"Hey, Charlie."

He looks up at me and his face lights up. "Paul, I was just thinking about you. Have you heard anything about the agent or Adam?"

"Yes, I have, but first I'd like to ask you a question."

"Shoot."

"Why didn't you tell me he was Black?"

"Black? Oh, well, I didn't want anyone to think I'm a racist."

"A racist? You know, Charlie, sometimes I see a little bit of Ben in you."

"Well thanks for the compliment, Paul."

"But not this time."

"And here I was about to offer you a Supreme on the house."

He tries to keep a straight face. "Just pulling your leg—one Supreme coming up."

Sorry, Grace.

"Thanks, Charlie. Just make it a small one."

Charlie begins to make his magic brew. "So you said you had some news."

"First, the Black fella isn't an agent."

"Well that's a relief. Then why would he ask me about you and my coffee?"

"He's a friend of Adam. He said even though Adam told him about you, he was still apprehensive. He thinks as we do, anyone could be an agent around here."

"I guess it makes sense. So we're back to peace and quiet."

I don't want him to get too cozy. "For the time being anyway."

"Now what the hell does that mean?"

"Tor has made a cottage available to Adam, so he's more or less tucked in out there."

"You got a speech impediment? What the hell is a Tor?"

"Sorry, Tor is the name of Adam's friend. He's from—never mind. Adam is still set on Alex's book, but he's very cautious. He doesn't want to end up like Alex and his dad."

"Can't blame him for that. If it were me I would have dropped the whole idea. The organization is filled with cutthroats. 'Course, if you had a plan to get him out of the country without them knowing it."

I thought I was all done with plans. "That's why I'll talk to Adam, to see what his thoughts are. Could you make it to go, Charlie?"

"Are you sure you want a small one? I made a little too much."

"I'm sure you'll find a way to dispose of it."

Charlie has an ear-to-ear grin.

CHAPTER 4

It's a perfect day for this drive, and I take my time with Charlie's magical, mystery fuel. It's not enough to take me back to Woodstock, but it sure mellows me out. I decide to lower my side window to get the pure country air and have the warmth of the sun fill me with vitamin D.

Here we are in Elmwood. Sandy Beach should be about a mile away.

About a half-mile in I can see another vehicle about to pass on the other side at a speed too fast for the likes of these roads. As it passes I'm hit with a strange, familiar feeling. It's black, and not just black—it's a Hummer. I immediately put my foot to the floor.

"Please, let it be a coincidence."

My core temperature rises. I glance in the rearview mirror to see beads of sweat have formed across my forehead. My mouth is as dry as the Gobi.

I see the sign *Sandy Beach Road*. Which way? I'll go right. The number is 528. Here's the first mail box—352. There's the second one on the other side of the road—354.

"Shit!"

With sweaty hands I wheel around as slow as I can go so I don't end up in a ditch. I back up then head in the other direction. There! 528. There's no car in the driveway but a motorcycle by a shed near the cottage. I can't get my seat belt off fast enough.

I race to the cottage door. "ADAM!"

I pause for a response—silence. A few hard bangs on the frame of the screen door have the same effect. I grab the handle and pull. The inside door is open.

I walk in to see what looks like signs of a struggle. A tornado-like pathway, as if someone had been dragged from one room to another, with scuff marks on the hallway walls that lead up to the front door. This tells me Adam didn't go quietly. I race out the door and hopefully there's a chance to catch up to those bastards. I start the car and hear—

"Paul!"

I look out the windshield to see Adam at the side of his house with a couple of old window frames. I exit the car.

"Adam, are you all right?"

"I think so."

He casually walks out to the front of the house and drops the windows on top of an old sofa, then steps up to me.

"Never mind me," he says. "Your face is as white as Tom Sawyer's fence."

"I'm not surprised. As I was coming up the road a black Hummer whizzed by me in the opposite direction and—"

"And you thought they were agents."

"Yes. I thought they had gotten to you."

"Well, in a way you were right."

"I knew it the minute I walked inside and saw the marks on the floor and the walls.What did they do to you?"

"They didn't do anything."

"They didn't drag you through the house?"

"No, that was me struggling to get this old couch out."

"Well, that's a relief. So, what did they say to you? What did they want?"

"It was weird. They pulled in front of the house and stopped just as I was dragging out the couch. I stood there staring at the Hummer for what seemed to be a lifetime. They must have been in a conversation."

"Probably about how they wanted to do you in."

"It did cross my mind. But then one of them got out from the passenger side and it looked like he was about speak when one of them reached out and pulled him back in. Then they quickly turned around and left."

"Sounds like they got a call with a change of plans."

"Exactly what I thought, but why? Not that I'm unhappy with the outcome."

"I think a bigger question should be, how did they find you?"

"The only one would be Tor, and he wouldn't say shit."

"What about neighbors?"

"Summer's over. I haven't seen a cottager in three weeks."

"Do you think you'll be safe here, or would you like a room at Rebecca's for a while?"

Adam ponders the thought as he looks about the area. "I think I should be safe here now. Like you said, they may have had a change of plans."

"True, but it doesn't mean it still wouldn't involve you."

There's a moment of silence as we take in the rustle of the trees.

"My other concern is you and Grace back in harm's way."

"I don't think that would happen. They seemed to have moved on from us." Good answer, but even I'm not convinced.

"Just to be on the safe side, I'll talk to Tor and see if he has another cottage available in a different area."

"And, hopefully, it won't leak out. By the way, what about the book?"

"Well, I just finished a Foreword about Alex's part and sacrificing his life in bringing the book to completion. I thought it was only right."

I place my hand on his shoulder. "I think he would have appreciated it."

Adam gives me his new cell number and promises to get back to me after he talks to Tor about another location. We say our goodbyes, and I drive away with my eyes fixed on Adam in the rearview mirror becoming smaller until he disappears. I have the awful feeling you get when you've left the house and wonder if the stove was left on.

—

As soon as I get home I don't falter in my promise to keep Grace in the loop. Her first reaction about the agents is the normal one of panic. I explain the part about them leaving without incident and she calms down, but wonders, as I do, if they will return.

"Adam will talk to Tor about another place he could occupy."

"Good, but isn't it possible they could find him again?"

"And who knows better than we do. They're relentless."

Grace grabs my forearm. "Couldn't we keep him here or at Rebecca's?"

"I mentioned it, but he said he didn't want to put it on us after all we had gone through."

"That's true," says Grace.

"After these last few months agent-free we don't want to bring attention back to ourselves."

She puts her arms around me and looks into my eyes with the same beautiful smile that captured me the first time we met.

"This is how I want our lives to stay."

She pulls back and says, "Now, we have fifteen minutes before supper, would you like a little brandy first?"

"Sounds great, it is chilly out there today."

"I trust it's a lot warmer in here," she says. Then gently rubs the inside of my thigh.

—

Dinner hour is over and now some quiet time by the fire. I must admit I did miss the TV. Some of the news, classic films, and a couple of sitcoms, but I would have no problem just having Grace to snuggle up with.

One bottle of wine has passed on and I am about to open a second when my cell goes off.

"People sure pick the most inconvenient time to call," says Grace.

I see it's Adam. I put him on speaker. "Adam, everything all right?"

"Paul, turn on the news in five minutes and then call me."

He hangs up.

"What do you suppose that's all about?" asks Grace, then bites the side of her lip.

"I guess we'll just have to wait and see."

With some anxiety we wait through the two minutes of local news.

The announcer looks into the camera and switches his best friend expression to a stern Ted Baxter expression.

Neil D. Burton

"And now a special report from John Myers at the head quarters of the FBI in Washington, D.C."

Reporter Myers stands in front of the FBI building.

"The FBI along with Homeland Security has been investigating a homegrown vigilante group of terrorists who have been spreading false information about our government. I talked to FBI agent Robert Brandon earlier, and here is what he said."

A close shot of Agent Brandon with a hand mic stuck in his face.

"These people will stop at nothing, even murder, to sway the American public into thinking there is a world government organization. The White House has said it is a total fabrication that was given credence through one man, Major Alex Miller. He was a disgruntled soldier in our military and landed a desk job. He stole top-secret information he used to distort and fabricate this hoax. After his death the group has expanded to the point where it threatens our democracy.

"We have confirmation there is a book about the fictitious United World Corporation written by his son, who is also deceased. If anyone receives a copy of this book, call your state FBI headquarters immediately. This book and these terrorists are dangerous."

"Bastards!" says Grace.

"Well, so much for the book now."

"But couldn't Adam still get it out? I'm sure once people read it they would change their minds and see the truth in it."

"Grace, they just branded Adam a terrorist. Any publisher who touches the book could also be brought up on terrorist charges."

"I'll call Adam back."

"He's not there?"

"No. I'll leave a message. Adam, it's Paul. Don't go anywhere and lock up the place. I'm on my way."

"You're going up there?"

I grab my coat. "I think he just had a short stay of execution."

"What do you mean?"

"I think those agents were told to wait until after the news report, so they could officially label him a terrorist. Then all they

28

have to do is go back, kill him, and who would object to killing a terrorist."

Grace is at her wit's end. "This is insane! The only thing he's done is try to get a book published."

"I don't think it's just the book anymore, Grace. They may want to connect him to all the killings."

I also have another thought I just can't divulge to Grace in her state of mind. They could let him go in hopes of leading them to other terrorists—meaning us, for one example.

"I just hope I'm not too late."

"Oh, my god! I'm coming with you."

Did I say that out loud? "Grace, this could be dangerous."

"If I stay here I'll go out of my mind with worry. I need to be there. I'll wait in the car. If you have to make a break for it all you have to do is jump in."

For a brief moment I look into her eyes and realize her mind is made up and it may be a good thing. "All right, let's go."

CHAPTER 5

"There's the cottage, Grace." I pull off the road a few hundred yards back. I reach past Grace to the glove compartment and pull out the Magnum that I shot Rigby with. I have a quick flash of that moment, but wipe the memory as soon as I picture it.

"Okay, you get behind the wheel."

"Be careful, Paul."

My mind is already ten steps ahead of my feet. I don't see any sign of Adam, and the place looks exactly as I had left it. The front door is still wide open.

"Adam! Adam!"

The silence leaves me with a lump in my throat. There doesn't seem to have been any kind of a struggle except the furniture that was moved around. I walk back outside and turn to the side of the house and think the worst. His car is still there and the keys are in it, and that's another red flag.

Grace gets out of the car and yells out, "He's not there?"

"No, and the place is exactly as it was before."

Grace moves in closer.

"Do you think he might have gone for groceries?"

"Not without his car, and the key is in the ignition. And not answering my message means he didn't get it."

"Paul, I'm scared. What can we do?"

"I don't know, Grace. For now, we go home."

—

All the way back Grace raises different scenarios and, like an idiot, I shoot them down until I realize she's doing it to calm her anxiety. And then it strikes me: "Since he wasn't there, they didn't kill him, so they might want to use him for publicity."

"I don't understand," says Grace.

"It would be a feather in the FBI's cap to have captured one of the terrorists."

"That makes sense."

"I think we should go home and wait to see what transpires on the news."

"And if they don't mention him?"

"I can't go there yet." My mind doesn't work that fast. It goes in sequence.

—

As we drive up the road to the house we see an unknown SUV parked in front. I pull off the road.

"Now who could that be?" says Grace.

"I have no idea, but at least it isn't a Hummer. You did lock the door, didn't you, Grace?"

"I sure did."

"Pass me the gun in the glove box. We'll start with the front door."

We walk to the car and see there is no one behind the wheel.

Grace becomes my shadow as we approach the door. I hold the gun at waist level like a gangster, not a cop. I try the door and it's still locked. I whisper to Grace to unlock it then stand back.

With one finger I open the door enough to see the living room and some of the kitchen, and it looks good, so far.

My shadow follows me in. Each of us checks a bedroom and thankfully we come up empty. The only other place to check would be the patio. Today is one of those rare occasions where we had closed the patio door curtains. I pull a small piece of fabric back enough to survey the backyard, and there sitting under the pergola reading a book is Tor. What a relief.

"It's Tor, Grace."

"Tor? Do you think he knows something we don't?"

"There's only one way to find out."

Hearing the patio door open, Tor turns to the house as we walk out. He stands to greet us.

"I knew you'd show up sooner or later."

"Is this sooner or later? How are you, Tor?"

Grace jumps right in. "We think some agents took Adam."

"What makes you think that, Grace?"

"Paul went to see him, and Adam said the agents had been there and then left without a word. We just came back from his place, and he's gone with his car still in the driveway."

"We think they came back after the FBI called him a terrorist and took him away."

"I had the same thought when I saw it, too," says Tor.

I can see by Grace's look and tone her anxiety level is back where it was a year ago.

"I can't believe we're going through this again," says Grace. "And there's nothing we can do. We don't even know where they've taken him."

Tor looks at her with a smile.

"Why are you smiling? This is serious," she says.

"What if I told you he's right under your nose?"

"What do you mean?" I ask.

"As soon as I saw the broadcast I did what you did, only I beat you. I rushed right over to see Adam."

"And he wasn't there?" says Grace.

"Oh no, he was there."

"So he's all right then?" I ask.

"Like I said, he's right under your nose. I booked him a room at Rebecca's."

"Oh my gosh, I could kiss you!"

Easy, Grace.

"I thought since the UWC seems to have moved on from Willow's End, it might be the safest place right now."

"That's perfect," says Grace.

"What a relief."

Tor's lips tighten and his eyes narrow. "There's one problem though."

"If it's about how long he can stay at Rebecca's, we don't have a problem with it," says Grace.

"I knew that. You two are great people. What concerns me is, how did they know he was at the cottage in the first place?"

There's a brief moment of silence. Grace and I look at each other with question marks on our faces.

"I think I know," says Tor. "During one of my meetings with the other members of my company I received a call from Adam about removing some of the junk from the cottage. When the conversation ended I did mention Adam's name in closing, and I think from that, I may have an informant in the bunch."

Now my face drops. "You mean you've got an agent working for you?"

"Exactly," says Tor.

I think my blood pressure just elevated to the top floor. "Any ideas?"

"Yes, the last salesman I hired. He's only been with me a few weeks. And now as I think back, when I hired him he seemed to know much more about me than real estate. I thought he was just trying to impress me—stroke my ego. But now I realize he had done his homework."

"I guess you won't have any more meetings at Rebecca's with Adam upstairs," says Grace.

"On the contrary," says Tor. "It's the perfect place. There's no way he would suspect it. We just have to make sure Adam stays in his room during any meetings we have."

"So I guess you'll be firing him."

"No, Paul, it would be the worst thing to do."

"That's right," says Grace. "It would tell him Tor is onto him."

"Grace, listen to you. You're becoming a little Columbo."

"Far from it."

"This way," says Tor, "I turn the tables and keep *him* in check, and I can feed him false information about Adam to take him away from any thought of him still being in the area or even the country."

Perfect, I think.

We decide to make dinner a foursome and invite Adam. Tor drives to Rebecca's to pick him up while Grace figures out the meal plan. At this point I take the opportunity to have a shower.

As the hot water begins to soothe my body, I let my mind drift and see a vision from my youth—fond memories of events that didn't mean much back then and just blew on by like a leaf in the wind. Some had life lessons, and even though it may take years to figure out, they do become part of who we are.

One of them was Al's Variety Store. When I was a kid, my parents were the oldest people I knew. We all thought of Al as an old man, but for all I knew at my age, half-bald with a low-lying trim of white hair wrapped around each side of his head, he could have been in his forties.

Back then I never got a cent from my parents. They struggled to keep it together. Like everyone else. We were scroungers who walked the streets searching for pop bottles to return for a few cents, or if we were lucky we got a onetime deal with a friend to deliver house flyers. Stealing was easier, and no one knew this better than Al. He would get really pissed off if we tried to rip him off—even a gumball—but for some strange reason he had no problem giving us three of them for free. Back then we all thought he was a little crazy for doing that, but as I got older I realized he just didn't want us to steal.

The front counter of his store had rows of precious bars of chocolate. If we were going to steal anything in the store, we'd plant ourselves there. For some of the older kids the only prize to dwarf those bars would be the skin magazines on the two top shelves of the rack leaning against the back wall, which meant less competition for those bars.

By the time I was eighteen, Al's Variety was just a memory. He had given up the business—probably too many missing chocolate bars, or maybe they closed him down when his special magazine library became a reality in the back room. Was Al a bad guy? I would have to say no. He was good to us, but as we all find out at some point, our weaknesses are manifested for all to see, and life has a way of drawing them out: lessons of youth —chapter one.

"Paul! Tor and Adam are here!"

"Be right out!"

I dry off and assemble myself, then head for the living room. I wrap my arms around Adam. "I'm so glad to see you safe."

"Not as happy as I am. Tor saved my ass once more."

"I think this calls for some prosecco," says Grace.

"By the way, Grace, did you decide on dinner?"

"Two pizzas, compliments of Rebecca's. They were frozen, but they've been in the oven with five minutes left to go."

"One of my favorites," says Tor.

"I guess we'll be switching to red later."

If the past has any influence on the future, our preference will turn to the truth serum—and that's when things open up.

Ding goes the oven, and after shoveling the pizzas to one huge platter, we eat on the patio, which might be one of the last times of the season. I light a fire in the pit to make it cozy.

We watch the sun do its magic as it tucks itself into the trees, igniting the sky with a wash of orange and gold that streaks and blends with a dark blue backdrop.

We chow down on the pizza like grazing cattle.

Adam asks the question, "Do you think they will still be looking for me?"

"I want to throw out a line of deception that stops any thought of them searching for you ever again," says Tor.

"And what would that be?" I ask.

"I'm not sure," he says. "Any ideas?"

I hope this doesn't turn into one of those plans *I* have to come up with.

"Before we start, let's finish up with dinner. I don't like to have indigestion while I'm eating."

Grace smiles and begins to relax. "It's never stopped you before."

The last slice of pizza leaves the platter as the sun disappears and the sound of a few night creatures begin their symphony. The air turns cool, but not enough to send us indoors when I throw more seasoned wood onto the fire.

It had slipped my mind that pizza, wine, fire, and those cozy Adirondacks angled in such a way will render us comatose. Will any of us be able to have an intelligent conversation?

Tor initiates with, "If I can convince this agent that Adam has left the country and won't be back, I think he will quit the same day and that would be the end of it."

Here I go, "What if you end it like you started it?"

"What do you mean?" asks Tor.

"You have this agent overhear another conversation between you and Adam. Adam tells you he couldn't take it anymore and has fled to Canada or Mexico or wherever."

"That should do it," says Adam.

I turn to Grace. "What do you think, Grace?"

Grace is out for the count. It must have been the pizza, because there is no way she would leave us with half a glass of wine clutched in her hand.

"Someone's coming," says Tor.

We look to the road and see headlights moving our way.

"Adam—why don't you slip into the house until we find out who this is?"

"Good idea." He quickly leaves us for the patio doors.

The car stops short of the house, and from that vantage point and the outside lights on, it's easy to spot us. The engine shuts down and a silhouette of a man gets out and cuts across the lawn heading our way.

Tor leans forward in his chair to get a better look. He announces to me in a whisper, "It's him."

My mind flashes back to the last time we had agents on the patio and it didn't go well, especially for the agents. Ben was still with us then.

"Sorry to intrude. Hello, Tor," he says in a jovial voice.

"What are you doing here, Ed?" asks Tor with a look he might reserve for racists.

"I asked at Rebecca's and they told me you were here. This must be the owner, Paul. Am I right?"

He looks at Grace. "And this must be the better half of that great establishment, Grace."

Hearing her name, Grace wakes with a jerk and squints. "What is it? What's going on?"

Tor stands up like a rising tree and towers over him.

"Would you answer my question, please?"

"Oh, yes. I um … I have some papers for you to sign in regards to the condos in Merrittvile."

"And it couldn't wait until tomorrow?"

He's not very good at deception. His face turns red, but it could also be the glow from the fire. "Well, as they say, I was in the neighborhood."

He looks over at the empty chair and an extra glass of wine on the table beside it.

"Sorry, I didn't mean to interrupt your party."

My turn. "I don't think three people would constitute a party."

"I thought I saw someone else rush to the house."

Tor's face remains the same, but his eyes do all the talking and right now he's having a fierce conversation in his head.

"Where are these papers?"

He raises his thumb. "Back in the car."

"I'll walk you back," says Tor.

I watch them head back to Ed's car until they disappear in the darkness.

Grace turns to me. "What's going on?"

"Tor's agent."

"Is that him? Where's Adam?"

"Safe in the house."

At that moment, Adam steps out and walks to the patio.

"So, who was that guy?"

"It's the agent," says Grace.

"Shit, I better get back in the house."

No sooner said, through the shadows Tor becomes visible.

"How did it go?" I ask.

"For me, fine; for him, not so good."

"You really gave him a tongue lashing, did you?"

I look to see the car hasn't moved. "Why is he still here?"

"I'm really sorry about this, but I had no choice. He won't be leaving the same way he came."

Grace puts her hand to her mouth while Adam's hangs open. My reaction is less visible; a sharp pain in my gut and my soft tone response doesn't reflect the compelling words I squeeze out between my lips. "You ... killed him?"

"If he found me here, he would find Adam, and unfortunately for him, he was right. And that put you both in danger."

I'm sure he's right. And I certainly wouldn't argue with him. His size being one, the other is the fact he just snuffed this guy. I have to justify this in my own head to move on.

"You don't think it was a little aggressive? I mean, couldn't we have just tied him up?"

"And then what? How long would you like to see him hang around, until the posse shows up? He was set to grab his phone and tell those bastards Adam was here. They would be here so fast you wouldn't have time to get a mile from Willow's End."

There's a look of fear and anger on Grace's face. "So now we have to figure out how to get rid of him *and* his car?"

I haven't heard the word *plan* yet, but I'm sure it will pop up at some point.

"I was hoping you might have the answer to that," says Tor.

There it is. The word isn't there, but the implication is clear. All eyes on me.

"Well," I clear my throat, "since Charlie owns Ben's store now, perhaps he could add Ed to the list there."

"And what about his car?" asks Adam.

Grace can't stand to hear any more, and without notice makes her way into the house.

"We could ask Mike to stow it in his garage?"

"Is he trustworthy?" asks Tor.

"He's one of us. He has a personal interest."

"It might be fine for the short term," says Tor. "But eventually the car will have to be destroyed."

"Eventually, but for now, I'll drop in on Mike in the morning."

"What do we do with the body?" asks Adam.

"We'll put him in the trunk of his own car for now, and tomorrow morning we'll transfer him into Tor's SUV," I said.

Listen to me, making it sound like a regular day with the Cosa Nostra, without the cement shoes.

"Mine?" says Tor.

"Well, he's too big to fit in mine. Besides, you did do the damage—will you like a hand?"

"As they say, *this isn't my first rodeo.*"

I smile and turn to the house. "I'll call Charlie right now to get the go-ahead."

After three steps, it hits me—*not my first rodeo.* That's a little scary, but I guess in a good way. Glad he's on our side.

In the kitchen I find Grace dishing out a plate of desserts.

"You're handing out pastry after a murder?"

"If I don't do this, I'll lose my mind and you wouldn't want to see that."

"That's a good idea, Grace, I forgot about dessert."

Things seem crazier by the minute. I kiss her on the cheek, then give Charlie a call and ask him about the burial ground, and of course he's all for it.

"You want to do what?"

"It's a matter of life and death."

"Yeah, yours and mine. I don't know about this."

Charlie had a lot of respect for Ben, and to will his store to him shows they were the best friends. So, in a case like this I have to play a little hardball.

"I know if Ben were still here he wouldn't hesitate. He would feel a duty to help rid this community and country of corruption."

It should absorb into his membrane in about one, two—

"Guess you're right. I'll have to call Sam with the digger. Funny, I just talked to him yesterday, and he complained about the lack of work and how bored he is. I would suggest you meet me at Ben's first thing. In the meantime, I'll look for a place that's unoccupied. Pretty soon we'll be giving Boot Hill a run for their money."

"Great, Charlie. We'll all be able to rest easier after this."

"Didn't I hear those very words a year ago?"

"I stutter a lot. Thanks, Charlie."

Grace has the island set with her usual overabundant fare.

"Looks good, sweetheart. Any liquids to go along with that?"

She reaches into the cupboard and hands me a grenade —the 40 proof and says, "I thought we had put all of this behind us, but here we are—another murder, another body to bury and back to looking over our shoulders and once again playing hide-and-seek with Adam. And now it's seeped into Rebecca's."

"He won't be here for long, sweetheart." I throw my arms around her. "Tor will have another cottage for him."

"How many times have I heard those words in the last year? But it doesn't end. You know what concerns me the most is I have to go into work every day worried about every new face that enters the place. Is this one an agent? Is he going to arrest me as a terrorist or wait for me to finish my shift and shoot me on my walk home?"

For the first time since we have been together I don't know how to comfort her because I can't deny any of it.

"Maybe it's time to leave. Sell Rebecca's and go back to the city," I said.

"I'm sorry, Paul. I don't want to leave this place. I just want to have a normal life and spend it with you."

"I know, sweetheart. I feel the same way."

All I can do is take her in my arms and hold her tight as she pours out the tears and frustration. Her heavy breathing begins to slow as well as the tears, and she looks up at me with fawn-like eyes. There is not a thing left to be said, we just hold each other for a while and realize with all the challenges we have faced, we have so many things to be thankful for.

From the patio doors, I see Ed's car is in the driveway. A couple of thoughts cross my mind. How did Tor kill him? No shot was fired. He didn't come back with blood on his hands from a knife wound, and not a scream, holler or peep from Ed. Perhaps it will all come out with the elixir—it usually does.

—

It's only 7:30 p.m., but it seems like we've been up half the night. The desserts have all but disappeared. After a third round of drinks I notice the change in expressions. I can't imagine how they'd look after one or two of Charlie's Emporium Supremes. This is the perfect time to ask Tor a few questions.

"I meant to ask how you disposed of Ed so quickly and quietly."

"Let's just say it's a survival tactic I picked up back home. In my country, as in most, there is widespread mismanagement, corruption, and terrorism. More than half the population live in poverty. About 60 percent of the urban population can't afford the cheapest house. So the care you give yourself has to be Number One. You can't save others, if you can't save yourself."

"It's a sad state," says Grace.

"It's been this way since the beginning of time—the haves and the have-nots. No middle ground." I pour my fourth and continue, "And with this president hooking his wagon to this United World Corporation—well, I don't see much hope for the future."

"No," says Tor. "It's not true. Things do look bleak, but the people are fighting back. It may not look like much right now, but you watch and see, we will prevail. There are uprisings all over the world. People are at their breaking point, and when this happens, change is inevitable."

"That might be overly optimistic, but I have to agree with you. Look what we did as a community. We got them out of Willow's End."

Grace picks up the last piece of carrot cake.

"We did do that. We all banned together, but what did it cost us? And what are we doing right now? Look what we have outside. Another life lost and another hole to dig."

"I'm sorry about that," says Tor. "I thought I would spare you a second round with these people, but I guess I may have put you back in the line of fire."

"I think this rests on my head," says Adam. "I may have bitten off more than I could chew. As I look back, I should have let the book die with Alex. Like you said, too many lives have been lost and we're still dealing with it."

I down the fourth drink and decide to calm the waves.

"All right, enough. No more blame game. Hindsight may bring out the mistakes, but when you're in the moment you do what you think is right, and you can never be blamed for that."

"You're right, Paul," says Adam. "We all did our best, and maybe once this situation is put to rest it will end there."

"It's late. Let's all meet back here at seven tomorrow morning. Tor, why don't you take Adam back to Rebecca's and grab a room for yourself."

We all agree to call it a night. Even though Grace's eyes float in her head, she still manages to blurt out, "I'll have breakfast waiting."

"Grace, are you sure you want to do all of that?"

"Oh, I won't be doing it alone," she smiles and looks away.

"Well, of course not," I say with a half grin.

CHAPTER 6

I wake to the smell of coffee and roll over to check the time—six-thirty. I throw on my clothes and head to the kitchen. With Grace it's like being mesmerized by a conductor with his symphony. She doesn't miss a beat and her hands are everywhere.

"Grace, I thought I was going to help."

"I knew you wouldn't be up," then she smiles. "It just felt good to say it."

"You're certainly cheery this morning."

"What's that saying about what doesn't kill you makes you stronger? Or in my case, crazier."

She's so damn adorable, I just want to squeeze her. Most women don't want the hug from behind when they're busy in the kitchen, but most women aren't Grace. I wrap my arms around her and look over her shoulder.

"You're making home fries, too."

She turns around to face me. "You gotta problem with that?" and gives me a quick peck on the nose. "Why don't you make yourself useful and pour yourself a cup of coffee?"

I hear the sound of a car. "Sounds like they're here."

"Perfect timing," says Grace.

After breakfast Tor goes out to drive his vehicle around back.

Adam and I help Grace with kitchen duty. No sooner have I washed up the cast-iron pan and there's a bang on the patio doors. I pull the curtain back to see Tor in a state of shock.

Through the glass he muffles, "Get out here!" and then heads over to the driveway.

Sounds serious if Tor gets rattled—I'm out in a flash. "Where's Ed's car?" I ask.

"You tell me."

Adam steps out of the house. "Everything all right?"

"The car's gone."

I look into Tor's eyes. "You don't suppose—"

"What, he wasn't dead and woke up from a deep sleep and drove away? Not in your life. Like I told you—"

"I know, this isn't your first rodeo."

Grace joins us. "Is there something wrong?"

"Just a slight glitch, Grace—Ed's gone and so is his car."

"You think he was still alive?"

"No, someone has been watching us and saw the whole episode."

"Oh no," says Grace. "I'm sorry, I can't deal with this." She stomps back into the house.

"Who do you think it was?" asks Adam.

"I think there could only be two answers. Let's go back in and try to figure this out."

Tor puts his large hand over my whole shoulder. "I don't think Grace would be up to our discussion. We're better off out here."

"You know her already, I see."

The boys sit around the fire pit while I grab kindling and start a small fire to warm us. Not long after we settled in, Grace steps out of the house with three glasses and a half bottle of the best.

"Here," she says. "If it stays with me any longer it will be gone by lunch, and so will I."

I look at my watch. "Grace, it's only just past ten."

"Well, there you go," she stomps back to the house as if she was wearing a pair of army boots.

"Is she okay?" says Adam.

"Too okay, she'll probably go back to bed for a while."

"That's probably best," says Tor. "Okay, my first thought is the easiest one. It's possible Ed told some of the agents where he was headed, and if he didn't make it back he'd be in trouble."

"That's possible."

Adam weighs in, "But if they did show up, why did they take the body and the car and not retaliate? They could have broken down the door in a second and whacked you both in your bed."

"That's true."

"There is one other possibility," says Tor. "What if it wasn't agents? What if it was someone who was on our side and tried to get rid of the evidence to save you the trouble and to keep you out of harm's way?"

"I think that's really stretching it. I don't have any idea who would have the capability to have a body *and* a car disappear during the night without a sound except for agents."

"Well," says Adam, "the job has been done for us and that's it. We're safe and don't have to look over our shoulders now."

"I wish I could share in your optimism. I'll have to call Charlie and cancel the dig. I'll be right back."

I enter the house and see Grace didn't quite make it to bed. She's out on the couch with an empty tumbler on the coffee table. Wow, she'll be out for a while.

I call Charlie. He'll be relieved.

"Holy Christmas! Now things are worse. Something is going on and we're in the dark."

"One good thing is it lets you off the hook."

"But this means now others know about Ed, and I'm just one arrest away with my private cemetery."

"If it hasn't happened by now, Charlie, it never will. Those bodies are resting comfortably."

"All right, I think my phone will ring again."

"Not if I can help it."

Back outside I see the boys have made themselves comfortable with everyone's friend in a bottle.

"You boys still with me?" I ask, as I lower myself into the Adirondack.

"Still here," says Tor. "We tried to come up with some answer other than the UWC but—"

"It all points to them except for the non-retaliation part," says Adam.

The next few minutes of silence seem like a lifetime. On occasions like this, I would ask myself, what would Ben do? Ben was good at human nature and women, but solving problems was something he did sparingly.

"Any ideas?" asks Tor.

"No, I'm afraid I'm bankrupt."

Adam has another concern. "And where do I go from here? I can't go back to the cottage because I'm considered a terrorist. They would love to hold me up as an example of the fine work this dictator does to keep his voter base happy."

"I mentioned to Paul, I can put you on another, more secluded lake. I have one cottage built, and the rest won't be up until next spring."

"Sounds good to me. Thanks, Tor, you've been a great friend."

That's one end locked up, but what about Grace and me? The whole event took place here. Sure, no altercation ensued to put us in danger other than the fact we witnessed a murder. That doesn't sound good either.

"What about Paul and Grace?" asks Adam. "Aren't they in danger?"

More sounds of nature. No one has an answer, which makes me think we could be in the eye of the storm, and one slight move in any direction could mean we're in their crosshairs.

"I—I think you should be fine," says Tor. "I think we all agree, if they wanted to harm you, last night was a perfect opportunity."

His opening hesitation tells me he wants to see my anxiety level down a few notches. "It makes total sense, but leads us to the other question, who was it?"

The continued conversation seems to sober us. They decide to head to Rebecca's for coffee and an early lunch, then visit the old cottage so that Adam can pick up his car before he relocates to his new safe haven.

—

I let Grace sleep. Finally about one o'clock she comes to life.

"Oh," she says as she sits up and puts her hand to her head, "my poor head. What hit me?"

"By looking at the tumbler, I would say a freight train."

She finally gets both feet on the floor.

"I just made some fresh coffee in anticipation of your return."

"Thanks, Paul. You're very good."

"Overindulgence is my forte, and it sounds more elegant than saying weakness." I pour her a mug and stress the fact having it black would be a good idea.

After five minutes of slow sipping, Grace begins her questions. "Paul, I don't know how we're supposed to take this. Are we in danger? Was it the UWC or—how the hell are we to live our lives with this over our heads?"

I sit beside her on the couch and hold her hand. "Grace, we didn't kill anyone. It was Tor, and he thought he was protecting us."

"But we were accomplices. We would have disposed of the body; and not only that, according to the FBI, Adam is a terrorist and we kept him at Rebecca's."

I can see I'm not much help. I have no answers, just the same questions and maybe a few more. Who is Tor? Is real estate his only job? He doesn't seem to have a problem exterminating people. Could *he* be an agent and snuffed out a fellow agent to keep him from exposing Tor? Or...could it be, as Tor said, some group that is fighting for our side?

"Paul, I just remembered I placed an order with the butcher shop in Campton and they can't deliver until tomorrow, but I need it at Rebecca's today."

"Okay, I'll go and pick it up."

"I'm sorry to have you go all the way out there."

"That's all right; it will give me some needed time to think."

"I'll have lunch ready by the time you get back."

—

The drive doesn't do much as far as any new train of thought, but the color of the landscape and cold air rushing through my half-opened window carries with it the smells of a variety of trees, and for the moment lowers my anxiety.

CAMPTON—even though just a town, they seem to have everything a large city would have—like a parking meter. One.

Before I hit the butcher shop my eyes zoom in on their library. I wonder if they've heard any talk of closing them down—I'm too curious to pass this up.

The automatic sliding doors give me some indication. Then, one thing completely unheard of or smelled in a library, the aroma of coffee and a Starbucks sign to the left with a glass counter and tables and chairs. What happened to the sign looming over every doorway—*SILENCE?*

The old library is now a thriving, commercialized donut hole. In my day the library snoopers, snitchers, or as Stephen King called them, the *Library Police* would be on you like flies on shit if you entered their sacred domain with so much as a stick of Juicy Fruit.

Next is no front desk. No one manning the fort and no mid-fifties woman who would sit there with nothing better to do than to stare at you with a stern, in-your-face look, as though you were there just to ruin her lovely demeanor. Their name tags always began with *Ms.*—I've never seen or heard of a librarian who was married. To me, the whole front desk scenario is the one part I don't miss. I walk through and see people upright by podium-like monitors with their USB sticks downloading a book. Another observation is the clinical look of the place. It leaves me with a cold, hollow feeling, not unlike the construction of new houses they put up today—no curved lines, no artistry, just straight-cut lines. Even though I knew it was inevitable, it's a sad testament to where we are and where we are headed, or aren't —and no Dewey Decimal System.

There are no shelves with books and no distinct smell libraries are known for, like the shoe stores when I was growing up. As soon as you walked through the door you were hit with the great unmistakable smell of leather—today it's rubber and plastic.

I leave the building with sadness and longing for the days of my youth. Then, I notice a small independent bookstore across the street, and I feel alive again.

I move on to the butcher shop and grab my order and hand the clerk cash. He looks down at my hand with an expression of contempt. "Don't you have a card?"

"A card?"

"Credit or debit?"

I refuse to stand here and argue about the implication of not using real money. I do the card ritual and head for home. The whole while I'm asking myself, how far can we take this planet before it all collapses? It seems like all that was tangible only exists in the air, and it can be turned off at a moment's notice.

CHAPTER 7

I deliver the order to Rebecca's, then leisurely head down the dirt road and into the driveway. Before I even get out of the car, my thoughts turn to the disappearance of Ed and his car. No matter how hard I try, I can't escape this glaring problem. I've gone full circle. Back to the questions I had at the start of the day and still have no answers.

I try to extinguish a dark thought with a more pleasant one, like, what has Grace planned for lunch? I walk through the door and my nose doesn't detect any cooking smells.

"Grace—Grace?" I look up at the kitchen clock. It's ten after one. Now where could she be? I notice a piece of notepaper on the coffee table.

> *Hi sweetheart.*
> *I've gone out with Tor. He has something in mind for us and wanted to get my thoughts on it. I should be home shortly. There is a corned beef sandwich in the fridge until I get back.*
> *Love you*

What the hell is this all about? I knew there was something about Tor that left me with a bitter taste, but I didn't think it was romancing Grace. I can hear Ricky Ricardo say, *"You haf some splainin' to do."*

Is this one more thing I have to add to my anxiety list? Well, I'll have the sandwich and a beer or two or—no, don't get started on the hard stuff. Might as well turn on the tube and suck in mindless corporate snake oil.

Just then the front door opens and there stands Grace. "Hi, Paul. Did you get my note?"

"Yes, I did."

"And the sandwich?"

"Yes, it was delicious. Thank you."

"I have some exciting news to talk to you about."

I'm sure you do. "You sound very excited. By the way, where is Tor?"

"He couldn't stay, but I have all the information I need. Just let me get my coat off and we can talk." She plunks herself on the couch beside me. "Well, let me start at the beginning. Tor called me and has a proposition for us."

"You mean some real estate investment scheme?"

"Not a scheme. He has a house—"

"We already have one."

"Paul, are you going to listen or not?"

"Okay, I'm sorry. Go ahead."

"Tor drove me to see this house, and it's perfect."

"Perfect for what?"

Her eyes twinkle and her smile stretches across her face. "A restaurant."

"A res—"

"Let me finish. It's very large and has a wraparound porch like Rebecca's, but it's a smaller version of Rebecca's. It sits in the middle of this town with a lot of senior residents. The town has a number of stores, but the one thing it lacks is a restaurant."

"It's a sad situation, especially in winter."

"Exactly, and Tor has done some research by talking to people around town, and he has discovered they are desperate for a family restaurant. He was thinking of us opening this house as another Rebecca's. He would put up half the money and we could partner with him."

"But don't you think we have enough to do now? How could we manage two Rebecca's?"

"This is the beauty of it. In the winter Rebecca's pulls in just enough to keep her going. The people of Bridgeburg are full-time residents and mostly retired seniors with plenty of time on their hands. They would be eating there all year round."

"But what happens in the summer when we get busy?"

"Tor said he will hire a manager to handle the staff and make sure it runs smoothly. What do you think?"

I was on the fence with Tor, but I look into her eyes filled with excitement and joy, like a girl on her first high school prom. How can I say no to that?

"I think it deserves some thought and we should meet with him to get all the ins and outs."

"Then you like the idea?"

"I'm not a businessman, but yes, I do like the idea. We could become the franchise of the north—a Rebecca's in every town."

We laugh and suddenly life doesn't look so dark.

"Grace, I had promised myself last year I would start to take you out places, but after the episode with Rigby that nearly killed us both, I've been hesitant to go anywhere."

"I've felt the same way."

"So—I'd like to take you out for dinner tonight. Let's just say, to celebrate our new business adventure."

"That would be wonderful, Paul. Where are we going?"

"I haven't figured out yet."

"Well, while you're mulling it around, I'm going to have a nice, soothing bath."

"I like the sound of that."

"Oh, no you don't. One customer per tub."

I hope she doesn't smell too nice or I'll have to give her a rain check on the restaurant.

While she washes away the cares of the last few days, I grab the *County Connection* newspaper to see what they have for dining. When I see descriptions like secluded or great ambience, I immediately think of that murderous rat Rigby leaving us with a time bomb in his briefcase. We were so damn lucky to get through it with a few minor injuries.

Ah, here's one, A Taste of Tuscany. It looks elegant, with great food, and it must be a popular place when they ask for reservations. I make a quick call to reserve a table that isn't close to the kitchen. I hate all the hollering and clattering when we are in a conversation and enjoying a nice meal. And if you're unlucky enough you'll hear an altercation while you're having soup.

Okay, that's done. Now, I'll watch some mindless TV until Grace steps out so I can step in. Whenever I have any quiet time to myself I seem to slide right into negativity—like an old black-and-white short made by a grade nine student with a 51 percent average in the *Introduction to Film.*

—

A Taste of Tuscany was better than I imagined, and for Grace, she was on top of the world. The place was to capacity as I expected, and we were able to enjoy the ambience and great food without looking for a bomb in a briefcase.

We leave the restaurant to a crisp, cold, starry sky and hold each other romantically close while we stroll to our car under the antique streetlights leading the way.

Five minutes into the drive I see headlights in my rearview mirror. They seem to come out of nowhere. Grace is oblivious to the fact. She is caught up in the new venture and hardly takes a breath as she gives me her view of what this new establishment will look like.

The road is a two-lane highway and we are the only cars on it. It's a leisurely drive and whoever is behind me could pass at any time. The distance between us is steady.

I negotiate a curve in the road, and for a moment lose the headlights. Now they're back. Each turn or dip in the road has me nervously glance at the glove box with the Magnum.

I turn off the main road and head for Willow's End. My eyes strain into the rearview mirror, waiting to see what will transpire behind me. The headlights disappear. I take a breath but only one, for the headlights quickly return—I'm being followed. I know Grace is still talking, but I don't know what she's saying. I can feel my blood pressure rise and my hands become slippery on the steering wheel. Just before reaching town, the mystery vehicle pulls off to a side road. I watch as it turns, hoping to catch a side vision of the vehicle. I can say for sure it's larger than a sedan. I know I promised myself I wouldn't hold anything back from Grace, but if truth be told, it could have been an SUV, van, or pickup truck, so why ruin this night with paranoid speculation?

Our romantic evening carries through to the bedroom. We lay there gazing out the window at the half-moon surrounded by a misty glow. The dark thoughts leave me, and this beautiful moment in time with Grace feels like a gentle wave reaching the shore. Tonight the world is a better place, a safer place.

The morning sun arrives later now and breakfast is made in the dark. By five o'clock in the afternoon the evening curtain falls and reminds us of last year with horrible flashbacks we try to shake off like mud on our boots. We have been anxiously awaiting Tor's call to get together to discuss our venture. Finally, Grace goes to her coat on the rack, pulls out a business card and hands it to me.

"Here, why don't you give Tor a call?"

The call response is, *I am not available at the moment, please leave*...I decide to give Adam a call, but end up with the same result.

Grace is frustrated and I'm uneasy. I try to sort this out in my head with the obvious, innocent excuses. I ask myself if these two phone calls are related. Is it just a coincidence, or are they doing something together, or worse, are they in trouble together? Did the agents pick them up? Then I go full: Is Tor an agent, which seems unlikely after his efforts to try to keep Adam safe, and wants to have this entrepreneurial endeavor with us. If I really want to screw up my head, I can throw in the episode of the vehicle following us. It wasn't a car, but I could let my imagination consider a Hummer or an SUV like Tor's.

"Paul? Paul?"

"I'm sorry. What was that?"

"What do you think we should do?"

"To be honest, Grace, there's nothing we can do except to carry on the way we have been until one of them contacts us. I can't drive out to Adam's new place because we don't know where it is."

"What about Tor's business card? Is his address on it?"

"It's only a box number. We need to keep busy by focusing our attention on Rebecca's."

"Out of sight, out of mind." I hope it works for Grace because it won't do it for me.

—

The next morning is coffee and pastries. Not the best breakfast, but it's simple, and that's what we want right now. Grace will go into work shortly and I should try to plan my day.

"So what have you planned for today?" she asks. Every time I hear the word *plan* my memory heads right back to last year: *What's the plan, Paul?*

"I think I'll drop in the garden center and pick up burlap to cover the rest of the shrubs. When I finish with that I would like to have lunch with a beautiful woman."

"Anyone I know?" she asks with a smile.

"I think you've met her a few times."

"Is she single?"

"Apparently, but hopefully not for long."

"Sounds like a proposal."

"Hmm. You could be right." I pick her up in my arms.

"Paul, what are you doing?" she laughs.

"Rehearsing," then I kiss her.

We usually walk the ten-minute stroll on the dirt road to town, but since the temperature has dropped and I have the run to the garden center, I take the car and drop Grace at Rebecca's.

I pick up the burlap and I decide to visit Charlie's Emporium to apologize for having to call Larry over to dig the hole. Of course, the thought of one of his Emporium Supremes with the weather change would sit well with me right now.

I open the door to the Emporium, and the first thing I notice is space. I don't have to climb over anything or anyone to get to the counter.

"Paul, you son of a bitch. You sure pulled a fast one on me."

"That's why I came over. I wanted to say how sorry I was for the inconvenience."

"I'm just pulling your chain. Larry ended up having to do a paying gig that day and couldn't make it anyway."

"That worked out well."

"Speaking of working out, what was the final result?"

"Well—"

"Just stop right there. Grab a seat at the back and I'll make us a couple of Supremes."

That's my Charlie. "Oh, I have to ask: Did you get a maid to come in and give this place the once-over, twice?"

"Smart-ass. We had a great summer. Sold a lot of shit."

"Give them Emporium Supremes first or after the sale?"

"Both." Charlie smiles.

I head to the back where we spent many hours the previous year discussing one plan after another on how to foil the UWC.

The chairs have been replaced with new secondhand ones. I guess things are looking up. "I see you have new lawn chairs."

"Not bad, huh?" he says, placing the coffees on the table.

Both chairs have the same response as the old ones. The fabric is either ripping or has the sound of squeaking one out. We raise our mugs and the conversation begins.

"So, Paul, are we out of the woods or in the thick of it?"

"I wish I knew."

While the brews settle in I explain the change of location for Adam. "We haven't heard from Tor or Adam, and it makes me nervous."

"I guess there ain't anything you can do until one of them makes an attempt to contact you?"

"That's what I told Grace, but we have no idea if they're safe."

"What about trying to contact one of Tor's employees? They might be able to give you something to go on."

"That's true. I'll look up his website and it should give me a list of them. Good idea, Charlie. Where did that come from?"

"It's amazing what a little mug of this elixir can conjure up in this wooden head of mine."

I smile. "Charlie, if it's wood, the fire's burning brightly."

—

I meet Grace for lunch and tell her of my conversation with Charlie. She reminded me that she gave me Tor's business card. I hadn't looked at it closely before now. I smile and shake my head when I read the name of the company, *Torrific Homes*. I look up the company name and it does give a list of salesmen. I call the first one on the list, John Burke.

"Hello, John? I'm a friend of Tor's, and I can't seem to get hold of him. Would you know where he might be or how I could get in touch with him?"

The answer is short.

"What did he say?" asks Grace.

"He said he couldn't give out that information and hung up."

"That's strange."

"More than strange. How do you run a business like that?"

"You know, Paul, it could have been an order from Tor because he may think the agents are onto him. By now they would know Ed is missing."

"That's true."

I decide to call one more salesman on the list and receive the same response.

"No luck?" says Grace.

"No."

"See, I'm sure that he's not taking any chances."

If she's right, which I think she is, the crazy notion of Tor being an agent doesn't even make sense. I tell Grace I'll wrap up the remaining shrubs and then see her back home.

—

Now there's a surprise. In front of the house is an SUV, but it's beige. Now what?

Before driving past the house and into the driveway, I peer into the backyard and there sits Tor with a small fire. I wonder if I should make him a house key.

I pull into the driveway then head to the patio and can't imagine what his story might be.

"Tor."

He jerks then turns to me. He must have been dozing, which tells me he may have been here for a while.

"Paul."

"Now that we've established who we are, what the hell's going on?"

"It's a bit of a story."

"Let's go inside before we freeze our ears off."

Once inside I ramp up the malnourished fire with a large log and a few shots of needed oxygen from Bellows Lugosi.

"I seem to be under surveillance," he states in a low-keyed tone.

"The UWC?"

"I think so. I'm sure they have been on my landline and my cell. I haven't gone anywhere near my personal computer."

"So that's why I couldn't get through to you."

"I'm sorry, Paul, but I told everyone at the office not to give out any information about me for the moment."

"You think they know about Ed?"

"I'm sure they expected some contact from him, and there's the possibility he told them he was coming here."

"And where's your SUV?"

"I couldn't have them track or follow me, so I rented one."

"Good idea. And Adam?"

"You haven't heard from him?"

"No. He doesn't answer his phone either."

"I don't like it. I gave him instructions on how to get to the new cottage, so he should be there."

"Let me try him once more." I call his number.

"Nope. Is it far?"

"Almost an hour."

"Are you busy?"

"Let's take the rental."

—

You can learn a lot about a person on a forty-five-minute ride. I'm not talking career, I'm talking about the person. From our conversation I find Tor has a few of Ben's traits—an honest, straight shooter, bent on stretching out a hand to your fellow man. If he's an agent, he's the best actor I've ever seen.

"In my country of Nigeria, before you could take a breath there would be another riot, massacre, robbery, or killings over ethnicity. My father and brother died in an uprising when I was in my twenties. I had to get out. A dear friend at the American Embassy was able to get me on a flight to New York. I had enough money to rent a small studio and took on every job I could find so I could send my mother some money and finish my law degree."

"A lawyer, I'm impressed."

"That was the goal, but the lawyer faded when I realized keeping my head above water was hard enough, and the racial obstacles certainly didn't help. I decided the city wasn't the place for me and moved up here, got my real estate license and never looked back. I stopped sending my mother money three years ago."

"What happened there?"

"I found out through my cousin she was crossing the street to go into a small market and a bomb went off as she was about to enter."

"I'm so sorry, Tor."

With watery eyes, "Now that my family is gone, I have no ties to my country."

"Most people on this side of the pond, and that's including me, have no idea of the plight of others around the world. They may see it on TV or read about it, but to live in that environment is beyond comprehension."

"I hate to burst your bubble, Paul, but it's here, too. It's more subtle, but still here. Just ask a Black, a Jew, an Indigenous person, or any immigrant. This New World Corporation will take this country down a similar path, if we don't act."

"I've always said, it's my own lily-white race that caused all of this."

"To some extent it's true, but there are plenty of white people who are poor, homeless, uneducated, and have no job as well. It's the 1 percent corporate machine steamrolling over all of us."

"Green is the dominant color in all of this, and like cancer it has no favorites."

—

We pull off the main road and I can see a body of water in the distance.

"Is that the lake there?"

"It's a river. I envision cottages on both sides."

"That's a big undertaking." I see one huge cottage standing alone farther down the river.

"Is that where Adam is?"

"That's where he's supposed to be."

"Wow, how many bedrooms?"

"Five bedrooms, three bathrooms."

A hundred yards from the house I see an old 1960s Ford Falcon in the driveway. "What's with the antique?"

"I picked it up for Adam, no computer parts to track."

"Ah yes, the old Nova routine."

"Nova?"

"Never mind, it's a long story."

We park in front of the cottage and step out. "Sure is a nice spot with the river on your doorstep."

"I could make more money if I crowded them in, but I give each lot half an acre: complete privacy. It's one of the big selling points."

The moment we pull into the driveway, Adam steps out of the front door.

"Well, this is a surprise," he says.

"We couldn't get hold of you, so we thought we would check in to see how you're coming along," says Tor.

"My cell's been acting weird."

"Like someone's hacked it?"

"Could be."

"Here," says Tor. He hands him another cell phone in a box. "Get rid of the other one. Use this one, it's brand-new."

"Thanks."

"You buy them by the gross?" I ask.

Tor chuckles. "Hopefully not. I have yet to set mine up."

"You got time for a beer?" asks Adam.

"Sounds good to me—Tor?"

"I'm good for one. Let's go inside."

To call it a cottage is an understatement. This is a summer home. All-open concept with solid wooden beams up to the pinnacle of the second level. The windows are floor-to-ceiling with a beautiful view of the river.

"And you completely furnished it, too."

"It's a model. Most people aren't very visual so you have to show them a physical picture."

"Adam, you'll never want to leave here."

"I know, and I thank Tor every day for taking such good care of me."

"I do have an ulterior motive. Adam is my security. He watches over the place."

"That's a great exchange."

"Have a seat," says Adam. "I'll get the brews."

We sink into a soft, tanned-leather sofa that hugs to the point it would be difficult to stay awake for any given period.

Right off our conversation begins with the disappearance of Ed and his car.

"There are two things troubling me," says Tor. "If it was the government, why did they take away the evidence? They had us right where they wanted us."

"It's too strange," says Adam. "I had something happen to me last night that I can't explain."

Tor and I lean in at the same time. "What kind of strange?"

"I thought I would sit by a fire and watch the sun go down. I didn't have a match so I came inside to grab some, and when I got back out a fire was blazing."

"Are you sure there weren't some hot coals in there from the last one?" asks Tor.

"No, I doused the last one with a bucket of water and it was two days ago."

I don't like the sound of this. "Have you noticed anyone around or footprints that would give you the impression you weren't alone?"

"Just the fire," says Adam.

Tor stands. "I'll be right back," and walks out the door.

"I wonder what he's up to."

Tor is back. "Here, take this," he says to Adam and hands him a gun. "Only use it if your life is being threatened. Don't shoot at a moving bush we end up having to bury."

I can see in Adam's eyes and the way he fumbles with the gun he isn't quite comfortable with this idea. He presents a half-smile. "I guess if I came by a wolf it would come in handy."

"Let's hope it won't be a two-legged one," says Tor.

"Would you like a drink with a little more bite?" asks Adam. "I have tequila."

We're all on the same page with that. I think it's more for his benefit to calm himself. I feel like Tor should have held back with the gun, but then again, you can't sugarcoat this shit.

"Just remember to key-in the alarm system as soon as the sun dips, and I think you'll be fine," says Tor.

Is handing him a gun then saying "you'll be fine" an oxymoron? Or am I just being the latter part of that word?

—

Reluctantly we leave Adam, and the drive back allows me to ask myself about Tor's dealing of Ed. I'm sure he had to protect himself in Nigeria to survive, but other than Ed, has he disposed of anyone else in this country? And if so, could it be why he's being watched? Do I ask him or keep it on the back burner —back burner.

—

Finally home and Tor hands me another business card with his new number on the back.

"I'll call you tomorrow," says Tor. "We should take a trip out to our new venture."

"I'm anxious to see it."

"I think you'll be impressed."

He drives off and I enter the house to see Grace with her eyes glued to the TV screen. "Hi sweetheart, how was work?"

"Shhh, come and see this."

"More government bullshit?"

"No. Listen."

"This parasite is normally found in birds, especially chickens. It's called the fowl mite and usually has no eoffect on humans, but recently they have found a breed of fowl mites at a chicken farm in Mexico that has now mutated into a super mite and has been killing not only chickens, but also infecting people with a deadly virus. It is rapidly spreading and is now infesting farms along the east coast of Mexico and appears to be moving north. The effects of these super mites are devastating. According to the CDC reports, 75 percent of people infected die from this virus."

I shut the TV off. "Sounds like a horror movie. I hope they can contain it soon."

"Do you think it could make its way up here?"

"I doubt it. That's in a whole different world, Grace. Besides, we have enough on our plates right now." I think we need a positive distraction. I smile. "Like a new restaurant."

"So we'll go ahead with it then!"

"Tor will meet us there tomorrow."

"Good, I really want that place, Paul."

"Me too. What's for supper?"

"I like your list of priorities."

"It was a long dusty ride on that buckboard all day, and it sure gives me an appetite."

"Did you feed the horses before you came in?"

"I sure did. I'll just mosey on into the saloon for a quick one. Are drinks still available at the bar?"

"You'll have to ask the bartender."

"I see."

I pull her up from the couch, hold her in my arms and kiss her. "How's that?"

"One or two?" she says with a smile.

"Shots or bottles?"

—

No sooner do we finish breakfast and I get the call from Tor with the directions to Bridgeburg.

CHAPTER 8

It's a beautiful morning and the drive is a delight, as the fall colors are at their best.

The sign up ahead—*BRIDGEBURG POP. 1,856.*

And of course there's a bridge. An old rusty, steel one with a gentle flow of a stream that at one point must have been a river. When we hit the other side there is a center island with a monument of a WWI soldier standing tall with his rifle and bayonet at his side. It has the character of Willow's End, but has more than just a pulse, it has a heartbeat. We can see it and feel it. The town is alive. Listen to me, a year ago I was crazy in a big city where so-called progress was everywhere. Tear that building down, put this one up—family businesses closed and new ones opening in the hopes of clutching a piece of the already thinly sliced pie.

"Isn't this wonderful!" says Grace. She points. "There it is, Paul, three houses down on the right with the For Sale sign."

"Good thing you added that. I might have gone right past it," I say with a grin. "It does remind me of Rebecca's, and it's on a double lot for parking as well as the street."

"I knew you'd like it."

I see Tor by his vehicle waving. I pull in behind him.

"Well, what do you think?" asks Tor.

"It's perfect, and right in the middle of town."

"That's what I liked about it. No matter which way you go, you have to pass it."

"Can we get inside?"

"That's why we're here," he says and dangles the key in front of my face.

The inside of the house is ghostly like in old haunted house films, only this one is exempt of furniture, but the ever-present cobwebs adorn the light fixtures and windows.

"Must have been on the market for quite some time."

"That's why we can have it for a song," says Tor.

"And what song are they singing?"

"Ninety-five and don't let the rooms fool you, Paul. Once we knock them out you'll be able to visualize it a lot better." He points to the living room window. "I think we should take out this front window and replace it with one huge picture window. Everyone that passes by will peer in, and when they see the patrons having such a great time they'll want to join in."

It appears Tor is quite the entrepreneur. Every room we enter he describes in detail what he envisions. He has really done his homework.

Grace is in la-la land. "It will be beautiful, Paul!"

I'm even having a hard time containing myself. I put my arm around her. "It sure is, sweetheart."

"The sooner we sign the papers, the quicker we can begin. We could have this up and running for Christmas."

"Christmas?" I can't see it.

"Sure," says Tor. "All my workers are idle right now until spring. They'd love to have the work. All you have to do is say yes and sign the contract."

When I see the sparkle in Grace's beautiful brown eyes I couldn't deny her a swamp in Florida.

"Do you have a pen?"

—

It's has only been two days and Tor's crew has already knocked out most of the walls that weren't weight-bearing. We don't want to be in the way, so we tell Tor we'll drop in once a week on a Sunday to see the progress.

Rebecca's slows to its pre-winter crawl, but we are pumped up about our new endeavor.

Then I get a strange message left on my phone from Adam, at least I think it was Adam. "Grace, listen to this."

"Hi Pau...I was out in the wo...found a de...as soon as you..."

"Play it again, Paul."

I play it once more.

"He didn't sound panicky, but very concerned or drunk. Sounds like he found something he wants us to see. Should we go out there?"

"I'll go, Grace. Can you call Tor and explain it to him? Tell him I'll meet him there in forty minutes."

—

The drive allows me time to analyze the call. His speech was broken, so either he was too far from the cottage or into his usual state. *I was out in the wo*—woods. That makes sense. *Found a de...*What the hell would that be; a decoy, a deep hole, a deranged bear? Why is this important?

—

There he is by the water with what looks like a tall glass of la-la land. So far, I'm not amused.

Adam doesn't move as I approach him. He turns his head to me with some effort. "Hi yah, Paul," he says with a slur. "Can I offer you a drink?"

I'm a little pissed to see him pissed. "I think I'll wait to find out why I'm here first."

At that moment Tor pulls up. Even from a distance he sees part of the problem.

"Looks like over-consumption. He doesn't seem to be too excited," says Tor.

"I think numbness has set in."

We sit on either side of Adam, and like pulling out a stubborn molar, we begin to extract the facts.

"You all right?" I ask.

"As best as can be accepted," he says, slurring his words.

Hmm, he's in good shape all right. "I think you mean, expected."

"That, too."

"Okay," says Tor. "Why did you drag us out here?"

"I'm not the only one out here."

"What do you mean?" asks Tor.

"He's sleeping."

"What do you mean, sleeping?"

"The kind you don't wake up from."

That I understand. "Can you take us there?"

"I don't think so." He points upriver. "See that [belch] big rock?"

Our eyes follow the slow motion of his arm to his half-bent index finger. It points to a large boulder a few thousand yards away.

"If you go there—"

He stops to gather enough information from his fermented gray matter to pull a string of thoughts together. "Turn to the forest and [belch] walk into the woods...can't miss 'im."

"Him?" I don't like the sound of that. "Are you all right if we leave you?"

"I've been good so far."

More than good. Tor leads the way as we walk along the river until we arrive at the boulder and reluctantly begin our walk into the woods. We can see the brush Adam had pushed aside on his walk, so we follow through. A minute in and we can smell what was ahead before we get there. Adam was right, it ain't Goldilocks. It's a man face down in swampy ground with hands that show signs of decomposition.

"That suit looks familiar," says Tor.

"I guess you should roll him over?"

"Me?" says Tor. "Why me?"

"You did say this wasn't your first rodeo?"

"From what I heard about last year in Willow's End, *you* seem to be the expert."

I can't dispute that. I squat down and turn him face up. "Oh shit!" I retract like a bungee cord and throw my other hand over my mouth. I'm one second away from tossing my cookies. The face is unrecognizable and covered in maggots and a few small beetles thrown in for an added touch of nausea. "Damn it, that's bad!"

"Now there's a familiar face," says Tor. "I saw a lot of that back home, and that was on a good day."

He sees a wallet floating on the surface of the muddy water. He carefully picks it up with two fingers and opens to reveal the driver's license.

"Are you ready for this?" says Tor.

"No, but go ahead anyway."

"Now I know why the suit looked familiar, it's Ed."

"What?"

"Someone is really trying hard to do a number on us."

"Why the hell would they dump him here?"

"I'll tell you one thing," says Tor, "whoever it is, they know this country."

"Why do you say that?"

"You see how muddy the ground is? This whole area is out-of-bounds for building. It's a patch of swamp that can't be used. So whoever put him here knows that, and knows the body would sink as it decayed and no one would find it."

"That leaves us with only one question: Whose side is this person or group on?"

"We may never know," says Tor.

"I guess we should go back and grab a couple of shovels."

"No," he says. "Turn him back on his face. Let nature do its work. We weren't here and that's the way it has to be."

When we reach Adam he has stopped drinking and is slowly coming around, which means if I mention Ed, it should sober him up in a hurry.

"We know who it is, Adam."

"You do?"

"It's Ed," says Tor.

"The dead guy we put in the trunk!"

I nod my head. "One and the same."

"But how is it even poss—"

"Whoever took Ed in the first place knows this area and must have had plans to drop him there the night he vanished from our house—where the body would never be discovered."

Adam raises his glass to his lips.

I gently take it from his grasp.

"I have to move again?" he asks.

I try to lower his anxiety level. "No, you'll be safe. If they wanted you we wouldn't be in this conversation now. For some strange reason I sense they may have done this to help us."

"By planting a dead guy in my backyard?"

"Like I said, it was already planned, and outside of Tor, there is not one thing linking Ed to us."

"Just leave things the way they are, and by next spring there won't be any trace left," says Tor.

I have seen enough for one day, but Tor decides to babysit Adam for a while.

—

Once again I'm confronted with the latest development and whether I should disclose it to Grace. Then there's Tor's violent background. When confronted with a problem he will eliminate it without batting an eye. Yet, he is a gentle, intelligent person who also wants to see a better world. This reminds me of what I went through with Ben. He was with me every step of the way, but once in a while I would have to reel in his *Wild West* way of thinking; and also, like Ben, Tor is someone I want on my side.

—

I'm home, and just as I get out of the car my thought is to tell Grace about the discovery by using that phrase, *I have good news and bad news.*

Grace is making magic on the stove.

"Mmm, smells awfully good in here."

"Well, I couldn't just sit around here wondering what was going on, so I made a big pot of beef stew."

"Does it include your world-famous dumplings?"

"Of course. Remember how Ben liked them so much he got all teary-eyed. He sure enjoyed his food."

"He crossed my mind, too." A moment of silence comes with the memory.

"So what's going on? Is Adam all right?"

I float my nose over the steamy stew to give the illusion all is well. "Yeah, he's fine."

"You seem too calm. Come on, out with it." It's like she has some special power.

"Okay, there's good news and—"

"Paul, just spit it out. I don't think there is much left that would surprise me."

I clear my throat and take a deep breath. "Adam found a body in the woods."

"What! I guess I was wrong about surprises. This is insanity! Who lives like this? You know something, we're in the wrong business. We shouldn't be catering to the living. I think we need to open a funeral home, not another restaurant." She takes a short pause to calm herself. "So, what's the good news?"

"It was Ed."

"Ed! The guy Tor killed then magically disappeared and that's the good news?"

"Sort of."

"Sort of?" Suddenly Grace's mood becomes somber. "Paul, could you be so kind as to get the bottle from under the island please, and a glass."

"This glass?"

"No, the large one."

Oh boy, this could be bad. As I continue to explain, her eyes focus on the fireplace and turning a full glass into an empty one. Like a magic potion her anger disappears, and to her credit, she understands my logic of not being in any danger, and it may be possible we do have someone on our side. Her demeanor also allows me to relax and enjoy a couple of rounds myself before dinner. Whether it was the liquor or my presentation, I may never know, but we got a lot closer by bedtime—just saying.

CHAPTER 9

Another Sunday and we're off to see how the new restaurant is coming along. It amazes me how different a place can look once the space has been opened.

"Paul, look at the beautiful new front window. It's almost the width of the house."

"Restaurant, Grace, the house is gone. Let's have a look at the kitchen."

"Yes, your favorite room."

"It's huge. I can smell food already."

"Why doesn't that surprise me?"

—

We take in the main street to get a feel for the town. At the far end of the street is a park with a playground and very nice garden areas. We rest on a bench and observe the people. In the distance we can see and hear the kids at the playground.

"Remember the carefree days of being a kid, Paul? Life was so simple back then."

"Now it's just simply terrible."

"That's not true. Even though we have gone through a lot together, I think in some strange way we are all the better for it. We appreciate the good that comes along so much more."

"That's true."

Looking around, I notice an old man with sunglasses and a walking stick by his side sitting on a bench across the park from us. He wears a long brown overcoat. His face covered with a full gray beard and matching hair topped off with a gray toque. Any other time I wouldn't have given him a second thought, but even though he appears to be blind, he seems to be staring at us.

"Grace, does that old guy on the bench over there seem to be observing us?"

"Where?" asks Grace.

"On the bench beside the tree."

"I don't see anyone on the bench."

I look back and she's right. He's not there. Is it me? Am I beginning to lose it? Are hallucinations one of the signs of dementia? I change the subject. "So, you're happy with the restaurant so far?"

"It will be fabulous."

"I think so, too. You know, we should come up with a proper name for it. How about Rebecca's Two?"

"Sounds like a movie sequel. I think it needs more thought. Let's go home, Paul."

We return to the car. I pull out to the street, and just as I'm up to speed the traffic light changes, and we wait for the pedestrians to cross. In the group I see the old man poking the pavement with his stick as he passes. He turns his head and stares right at me, like he sees me. I won't say a word to Grace again, but it does seem a little odd—or I am.

"Paul, the light's green."

All the way home Grace is at her best. She describes the furniture she wants to buy for the new place and the food she wants to serve and on and on. When Grace is this happy, I am, too. Whoever said, *if momma's not happy,* nailed it.

—

It's been two weeks now and we just had our first overnight snowfall of the season. It's only an inch, but for Grace looking out the patio door—

"Oh, Paul, come and see how pretty it looks."

"Does it look the same as last year?" I ask as I pour my first coffee of the day.

"Yes, it's spectacular."

"That's disheartening," I say under my breath.

"What was that?"

"I said, let's have a party."

"A party?"

"Sure, to celebrate the first snowfall."

"Who should we invite?"

"Do we have to invite anyone?"

"Oh, you just want me to be a party to your madness."

"Those are the best ones and the most memorable," I say as I snuggle up behind her while she gazes out the door.

She turns to me, opens her robe and wraps it around me along with her body. "I can't argue with that," she says.

Sometimes breakfast has to be put on the back burner or the main course will get cold.

Eventually we were able to add in breakfast and leave the house for Rebecca's.

Even though it's a minor snowfall and business is slow, Grace decides to waitress the few locals we get in for lunch to keep her busy.

I take the helm of washroom duty with a mop, a bucket of soapy water and a hint of bleach added. Next is the hardest part of my day. I slip into the lounge for a beer and some news on the big screen.

"We interrupt this broadcast for this Special News Report. There has been another mass shooting in—"

I can't handle this. I shut off the TV. What the hell is going on in this world? This is why I left the city. I said I'd never involve myself with the media again, and look at me. It's not like I want to bury my head in the sand, but I can't change what's going on out there—all I can do is live my life as best I can and, hopefully, others start doing the same.

Here comes Grace, so I better switch gears and put on my happy face.

"Hey, young fella," she says. "Care to join an old lady for lunch?"

"Old lady? Sure, you know where I could find one?"

"You're right on the money when there's food involved."

We take our favorite window table which Grace prefers, so she can admire the wintery street scene.

"Isn't it beautiful?" she says. "It looks like a scene from Currier and Ives."

"I must admit it gives a warm, cozy feeling." No one would have heard that from me a year ago, but Grace and Willow's End have given me a better outlook on winter—it's almost tolerable. I hardly mind the cold when I look at Grace's happy face.

We enjoy our lunch and conversation about the new restaurant and are about to have a last cup of coffee to end our meal when a patron walks in and startles me—he looks like the old blind man from the park. How did he get here? Bridgeburg is miles away. And most importantly, why is he here?

"Grace, you see the old fella who just came in?"

She looks up from her coffee. "You mean the blind man?"

"What if I told you he's the same guy I saw in the park at Bridgeburg?"

"Isn't it nice he came all this way just to have lunch? This just proves what Tor's research showed, the people in Bridgeburg need a restaurant."

Sure—why do the things I see have to be suspect? "I think you're right, Grace."

"Of course I am. Are you ready to go home now?"

"You're finished for the day?"

"That's it. There's nothing else going on until dinner. The staff can handle that. Did you want to walk or take a snowmobile?"

"The weather report said snow overnight, so it would be nice to have it there for the morning, if we need it."

We get up to leave, and through the corner of my eye I see the old man turn his head my way. I decide to stare back and he immediately looks down at his bowl of soup and crunches in a few crackers. Either he's only partially blind or not at all. Here I go again, falling into the trap. The first thing that hits me is the UWC. I watched a lot of TV when I was a kid, and my ability to create scenarios with a hint of paranoia is world-renowned.

—

It's a quick minute to get home, and at this time of year the fireplace needs constant attention. "I'll go out and grab some wood."

"Good. Bring enough in for the night would you please, Paul."

"I'm on it."

I lift the tarp and pick up a few logs. As I grab the last one I notice a shiny object in the pile. It looks like a cell phone. I drop the logs and pick it up, wondering how it got there and who owns it. Examining it further, I'm stunned. I never thought I'd see the likes of one of these ever again. Right there, at the bottom of the device, the nightmarish, unmistakable—Q4. Must be an upgrade. Right away my mind goes back to last year when I had the Q3. It was a powerhouse. I can't even begin to imagine what capabilities a Q4 would have.

Now comes the paranoia—but for a good reason. The UWC agents are the only ones I know who have these. Why was it left here? Wait a minute. Maybe it does make some sense. Both Ed and his car disappear without a sound, and the only way it could have happened is by implementing one of these. I slip it into my pocket, pick up the logs and head inside.

"I used the bellows to get those coals red-hot for you," Grace says.

"Thanks, sweetheart. That always helps."

After a great dinner, to sit around a blazing fire with a nice brandy and an old classic movie like *Inherit the Wind* is divine. I'm not a religious person, so that kind of debate is right up my alley. Since Spencer Tracy can't compare to Marlon Brando in the looks department, Grace falls asleep in my arms, and soon after my thoughts zoom in on the Q4. It would have to belong to an agent, which completely lies to rest the fairy-tale idea someone is protecting us. So I'm back to square one as Paranoia Paul. But then again, if it were the UWC, why didn't they arrest me or kill me when they had the chance? And why did they dump one of their own in a swamp?

The movie's over and Grace is still out. Even in that state I still find her such a beautiful treasure. I gently pick her up and put her into bed. I'll watch the last of the nightly news and indulge in one more brandy.

"The latest news out of Mexico on this deadly invasion of Super—"

They sure make a lot of noise about a bunch of fleas. I shut the TV off, down the rest of the brandy and head for bed. I hope I can sleep with all these thoughts dancing in my head.

—

It's a new day, a new snowfall, and still old questions with no answers. Should I mention the Q4 to Tor, or keep my cards close to my chest? I've already established that he's on our side, and who knows, he may have some thoughts or insight about it. *What about Grace? You said you weren't going to hide anything from her anymore.* Hmm. Okay, I'll tell her after I talk to Tor. Maybe by then I'll have a clearer picture.

"After you drop me off at Rebecca's, how would you like to take a trip to Bridgeburg? The tables and chairs will be delivered, and I want to make sure they are what we ordered and don't have any defects."

"Sure, I can do that. I don't detect any breakfast smells."

"I thought I'd make it easy this morning." She opens a small cardboard box. "Two-day-old Danish pastries, compliments of Rebecca's, but the coffee's fresh."

"What's this poor, lonely, little bran muffin kicking around in here?"

"That's for the sad little maid you hired."

—

On my way to Bridgeburg I try to relax and not become overloaded with scenarios. Even though winter is not my favorite time, I have to admit, the scenery is breathtaking. I pass a billboard planted in a farmer's field—an advertisement about helping war veterans, and my thoughts whisk back to the day my old man passed away. He had been drinking since breakfast when I arrived at noon. It was a behavior he developed after my mother died. We sat in the living room, him in his recliner and me straight across on the sofa. I heard all the war stories and about all the friends he lost then and since.

For years he would sit in his chair and lift one leg and point his big toe at some object in the room. One day I got brave enough to ask him. "What are you doing with your foot, Dad?"

"Just an old habit from the war. I line up my toe like I would my rifle barrel to shoot one of those Nazi bastards."

I was always hoping at some point I would hear something a father might say to his son, especially when I'm the only child, like how proud he was of me or how much he loved me. Instead, he asked me, *How old am I?*

I said eighty-five. A grin appeared on his face. I hadn't seen one in quite some time. Then he said, *I beat 'em all.* Right after, he raised his leg and pointed his toe around the room and finally rested his aim on me.

A few moments later he collapsed and took his exit while still holding on to his glass of rum. What he meant by *I beat them all,* I'm not sure. Was it his siblings or his war buddies? I'll never know...but the pointed toe—I got.

—

Bridgeburg—the more I see this town the more I like it. Before I get out of the car I pull the Q4 from my pocket and place it in the glove compartment next to the Magnum—like salt and pepper shakers.

As I enter this old house that will soon become a great eating establishment for this community, I can't help but feel a sense of pride. It's not like Rebecca's, having had a great reputation for years. It's brand-new from scratch—bare walls and a dream.

I see Tor standing next to large boxes in one corner of the room with a smile on his face. "Well, what do you think?"

"I'm amazed at the transition already."

"So am I," he says and points to the boxes. "I'm sure these must be the new tables and chairs."

After we checked the contents of boxes, I ask Tor if he has some time to talk. He looks around the room with painters and electricians. "We need some privacy."

We walk out to my car.

"So, what's up?" he asks.

"Have you ever heard of a Q3?"

"Q3? Funny you should mention it. Awhile back when we had our meetings at Rebecca's we broke for lunch, and I decided to take a stroll around the property, and in the back of the building I found what looked like a cell phone, but it was totally different and had Q3 written on it."

"Did you have any idea what it was?"

"I thought it might be some new type of phone."

"Do you still have it?"

"Sure," he says and reaches into his coat pocket. "It's right here. I don't know why I kept it. Looks like some child's toy his mother picked up for him at the supermarket to keep him quiet." He hands it to me. "So, what is it?"

"It doesn't have any power now, but last year it could move mountains."

He looks perplexed. "That little thing?"

"This little thing helped us save Willow's End."

"So why doesn't it work now?"

"Best I can tell, it ran off two huge coils underground and they were destroyed by fracking."

"So it's completely useless?"

"This one is, but I found this other one in my woodpile. This is what I want to talk to you about." I reach over and open the glove box.

Tor sees the Magnum. "You seem to be nicely equipped."

"I try to be." I pull out the Q4. "This is a Q4."

"In your woodpile, but how—"

"That's what I'd like to know. Was it left by some agent, and if so, why? I can't see anyone being so incompetent. It's completely not their style. It doesn't matter how many times we go over this, we just don't have any answers, only more questions. Like who, and why put Ed in the swamp close to your building lots?"

"Because it wasn't them," says Tor.

"Right, then who did it?"

There's a long pause. "How 'bout a beer?" asks Tor.

"I've got something better."

"What's that?"

"The infamous Emporium Supreme. It won't answer our questions, but it will make them easier to talk about."

A huge smile ignites on Tor's face. "I've wanted to try this legendary brew for quite a while. Lead the way."

—

I pull up to the Emporium. We get out of our vehicles and Charlie meets us at the door with his shotgun by his side.

I point to the shotgun. "You plan on using that, Charlie?"

He looks down at the gun. "When I see two vehicles pull up at the same time it makes me edgy. At this time of the year business is pretty sad. I don't expect much buying, so I'm always ready for someone to come in and take advantage of the situation."

"Makes sense." I point to Tor. "You remember Tor?"

"Sure, the Black fella."

Tor looks at me.

"Charlie, we don't consider that polite. It's racist."

"Racist. Now hold on there. Last time you said I should have told you he was Black. Now I say he's Black and I'm back to being a racist. I just don't understand this world anymore." He looks at Tor with firm lips. "Tor, as far as I'm concerned, we're all the same, stuck in this, the inhuman race."

Tor smiles. "Well said, Charlie." Tor reaches out to shake hands and Charlie grabs it and shakes it with vigor.

"So, what can I do for you boys, or do I need to ask?"

"Two large ones, Charlie."

"Is that to go?"

"Two large ones? Hell no. You still have seat belts on those chairs, don't you?"

Charlie laughs. "I'll meet you in the reserve section in the back."

Tor makes a quiet comment heading to the back. "Wow, this place is incredible. Is there anything he doesn't have in here?"

"If there is, I can't imagine what it would be."

As we sit down in the old lawn chairs, fart-like sounds tear through the quiet. Tor laughs, "And entertainment, too."

Charlie drops three mugs of the magic brew on the table and pulls up a chair.

"Okay, Tor, put that mug up to yours and let me know what you think."

Tor takes a sip then pauses and then another. "Wow. Is this legal?"

"The way I see it, who's going to complain?"

"Certainly not me."

"So," says Charlie, looking at me, "last time I heard you had a visit from Houdini."

"Houdini would have been easy to understand, but I'm leaning toward the UWC. They could have used a Q3 or 4."

"Four! I thought the Q3 was a doozie."

"I did, too. But it looks like they've upped it a notch—I found a Q4 in our woodpile at the side of the house."

"So it *was* those bastards," says Charlie.

Tor steps up. "That's what complicates things. Why would they destroy evidence that implicates Paul and Grace, and in the process not arrest them or even question them?"

"And they would never leave a Q4 behind," I add.

"Well, I guess as long as the evidence is gone, it's a done deal," says Charlie.

"Not quite. Adam found the body in a swamp near Tor's cottage lots."

"What the hell? This is starting to feel like two Supremes now. Why would they dump the body there?" asks Charlie.

"That's why we think there is something else at play. Another faction or person involved," says Tor.

"This is getting crazier by the minute," says Charlie. "But it could mean you have someone on your side of the fence." Charlie's eyes narrow. "So what happens with the body now?"

"Don't worry, Charlie. We don't need your help on this one."

"Well, that's a blessing."

"It's a swamp. It will disappear by spring," says Tor.

"Sounds to me like you boys have everything under control. How's the Supreme, Tor?"

"Very exciting, I've never had anything like it. I feel like singing. Is that normal?"

Charlie laughs. "By the time you finish you'll want to join a rock band. Well, maybe one of those soul groups. We had our own Woodstock last year at Rebecca's with those agents, remember, Paul?"

"We sure did—Supremes all the way around."

"Adam told me it went very well. He said it was a sold-out performance," says Tor.

"The kicker was seeing the trailer disappear. In a flash it was gone with all those flower power agents inside," says Charlie.

Tor looks at me. "And what happened to them? You didn't—"

"They were fine. I just sent them a few hundred miles away."

Whenever we get together for some special coffee I can't help feel the emptiness of not having Ben here with us. It must get lonely for Charlie in the off-season without him. They were more like brothers than friends.

"Guess I should head for home. If the timing is right I should meet Grace at the door."

"I think I'll go back to the restaurant and see if they've assembled the tables and chairs," says Tor.

"You boys want one for the road?"

"Charlie, you're too generous. It'll be hard enough to remember where I live."

"I will say," says Tor, "this brew has quite a kick. I hope it doesn't affect my driving."

"Just don't play any Jimi Hendrix," says Charlie.

—

With the brew in my belly and the effects on my brain, I head for home. The window comes down and the cold air slaps my face like a washcloth. Up ahead I see a figure along the roadside. I begin to pass and look through the side window. What! It's the old blind man. What the hell is this? He sure covers a lot of territory for a guy who's supposedly blind. Why does this old man keep popping up? Once again, he stares at me. I'll pull over to see if he needs a lift and possibly find out who he is. As soon as I stop he turns into the forest. I've had enough of this. I back up to where he turned in and he's nowhere to be seen. Does he want to lure me into the bush where agents will do me in? Or is it a slight hallucination from Charlie's coffee? But Grace did see him at the restaurant.

CHAPTER 10

Grace's white wonderland all but melts away with the morning sun and I'm delighted.

"Grace, your snow is gone."

"Oh, no."

I look at her with a straight face. "Yeah, what a shame."

She stares back knowing I'm not sympathetic and waits for me to crack. As hard as it is to keep a straight face, I finally break into a smile and try to hide it with my hand. "I'm sorry, Grace; I'm from the big city. We hate the snow. Traffic jams, sliding all over the place, accidents."

"Understandable, but you are not in the big city now, and where do you think I came from, Mongolia?"

I change tactics. "Actually, I did like the snow at Christmas. It was nice being snowed in and cuddling by the fire." Then other thoughts creep in. "And wondering if we would starve to death waiting for Mike to dig us out."

"You're a humbugger."

"Are you sure you don't mean humdinger?"

"That, too."

"I think I'll put on a jacket and enjoy the morning sun with a coffee. Care to join me?"

"Sounds like a great idea. I'll heat up the muffins I brought back from Rebecca's and meet you out there."

I step outside and my nostrils fill with fresh, cool air with a hint of pine and poplars. I take a sip of steaming coffee. We just need a small, cozy fire to complete the picture.

As I wait for Grace it dawns on me—Rebecca's. Ben gave us the place as a wedding gift, and I haven't held up my end of the bargain, and Grace hasn't mentioned marriage. She's waiting for me. I *am* a humdinger.

Now I have a new priority: marriage. I've got serious planning to do. Did I say plan?

I wonder what's taking Grace so long. She just had to warm those muffins. I'll see what's going on. I could use more coffee anyway.

The muffins are on a plate by the microwave. Where's Grace?

"Grace!"

"I'm at the front door, Paul."

"What's up?"

She turns to me with a package. "This was outside."

"Mail already? He never shows up until noon."

She looks at me with concern. "It wasn't the mailman."

"Who else could it be?"

"I don't know. There's no label or markings on it so it didn't come from the post office."

"It might have been dropped off by mistake. Remember the time we received the case of shrimp labeled for Nebraska?"

"Remember it, how could I forget? It was a scorcher of a day in the middle of August. We had every bear in a fifty-mile range on our doorstep."

"Yeah, I had to wash my clothes twice. Then I buried it out in the bush, and I swear I could still smell it a week later."

"Well, I don't think we have to worry about shrimp in a small, thin package. The only way to find out would be to open it. You don't think it could be a bomb, do you?"

"Before we go there, let's take off the brown paper first. It could be a gift from someone."

She hands it to me. "Here, you do it. I'm too nervous."

"Tell you what. I'll step outside and close the door."

"Be careful, Paul."

I slowly peel away the paper and see it's only a manila envelope. I know people have opened up packages to find ricin inside. Slowly I open it with stretched-out arms and carefully tilt it to see what's inside. It looks like a photograph.

"Did you open it?"

"Yeah, you can come out now."

"What's inside?"

I pull out the picture and we stare at it for a moment. There are three men in the picture with two standing over what looks like a freshly dug grave, while the third holds a shovel.

"Why would someone send us a picture of a gravesite?"

"And who are the three people?" says Grace.

"I don't recognize any of them."

"What if it's a warning?" Oops. I have to nip this in the bud. "It may be as we thought before—someone on our side trying to warn us."

"You warn someone by showing them a grave? This looks like a threat to me, Paul. I think we're in someone's crosshairs."

"Crosshairs, listen to you."

"I've watched a few movies, too, you know."

"But you're right, Grace. Either way, a threat or a warning, it's not the best news we've had. I'm sure if Alex were here with his knowledge of the UWC, he would have been able to tell us more about this picture. Let's go inside, it's getting chilly."

"The best place for this picture is right here." I stick it to the door of the fridge. "This way each time we pass there maybe a new discovery."

"So, you think there's a message in there or a hidden story?"

"I don't think it's hidden. I think we haven't discovered it yet."

"Paul," Grace looks at me with watery eyes, "I don't want it on the fridge. I want it put away. It makes me nervous, and to constantly be reminded of a possible threat doesn't make me comfortable. Our home is the only place we can feel any level of safety and security."

I can't disagree with that. "You're right, Grace." I place it in our junk drawer.

This new event puts a bit of a damper on my marriage plans. No, I won't procrastinate. I'll still move forward, but will have to do it with an extra set of eyes—most likely in the back of my head.

—

For the next couple of days, each time I go by the junk drawer I want to open it and study the picture. But I try to console myself with the fact there is a fifty-fifty chance it's not a threat, and I guess those odds aren't too bad.

The main part of a wedding is the ring, and today I have to find an excuse to leave Grace to hunt for one. I open our mail and thankfully no graveyard pictures, but a little good luck: a notice from the car dealership, there has been a recall on one of my airbags. Now there's the perfect excuse to get out.

"Grace, I'll drop you off at Rebecca's. I have to go to the city to my dealership. There's been a recall, and I have to get a new airbag."

"Can't Mike fix it?"

"Unfortunately, it has to be the dealership."

"Would you be back in time to dig out the small dead tree from the side of the veranda at Rebecca's? You remember, the one I asked you to do last week before the ground freezes."

Damn it. "You sure are a mind reader, exactly what I was going to do."

"Keep an eye on your nose."

"My nose?"

"Don't let it get too long."

Women are so good at this game.

CHAPTER 11

I drop the car at the dealership with my usual reservation—what will they find wrong with the car to squeeze a few bucks from my worn-out wallet? When I bought the car it was all smiles in the showroom, but as soon as I made the leap into the dreaded dark side—the SERVICE DEPARTMENT—it was a different world. There's a hideous smile when I walk in, which has me sitting nervously for a span of ten minutes until a guy in a lab coat comes out of the shop. His face has a look of constipation as he gives me the diagnosis on what I thought was a mere recall issue.

I walk the three blocks to the jewelry store. You can't miss the sign out front, *Reuben's Jewelers—since 1909.* Of course Reuben isn't there anymore, neither is his son, Saul. It will be his grandson, Rodney. That's right, Rodney; there's a misstep there somewhere.

Beyond the malls and box stores, Reuben's is the old-style jewelry store squeezed between other independent proprietors. Inside are long and narrow, scratched glass counters with the expensive stuff on one side and the cheap—mainly costume jewelry—on the other.

The sentinel tinkle of the little bell over the door announces my entry. Rodney is at the far end of the counter with his eyepiece band around his head examining a stone.

"Paul, how the hell are you? Long time no see. Let me guess. You finally found someone and want to lavish her with a very fine necklace."

"Close, but no lox and bagel for you. I'm here for an engagement ring."

"Engagement!" He places the gem on a soft cloth, covers it and rushes over with an outstretched hand. "Well this has to be celebrated. Congratulations. Come with me."

Ever since I received my parents' inheritance and gave Rodney $1,000 for a well-needed charity, we have become good friends. A philanthropist and sometimes comedian is how I see him. They have a word, *Natan*, when spelled backward, is the same; which is to say, *to give* is also *to receive*. Makes sense.

Just before he takes me to the back of the store, the little bell sounds and we both look to see a plainly dressed man in sunglasses. "I'll be with you shortly," says Rodney.

We head to the back and he draws open the curtain where he has a tiny office.

"We need a drink." He pulls out the bottom drawer of a filing cabinet to reveal a bottle of red wine. He places it on his desk then reaches up to a bookshelf and retrieves two glasses.

"It's not Mogen David, is it?"

"Mogen David? No, not that shit, this is Portuguese. It's a good wine for half the price."

"You think like me, Rodney. You may convert me yet."

"I've already converted you. You always come back." He pours two substantial amounts, "Cheers to Paul and—"

"Grace."

"To Paul and Grace, may you have a long and beautiful life with health and many child—"

I clear my throat.

He shakes his head. "A beautiful life with health, wealth, and happiness."

"Now, I'll drink to that."

When we walk back to the front of the store the man is gone.

"Well, he didn't stay too long."

"It happens a lot. They do a bit of window shopping from the inside, and either they don't see what they want or it's too expensive."

Rodney is a gem himself. I walk out with a good-sized rock inside a blue velvet ring box, and a 40 percent discount. It may be less, but it's the thought that counts, and I know for a fact his regular Gentile friends only get 15 percent.

A few more miles to Willow's End, then I must deal with the tree that Grace wants me to take out. What the hell is this? A large tree branch is right in the middle of the road. I stop the car and step out to remove it. I pull it off to the side of the road. Funny, there isn't one tree anywhere near the road.

I FEEL A SEVERE PAIN at the back of my head.

—

My eyes open to a cloud-filled sky and a bad headache. I slowly get to my feet and find myself in a ditch, only a few feet away from my car. The back of my head is sore. With my fingers, I feel the area and discover a substantial goose egg and a little blood on my fingertips. I had the same treatment from the agent in the Nova last year; must be standard procedure around here.

I get back into the car and check the time, and I've lost fifteen minutes. I continue home with more questions added to my over-extended laundry list—who hit me and why?

At least Grace will be happy when I show her the ring. I reach over and open the glove box to retrieve it. It's gone! Shit! Bastard! How the hell did he know I had—. The guy with the sunglasses who came into the store. Sure, and the tree branch across the road. I can't do the knee drop without the ring.

—

I make it back to Rebecca's, and I'm so angry by the time I get there that I don't bother using the shovel on the tree and just pull the damn thing out with my bare hands. Walking into Rebecca's I try to compose myself. Better she doesn't see me in this state.

She's in the office shuffling papers. "Oh," she says, "you're back. How's the new airbag?"

"Hopefully, I will never have to find out."

"Are you okay?"

Here she goes. "Me? Absolutely." She's the one who could detect a fart in a windstorm.

I stare at her working away and think how I could have brightened her day with a proposal and the ring.

She looks up at me. "What is it, Paul?"

"Just taking in your beauty and how grateful I am to have you in my life."

She wheels her chair around to me. "Come here," she says, then pulls me close and puts her arms around my waist and rests her face on my stomach. "And you mean the world to me." She looks up at me with concern. "Are you sure you're all right? You seem a little solemn."

Boy, can she read me. I have to be careful now. "One of those heart moments, when I feel so much love for you, I can't let it go." Grace can extract things out of me like a dentist on a molar. I can't cave and tell her about the ring and have us both feel bad on a day that is supposed to be the highlight of our lives.

"Thank you for saying that, Paul. And as we use to say when we were younger, ditto."

"I'm going home now to make us a beautiful dinner."

"Boy, you really do love me. What were you planning on making?"

I kiss her on the forehead. "It's a surprise. See you when you get home."

It will be a surprise to me, too.

—

One of the few dishes I know how to make is lasagna, and we have all the ingredients at home. First is a stop at the liquor store. Pasta means red wine, and I think this calls for two bottles. We will end the evening with...no, not prosecco. It will have to be a nice bottle of champagne. Okay, the hard work is done. Oh, and a nice bouquet of roses from the flower shop.

I have three and a half hours to get this done before Grace gets home, but the anxiety I have reverts back to the ring. I slide the bottles of wine along the island and hear something fall to the floor on the other side. I walk around and I'm dumbstruck. I rub my eyes in disbelief, for there at my feet rests the ring box. How is this possible? I take my time bending over to pick it up as though it were a bomb to go off in my face. I place it on the counter and pause. I'm almost ready to spew out a little prayer to St. Anthony, the finder of all things, but it would put me in the hypocrite column. I open the box like I would open my hand in a poker game. Slowly...slowly—"It's there! I'm back in the game!"

Then I have a knee-jerk reaction, how is this possible? Who got in here? Then the imminent question is, are they still here?

I pick up a knife from the counter and think, would I use it? I don't know, but it feels right to have it with me. Through the house like a madman I go, even checking under the beds, and do a little *Psycho,* raising the knife as I check behind the shower curtain —free and clear.

As I rewind the memory tape I realize the door wasn't locked when I entered. We've let our guard down. So who brought it back? I'm so damn excited about it I can't entertain the thought right now. I have an engagement dinner to prepare and practice my knee bend.

I made it. The dinner's ready; and with a few minutes before Grace arrives, I bring out the card table, throw a white tablecloth over top, set it up just like Rebecca's, and even complete the picture with garlic bread. She should be here any minute.

I crack open the front door and there she is up the road. I grab a white tea towel and place it across my forearm and stand at attention by the door.

"It's getting colder out there," she says, taking off her coat. "I bet we'll see more snow by morning." She finally looks up. "Oh, my gosh," she chuckles. "What is *this?*"

"May I take your wrap, Miss Grace?" I take her coat and throw it over a chair. "Your table has been reserved. Right this way, please."

I pull out her chair and she sits to a completely set table with softly glowing candlelight.

"Did you make a stop at Charlie's today?"

"And still arrange this? I don't think so."

"Paul, this is so nice of you to do this. What's the special occasion?"

Oops! "I want to show you how much I love you."

"Well, you sure have."

"I hope you still feel the same after the lasagna."

"I already know it will be fabulous."

"With garlic bread and red wine, too."

"Now there's the clincher."

Grace was her gracious self. She said the lasagna was exactly how she likes it, even though I felt it was a little overbaked. How can I not love this woman?

We finish with a cappuccino, and now my throat becomes dry, my palms are wet and I'm sure my face is slightly pale.

"Paul, are you all right?"

"Couldn't be better, but I do have a little business to discuss with you that I've put off far too long." I pull my chair close to hers.

"Oh, like what?"

I hold her hand. "There's a special occasion we have to plan."

"What special occasion?"

I feel as awkward as Barney Fife. "A wedding."

"Wedding?" She jumps to her feet. "Whose wedding? Has someone reserved Rebecca's for a reception and you didn't tell me! When is it? How long do I have? Please, don't tell me it's on Christmas!"

She's not getting it.

"No, it's not on Christmas. I'm thinking June."

"You're thinking June? They haven't given you a date yet?"

"No. He hasn't asked her yet."

"What! That's taking a lot for granted, don't you think?"

"On the contrary, he's very nervous about asking her."

"Well, I would tell him to pull up his socks and go for it. A woman likes a strong man with conviction."

There's my opening. I grab her and pull her close. Then pull the boxed ring from my pocket and conceal it in my hand.

"Grace." I look deeply into her eyes. "Will you marry me?"

She looks at me with a tilted head and an expression of uncertainty. And then—

"That's it. Exactly how he should do it. But he should get down on one knee."

I assume the position and repeat the question.

"Perfect," she says.

"Not quite." I open my hand, exposing the box, and with all the bright Christmas lights all around the room, the diamond sparkles like the star over Bethlehem that even has me in awe.

Grace's eyes explode the size of silver dollars. Her bottom jaw drops and her eyes look into mine.

"Paul, is this—are you—"

I can feel my mouth stretch from ear to ear. "I am."

She reaches down and pulls me in close. Her bottom lip begins to quiver as she wraps her arms around me and holds me so very tight. Her body begins to jerk as she sobs. I pull her back just far enough to see her face.

"Grace, are you crying?"

"Of course I am. This is the happiest moment of my life," she says and cuddles into my shoulder. "Paul, are you sure of this? I mean, this is what I want."

"I've never been so sure in all my life."

I race over to the fridge, open the door and scramble through the food containers to the back and pull out a bottle of Krug Grande Cuvée that I had hid, and raise it in the air. "And now the celebration begins!"

"Oh my god, it's so expensive."

"Not for my girl. This is just the beginning, Grace. Whatever the rest of our lives has in store for us, we'll be doing it with a bang! How would you like to go to Europe on our honeymoon?"

"Oh my god, is that something we can do?"

"Absolutely, and once we get Ben's Place off the ground, we are gone."

"So when and where will the wedding be?"

"How does the first Saturday in June at Rebecca's sound? It's the first time we met."

"You're so romantic."

"The flowers will be in full bloom, the perfect atmosphere for creating a new beginning in our lives, or at least another chapter. And we'll do it up right. We'll fill the dining room with all kinds of flowers and invite all of our friends." I'm giddy.

"I'll do the menu. Oh Paul, it will be wonderful."

"Like I said, it will take some planning."

"I'm so excited."

"Me too. And of course there's the honeymoon."

"Yes, Europe. And you're sure about this?"

"I'll tell you one thing, it won't be Mexico."

Grace was like a schoolgirl, and me, I don't know what I was, but I know where I was—cloud nine and climbing. It took us until two in the morning to finally settle down. Between the wine and the lasagna, we finally called it a night and slept like babies.

The sun is up and we are still flying high, and neither one of us wants any more than coffee and conversation about the wedding. Grace moves the conversation about the wedding to the honeymoon. Somewhere in there I think of how I got the ring back. What was the purpose? Knocking me out, taking the ring and then not just giving it back, but coming right into the house? Of course it doesn't make sense. Someone got to the thief and brought the ring back. Why? Because someone *is* on our side.

"How do you want your eggs, Paul?" says Grace, cracking a couple into the pan.

"Sunny-side, just like you." I kiss the side of her neck.

"Don't make any more moves or they'll end up scrambled."

"Okay, I'm out of here."

I turn on the TV and flick channels until I come to a news report, which I would never have done two years ago. After a while it becomes an addiction or obsession.

"—and the deadly surge of super mites is now within reach of the U.S.-Mexican border. So far there have been no reports they have entered the U.S., but moments ago the President ordered stepped-up security at all border crossings to and from Mexico. The Mexican government denies any knowledge of the existence of the mites and claims the American government is trying to prevent any Mexican citizen from entering the United States."

"Did you hear that, Grace? Those fowl mites are at the southern U.S. border."

Grace comes with the coffee pot and gives me a refill.

"It's worrisome. But what about the part where the Mexican government denies it?"

"Governments are the last to admit they have a problem in their country. It's always bad for tourism, and that means money. Grace, don't you remember the mad cow disease in Britain? They tried to keep the information suppressed as long as they could."

"I guess we have to choose one government over the other. Knowing our government, especially with this new president, who do we choose to believe?"

"I guess we consider it a draw, fifty/fifty."

"That's not much help. Okay, I'll go with the Mexicans."

"And your reason is—"

"They beat us at the Alamo."

"What?"

"I'm just teasing. It sounds very serious. If it's true, I just hope it doesn't bleed to our side."

"Right, because we have important items to address."

"Like a new restaurant, a wedding, and a simply wonderful honeymoon."

"June can't come soon enough."

The weather report called for snow, and I have certainly found out how unpredictable the weather can be up here. It could be an inch or a couple of feet.

I tell Grace I'll take a trip to our new establishment to check out the situation and I should be back at Rebecca's for lunch. She leaves me with one thought as she gets out of the car.

"Remember, we're supposed to get snow today. Are you sure you want to go?"

"No problem. I had Mike put the winter tires on last week. I have 'snows to go.'" At least I didn't procrastinate and wait until February this year.

CHAPTER 12

Almost to the town of Bridgeburg, I become aware of small tree branches blowing past the front of the car. The sky ahead becomes dark and ominous. A sign alerts me, only five miles to Bridgeburg, and I feel confident I'll at least make it there.

One minute later, like taking a dip in the ocean, and when you pop up out of the water you see a tsunami headed your way, and all you can muster is *holy shit!* Only this one is a huge wall of white right in front of me. I don't know why I have this instinct to hold my breath, and as I do, these tiny, unassuming white flakes engulf my car like a swarm of killer bees. The loud, intense sound swirls around my ears like a Hoover attached to a Leslie speaker.

It's a dry snow, and at this point the wipers are useless as the flakes just blow right off the car. The landscape and the road disappear. I try to see through it only to be hypnotized. When it's this bad the only recourse is to pull over, if you can.

But the question is, how far over? Will I land in a ditch? These country ditches are more like gullies—they could be three feet deep. Another scary thought, what if there is someone just ahead of me who has done the same and I slam into them or someone driving behind me? I turn on my four-ways and gingerly pull off to what I hope is the shoulder of the road and not the infamous ditch.

Good. I've made it. Now what? I reflect on the warning from Grace, *Remember, we're supposed to get snow today. Are you sure you want to go?* Of course, I'm just so smart. I'll be fine. I'm prepared. I've got snow tires and they don't do a damn thing in a blizzard. I want to hit myself over the head with a tire iron.

The only way to prepare for this is to have at least two extra layers of clothing, a blanket, matches, an abundance of candles and a Bible, if you're so inclined, of which I'm not. I lean more toward my old heat warmer in a bottle that I don't have. The best advice is to listen to your better half in the first place—they aren't called *better* for nothing.

The next item is to turn on the local radio station for the weather to get some indication of how long I may be here.

"And the latest books to be banned... The Great Gatsby, The Catcher in the Rye, The Grapes of Wrath, and The Color Purple."

Banning the classics that have been read around the world for years—what's next, *Alice in Wonderland?*

"Looks like I missed one, folks—believe it or not, Alice in Wonderland."

"Have they all gone insane?"

"Now your local weather forecast. As the storm moves east we can expect about a foot and a half of snow with three-foot drifts. At times visibility will be zero. So please, stay home, and for those on the road find a safe place to park, and I'm afraid you may have to wait it out, which could be early evening."

Do I need to hear more? I shut the radio off to save the battery, and I have to let Grace know. I reach into my jacket pocket and take out my cell phone. Before I dial the number I suddenly feel sick—I have no charge. It's dead! There's the procrastination again. I knew it had a low charge last night.

I do have a collapsible shovel in the trunk, but it's absolutely useless in a storm. Another shovel enters the picture—the dreaded snowplow. If it comes by it could cover the car enough I wouldn't be able to get out. It could take a day for me to get out, unless I suffocate in the meantime. Worst scenario—my calculation is wrong and I'm still on the road and I get plowed into the ditch.

I check my gas gauge and it's down to half. It will keep me warm for a while, but after that—I'll have to shut it down and wait for my ears to fall off. The extremities go first. Oh shit! All I need is snow to plug up my exhaust pipe and I become a memory.

Panic steps in with shallow, rapid breathing. To add to my anxiety I recall the Storm of '77. It was paralyzing. Pictures in the paper showed cars being buried, and when they eventually pulled them out, there were other cars beneath them.

The cold is starting to settle into my bones, and in the distance I hear the sound of a snowmobile. Why the hell would anyone be out in this? It's getting closer and I can just make out a hooded figure approach my side window. Then—a blast of light.

—

What happened? For some reason I blanked out. I'm still in my car, but the snow has stopped. Have I been out here all night? I look outside and at first glance I'm disoriented, but then something shocking: I am parked in front of Rebecca's. Oh no! Is this some sort of relapse from the pink shit that was given to me last year, or was this done with a Q3 or 4?

The dash clock reads 11:55. Does this mean I made it back for lunch? I get out and see there is only about an inch of snow cover on the ground. I walk up the porch steps and hope when I get to the dining room Grace will be there and all is normal.

There she is serving a couple. She looks up and sees me.

"You made it. I was beginning to worry. I heard it was quite nasty in that neck of the woods and thought you might have had to stay there overnight. We just had a dusting here. I did say maybe you shouldn't go."

Yep—it's all normal. "I saw how bad it was and decided to turn back."

"Wise choice. Would you like to start with a coffee or a beer?"

"How about a coffee and a scotch?"

She laughs. "One to wake you up; one to put you to sleep."

That brings back a flash of Ben when I was in his small, but cozy house adjacent to his store and he asked me if I wanted a shot along with my coffee. I responded with, I need something to wake me up, not put me to sleep. He laughed and said, what's the matter with you? They cancel each other out. Ah Ben, you're never far away.

I gaze out to the street and see my car parked there and replay those last few minutes of the storm to understand what happened. I remember the sound of a snowmobile and a hooded figure at my window, but that's about the extent of it.

Here comes Grace with two plates.

"I thought I would join you. Brought you one of your favorites, toasted western with a dill and ketchup on the side and, of course, I love my grilled cheese."

She sits down and then stares at me for a moment. "You look troubled, Paul. You're not getting cold feet about the wedding, are you?"

I have to smile. "The only cold feet I would have would be due to poor circulation."

She smiles. "That certainly isn't your problem." Her face turns serious. She reaches across the table and holds my hand. "Then, what is it?"

"Grace, I didn't make it back, at least not on my own."

"Now that's a little vague and confusing."

"For me, too. I got stuck in the storm and had to pull over. I was all set to call you but my phone died, and I thought I would, too. Then a strange thing happened. I heard a snowmobile pull up beside me. I couldn't believe it. How could anyone be out there? I couldn't see the hood of the car. All I could make out was someone with a hood over their head and scarf wrapped around their face beside my window. Right after that a blinding light hit my eyes and I must have passed out. I woke up in my car in front of Rebecca's, and then you saw me walk in."

She sips her coffee then states, "This sounds awfully familiar."

"I had the same thought, a Q4. It adds to the mystery as to why the UWC is not only leaving me alone, but is actually helping me. I could have easily died out there."

"I find it hard to believe they would be helping you. How would they even know you were there?"

"I could do with another shot."

"Why don't you have some of your coffee first, you know, for balance."

I take a sip then add, "There's one more item I haven't mentioned to you, Grace. Remember the old blind fella we saw in Bridgeburg?"

"You saw him, I didn't."

"Okay, but you do remember him at Rebecca's?"

"Of course, I remember. Now don't tell me you think he had a hand in saving you?"

"I don't think so, but it's strange. Both in Bridgeburg and at Rebecca's he seemed to acknowledge me as though he wasn't blind."

"You do have a tendency to make up some strange scenarios at times."

"I'd call them hunches."

"I'd call them guesses."

"And what do you call it when *you* have a hunch?"

She smiles. "Intuition."

"Hmm, I forgot about that one. No one could have zapped me back here unless they had that little tool. I remember Charlie saying that it could mean I have someone on my side of the fence, like an ex-agent or a person with a grudge against the UWC."

"Now that I'll believe," adds Grace.

There's a quiet moment. "I'll go back to the restaurant tomorrow. The roads should be clear by then."

"Wish I could go with you, but I have a big order coming in and I should be here. By the way, make sure your phone is charged."

"I will, and to be on the safe side, I'll see if I can pick up a charger for the car."

"That's my boy."

—

The roads are clear, salted and sanded. One thing I can say about the North, they plow immediately after the snow falls. Not like the city, where you could wait a couple of days to get your street done, and only if you're on their designated route.

Here we are in Bridgeburg. The main street and sidewalks have been plowed and shoveled. I park and walk a few car lengths to the restaurant. Each time I come to this town there is a sense of community and that what we are doing is right.

As I reach the front door I'm stopped cold. There's splattered red paint on it with the words, *WHITES ONLY.* "What the hell—?"

I thought this was the North, not the South. Then it hits me. Some racist has seen Tor and found out he has a vested interest in the place. I never imagined that I would see the ugly head of racism seep through the fabric of this town. Now I feel deflated. What I don't understand is the people of this town seem so friendly and excited about a nice family restaurant here and have been very excepting of Tor.

"Excuse me."

I turn to see a short, older man beside me with a bucket of soapy water and a brush.

"Don't let that bother you," he says. "This doesn't represent our town. It comes from an outside source. If you'll allow me, I'll get rid of it. I think it was put there sometime during the night, and hardly anyone has seen it yet."

"Well, thank you. I was really starting to have a change of heart about Bridgeburg." I hold out my hand. "I'm Paul."

"Gus, Gus Ferguson. Nice to meet you, Paul." We shake hands. "From time to time we get some backwoods boys who aren't happy with change and try to disrupt the atmosphere of the town. It's times like this that I wish I could hide my whiteness."

"I know what you mean, Gus. People think that progress means financial, when the reality is that humanity comes first, and sometimes it's one step forward and two back."

"It sure seems that way, but as soon as you open your doors, my wife and I will be your first customers, and I expect to see your wife and the other owner here, too."

"Actually, we just got engaged."

"Now there's another good reason to celebrate."

"I appreciate you doing this, Gus."

"Don't give it another thought. I have one request, though."

"And what would that be?"

"I'd like a table by the front window."

I smile. "I'll have a reserved sign on it."

I unlock the door, walk in, and the place looks great, it hasn't been trashed. Just a couple of items to hook up in the kitchen and we are good to go, except for staff and to come up with the name, which I think I have. All I need is Grace's approval. I've already been calling it Ben's Place.

On my way out Gus's handiwork is done.

"There you go, Paul, just like nothing happened."

"That's great, Gus. Thanks so much."

"By the way, I own that little secondhand store right across the street. I'll keep an eye open for any more mischief. If you have a business card, I can call you right off."

"Business cards is one more item I have to add to the list. I'll write it down for you. Do you have a piece of paper?"

Gus reaches into his wallet and hands me a business card.

"Here, put it on the back of my card."

"This is very nice of you, Gus."

He hands me a second card. "Just in case you have a need to shop my store. Community, you know. We take care of our own."

Hearing those words brings back Ben's voice once more. It echoes those exact words, and a warm, emotional feeling washes over me. I can't help but think Gus is also a man of his word.

Gus has reassured me that Bridgeburg will serve us well, as we will serve it. I'm hoping the racism is what he says, just an isolated case. I don't think that Tor, being a silent partner, will escalate the problem. His physical presence will be limited due to his other duties, and I have no doubt he can take care of himself, if need be. Besides, it isn't likely that anyone knows he's a partner, they just saw him go in and out of the building.

—

Always a welcome sight are the billows of smoke rising from the chimney, informing me that Grace is home.

I find her asleep on the couch, and it allows me a rare moment to focus on her beauty without her feeling self-conscious. She's so beautiful. I don't know how I lived all these years without her and, I guess, in a way I didn't.

There is one little spot somewhere on the floor by the entrance to the living room that creeks when you step on it—I found it.

"Oh, you're home," says Grace, sitting up and pushing her hair from her face as she shuffles over for me.

"Do you know how much I love you?"

She smiles and pinches two fingers together. "This much?"

"That's one hair on your head, what about the rest?"

Neil D. Burton

She reaches out and puts her arms around me. "Come here, my handsome man," then kisses me.

"So, how's our new restaurant?"

Shit, the racism part. Think fast. Do I leave it out? She only asked about the restaurant.

"It looks fabulous. All we need now are employees."

"And a huge sign with a name," she says.

"I''m glad you brought that up. I think I have one. I hope you like it."

"Okay, lay it on me."

"Ben's Place."

"Ben's Place—I never thought of that, but it's perfect, Paul. He gave us Rebecca's, and this is sort of a payback and it honors his memory."

"That's what I thought."

"You're so smart and sensitive, too. That's why I love you so much." For that one I receive a peck on the cheek.

"Now we can order the sign. You don't think Tor would have a problem with that, do you?"

"Tor?"

If there is, I hope that's his only problem. "I don't think so. Besides, it's two-to-one on the vote."

—

Another beautiful start to the day, but that can change with a stir of your coffee.

"Grace, I can drop you off at Rebecca's."

"And where would you be headed on this delightful morning?"

"I'm going back to Bridgeburg. They have a sign shop just outside of town. I'll see if they can come up with a few designs and give us some quotes."

"That's an excellent idea. Did you want to meet me at Rebecca's for lunch?"

—

No sooner do I hit the highway than I get a call from Tor. He's about to leave for the new restaurant to see the latest developments and wants to know if I could meet him there.

"There's a sign shop close to town, after I see them for a few quotes I'll meet you at the restaurant."

For being out in the boonies I am more than surprised with the sign shop. The quality and creative talent of their work is top-notch. They give me a couple of reasonable quotes and will have their artist do a few designs. Before I get into my car I get another phone call from Gus, but since I'll be there in five minutes I don't bother answering.

CHAPTER 13

Pulling up to the restaurant I spot Tor's rental just ahead. I walk up the restaurant stairs and notice Tor has left his keys in the door, and that's not something he would do.

"I tried to get you on the phone, Paul."

I turn to see a worried-looking Gus. "What is it?"

"Just as Tor was about to go in, two men came up behind him. They talked for a minute and then they escorted him to their car. At first I thought they were businessmen that he knew. Then I noticed how stiff he looked, as if he was hesitant to go along. It's possible they had a gun because I don't think a big man like him would go otherwise. He was sandwiched between them in the back seat while a third man drove off. Sorry, Paul, it happened so fast."

"You didn't happen to get the license plate, did you?"

He pulls out a folded sheet of paper from his shirt pocket. "I have it all written down here. The license plate number, make and model, and a somewhat foggy description of those bastards; the eyes and mind don't work together as well as they used to. They headed east out of town, then made a left turn north on Derby Road."

"Boy, you sure covered all the bases, Gus."

"Community, Paul."

I jump back into the car, and with a short squeal from the tires, take off for Derby Road. My hands shake and sweat from my forehead is now an issue for my eyes. My heart pumps faster than the cylinders under the hood. I'm starting to feel queasy. What the hell am I doing? I'm no superhero. I must be insane. *Take it easy, Paul. You can do this. Think it through. Put a plan together.* Not the plan thing again. I do have the Magnum in the glove compartment, but do I have the guts to use it? I did shoot Rigby. I did have the balls to do that; but it was him or me.

There it is, Derby Road. That sick feeling in my gut intensifies and tightens like a vice. I pull over and check the paper that Gus gave me—a big, white older-model Cadillac. I grab the Magnum and rest it on the seat beside me.

Thanks to Gus, I find the Caddy parked at a house about four farms in. Now what? I'll knock on the door and say I'm a salesman. No, I'm lost and need directions. That's the one. It's a typical country driveway that seems like a mile from the house and, of course, only one lane. If I have to leave in a hurry, my backup skills at 50 miles an hour may be hazardous to my health. I should drive slowly, as if I have no idea what's going on.

Reaching the house I make one good move. There's just enough room to swing the car around to make a quick exit. I grab the Magnum and slip it into the deep pocket of my winter coat, then nervously walk up to the door. I knock with my left hand while I grip the gun with my right. I wait, but for how long? I knock harder. The longer I wait the more chance that I may be too late. Guess I'll do the old movie bit and kick it in. Raising my leg I give it the hardest boot I can. Shit, that felt like my ankle went up to my kneecap. In desperation I grab the doorknob and turn it, only to discover it wasn't locked; Barney Fife at your service.

Pushing the door enough for it to open on its own, I can see part of a leg on the floor. I pull out the Magnum and cautiously walk in. What I notice first is the leg isn't attached to anyone! Passing out is not an option. I can see skin above the sock line of the leg, and it's white. That's a relief. I force myself into the room and see what might have been the three men, and it ain't pretty. I feel the cookies coming up. It looks like they swallowed hand grenades, with body parts splattered on the walls and hanging flesh on a light fixture. Puddles of blood are everywhere. I take each step with care so I don't slip and fall. The last time I saw a mess like this was when Ben zapped Wagner with the Q3.

And where's Tor?

"Tor! Tor, are you here?" I hear shuffling on the other side of a door. My whole body tightens as I grip the doorknob. I turn it and pull. My eyes squint under the pressure, expecting to see a similar fate for Tor.

There he is, sitting upright in a chair. His face isn't as bad as Rocky after the first fight, but bad enough.

"Tor, are you all right?"

He slowly lifts his head. "Not bad."

Not bad? I'd be crying, moaning and groaning. I untie him and help him to his feet.

"I thought they would be coming back to do me in. I heard a lot of noise and screaming out there earlier," he says. "Then it all went silent."

"There's a reason for that. You won't have to worry about them anymore. Come and have a look."

"What the hell? Looks like a bomb went off. I sure underestimated you, Paul."

"Me? Eating a truckload of spinach couldn't bring me to this. I think it was the work of a Q4. Let's get the hell out of here before the neighbors or the cops show up, or even worse, more agents."

Tor is a tough nut. He walks to the car like nothing happened. "If I didn't have a couple guns in my ribs, this would never have happened. They'd still be dead, but at least there would be enough left to box them."

My tires spit gravel as we head down the driveway to the main road into town. Tor seems more at ease than I am.

"At first I thought it was racial, but then they asked me why I was doing business with you and how long I had known you."

"They didn't ask about Ed?"

"They only asked if he was still in my employment. I said he quit and I never heard from him again."

"I guess they're not as smart as we thought."

"Don't be too sure. I think they left the room to consider another strategy. Moments later I heard all the screams."

At that moment I notice the back of a figure by the road. Passing, I look into my rearview mirror and can't believe it. It's the old blind man.

I slam on the brakes.

"What's the matter?" asks Tor.

"It's that old man!"

"What?"

I jump out and run to the back of the car—he's gone.

"What's that all about?"

"Did you see that old blind man?"

"I saw someone, but didn't notice what he looked like. So why the interest in some old blind guy?"

"Because I think he's interested in me."

"What interest would he have with you, if he can't see you?"

"I don't know." Tor must think I'm losing it. "Never mind; it's probably all this murder and blood is taking its toll on me."

"Now, that I understand."

"By the way, how are you feeling now?"

He smiles. "Better than you, if that eases your mind."

—

Back in town I park across the street from Ben's Place. Ben's Place—I like it more each time I say it. I should mention the name to Tor and see how he feels about it.

"Ben's Place. I like it. It's short, which makes it easy to remember, and it has a rugged country feel."

"That sign shop I mentioned does great work. They're going to do up a couple designs for us."

"Good job, Paul. I can't wait to see it out front."

"So you have no problem as a partner after what just happened?"

"No, I would just like to know why."

"From what Gus told me, it isn't any different than Willow's End. Once in a while, like any other town, you may get one or two that just like to go against the grain for the attention."

"So it may not have anything to do with me or the restaurant?"

"That would be my understanding, and since the problem has been eliminated—"

"We're back on track."

I hope.

—

I decide not to mention the incident to Grace. I know, I know, I promised not to hold back, but I just can't throw that at her now.

I turn the TV on low to watch the morning news, so Grace doesn't hear it from the bedroom. I thought this massacre at the farmhouse would be all over the news, but not a word. I decide to call Gus, but leave out the gory details, and that's when I find out why.

"I saw a black Hummer and a couple of trucks ramble through town headed in the direction of that farm," he says.

Bad news travels fast when you're the UWC. Since that question has been answered, the next one is always the same: Why are they on us again? Or is it Tor they're after for killing Ed? That seems logical. Logical—when have I used that word in the last year? Wait a minute. If that mess at the farm were the agents, then who zapped them?

This is all we need right now while with Ben's Place underway. Everything is bunching up and I can't figure out how to unravel it. Hold on, maybe there isn't a need to get my shorts in a knot. So far all that's happened has been fixed or altered and it has benefited me, except for Tor. He was roughed up, but someone stepped up on his behalf, too. That could mean anyone who is affiliated with me is also protected. How else can I explain it? And who it may be might not be as important as knowing I was being protected. I feel better already.

I leave the couch for my second cup of coffee. I check the photo in the drawer that appeared on our doorstep. Three men stand by a gravesite—it makes no sense to me. I pull it out, grab my coffee, and back to the couch to study it further. Three men and a shovel sounds like a movie. And the shovel is there because...it's a newly dug grave. Okay, so why only three people for this burial? Is it because the person had no friends, or was it something sinister—like a cover-up? There's more to this, I'm sure.

Grace enters from the bedroom.

"You see something in that photo?"

"Not really. But I don't think it was given to us by mistake."

"And your reason is—"

"I don't know. What if there are clues that we are supposed to figure out?"

"You mean like the Hardy Boys?"

"I loved those guys."

"Paul, this sounds more like your adolescent fantasies playing out, and I'm left with Nancy Drew."

"I'm serious, Grace. It could be the connection to all that's been going on. We just haven't been able to piece it together yet."

"Or, we could simplify it and go back to the original theory."

"Which was?"

"It's a death threat."

"Is there any more of that bottle left in the cupboard?"

"It's a little early for that, isn't it?"

"Just a little for my coffee."

Grace raises the bottle to the light. "There's half a bottle left."

"That should do it."

"What happened to balance?"

"Being a Libra doesn't mean I can't tip the scales from time to time."

—

Here we are, outside of Ben's Place just one day before we have our grand opening. Even though Ben is a memory and a great one, I think having named the restaurant after him makes me feel that even in death he continues to give to the community. Tor was great with the advertising, even though it didn't need much. In a small town good news travels almost as fast as bad rumors, and tomorrow we will see the results, and hopefully it worked.

Of all the commercial signs on the main street of Bridgeburg, the one that stands out is, clearly, Ben's Place. It rests on the roof surrounded by twinkling lights. A little Las Vegas perhaps, but it's a wake-up call to the town saying, *we're here!*

Grace looks up at the sign. "That is a beautiful sign! It makes you feel proud, doesn't it?"

"Sure does. I think Ben is smiling, too."

I open the door and there, like an oak, stands Tor.

"Good afternoon and welcome to Ben's Place. Seating for two?"

We chuckle. "I see you'll be wearing a number of hats in this place."

"No thanks, Paul. Besides, no one wants to see a Black man of my stature greeting them at the door. A little intimidating, don't you think? We have a nice, unthreatening pretty girl for this job."

I turn to Grace. "You didn't tell me you were going to be the hostess."

"Thanks for the compliment, but been there, done that."

After our meeting with the staff, a small celebration begins. Everyone wants this venture to succeed. For the most part Tor's job is done, and he can go back to his real estate and will only be needed for our once-a-month catch-up meetings.

"I won't be here for the opening at breakfast," says Tor. "But I will be here for dinner. And it won't be freebie, either, full price."

"And don't forget the tip."

If this goes as planned, tomorrow will be a long and hectic day. From the three owners, right down to the dishwashers, we all share the same nervous excitement.

The staff is well prepared, and who would know that better than Grace. We will be right in the mix for what we anticipate as a large breakfast crowd. Our adrenaline should keep us upright and moving. And hopefully a great day will be had by all—especially the clientele.

—

Up before the crack of dawn is Grace's forte. For me, I sit in the passenger's seat with my eyes closed and my half-filled coffee cup wedged between my legs.

"Paul, we'll be there in five minutes, will you be okay?"

"Absolutely," I say with conviction.

"How about sipping your coffee and allow those eyes to come to the surface?"

I think the first step is to raise my eyebrows and hope the eyelids follow. Ah, there we are.

"That's better. Now finish up your coffee and be prepared to have another one when we get there."

Boy, she's tough. I can feel her owner energy already. If anyone can make a go of this place, it's Grace. I hope I don't get fired.

"Paul, look, it's snow. That will add some color to the atmosphere."

Wonderful. "By the way, Grace, snow is white. It's a tint, not a color."

"Well excuse me, Mister Humbugger."

I knew the art class I flunked in high school would come in handy.

—

Once again, she's right. With all the Christmas lights and decorations on all the lampposts and store windows along the main street, the gentle snowfall adds a magical backdrop to the first day of December.

We leave the car and can't believe our eyes. Six car lengths from the restaurant and we're passing people lined up to get in.

"Isn't this exciting?" says Grace.

"What a great response. It looks like the whole town has showed up."

"All we need is Jimmy Stewart," says an exuberant Grace.

Up the steps to the front door, and the one thing that isn't a surprise is Gus at the head of the line.

"Good morning, Gus. It's great to see you here."

"I wouldn't miss this for anything, Paul. The most excitement our town has had in the last twenty-five years." He looks at Grace. "Is this your lovely wife?"

"Soon-to-be; this is the lovely Grace."

"It's a pleasure to meet you, Gus. Paul has told me you're the hub of Bridgeburg."

"I would say more like a cog, but I'll take hub until further notice." He turns to his wife. "And this is my honey, Vera."

"This is so exciting. We can't wait to see the inside," says Vera.

I lean over to Gus's ear. "Eat all you can handle, Gus, this one's on me."

I check my watch then turn to the line of enthusiastic patrons. "Five minutes, folks, and we'll be open."

The patrons respond with applause and cheers while we head for the warmth inside.

"Grace, can you bring out the kitchen staff and I'll say a few words?" She beelines it to the kitchen while I take a head count of our dining staff.

Grace re-enters the dining room with the kitchen staff in tow and takes her rightful place beside me.

"Grace and I would like to take this opportunity to thank you all for the hard work you've done to bring Ben's Place to this point. You are the best people anyone could have."

Grace adds, "All your friends and neighbors are waiting outside, and we want them to feel like this is their second home. A family place for them as well as us."

They erupt with applause and smiles.

"Now, let's get this show on the road," I urge.

They scatter like field mice.

Bees couldn't have been busier, but no one seemed to mind. We were all caught up in the excitement, and our adrenaline was through the roof. I've never seen Grace happier.

By two o'clock the patrons had all but dispersed, and the changing of the guard was well underway for the dinner crowd. Thank God the staff is all under forty and has no problem keeping the momentum going. Grace and I take a much-needed break, and even though we could use two-by-fours to keep our eyes open, we sit at one of the tables sipping the only remedy we can think of—caffeine.

Dinner hour is as smooth as a Swiss movement, until I notice one customer sitting in a corner alone—the old blind man. I'm just about to confront him, when I'm summoned into the kitchen to assist one of the waitresses with a large order. I hurry as fast as I can, but once again as I enter the dining room—he's gone. I walk to the cashier to see if he paid with a credit card.

"Judy, can I have a word with you?"

Her face turns grim. "Have I done something wrong, Mr. Fenton? Am I too slow? Did I forget a table? Was it—"

I have to smile. "No, you are the perfect waitress. I want to ask you about the old blind man that you served."

"He didn't complain, did he? I treated him just like any other customer."

"As you should. No, I want to know if you've seen him before. Does he live in Bridgeburg?"

"I saw him once sitting at the park, but I have no idea where he lives. If he was a local I would have seen him around more."

"Good point. Thanks, Judy, and you're doing a great job."

She smiles. "Thank you, Mr.—"

"Just Paul—makes me feel younger."

"Got it. Oh, I didn't mean that you're—"

"Got it."

—

It's one in the morning. We are finally home and practically fall on our faces through the front door. The last time I was this exhausted was in my previous life of a double shift on the treadmill. I barely make it to the bed with my clothes still on. I hear Grace running the shower in the bathroom—another distinction between men and women. Taking care of the physical outweighs any mental fatigue for them. For me, even a morning shower seems too early. I do manage to shake my shoes off and they hit the floor at precisely the same time I pass out.

—

I hear the phone ringing and open my eyes to a morning sun.

"Who the hell could that be?" I roll over to see a vacant spot. Grace must have gotten up to answer it. But why is it still ringing? Still feeling the effects of Ben's Place, I stagger into the living room. Grace is nowhere to be seen. I pick up the phone.

"Hello."

"Paul, it's Adam. You need to come over right away," he says, slurring his words.

Before I can ask him why, he hangs up.

I'm in such a state that I arrive at the cottage with no recollection of even getting into my car. I'm getting some déjà vu. Adam is slumped in a chair outside with a half-bottle in his hand hanging over the armrest. His eyes are shut.

"Adam!" His eyes pop open like a kid's doll. "What's going on?"

"You made it," slurring as he speaks. "Great to see yuh."

Now I'm pissed. "Why the hell did you call me!"

"Call you? Oh yeah. It's Ed."

"Ed! What do you mean, it's Ed? Ed is dead!"

"Well, somebody forgot to tell him."

"Adam, you're plastered. You don't know what the hell you're saying."

Neil D. Burton

He takes a swig from the bottle. "Go see...for yourself. Give um my best."

He passes out. His hand loosens its grip on the bottle and it shatters on a patio stone.

I know he's drunk, but I have to eliminate any crazy thoughts of Ed being alive.

I reach the swampy area and one thing is for certain, there is no sign of Ed's body. It must have already sunk below the surface, which would make Adam think he got up and walked away. I grab a stick and poke the area. For some reason the area becomes deadly quiet. No birds, not even a breeze to rustle the leaves.

"Looking for me?" comes a raspy voice.

A bolt of fear screams up my spine to my brain where rational thoughts explode into tiny particles. I can't look up, but my dread is overpowered by my fascination for the macabre. Like the slow pan of a camera, my head and eyes raise up. It's madness! Threads of clothing clinging to legs of bone and rotting flesh. The groin is a gaping hole, and the torso like a birdcage has organs partially hanging like meat in a butcher shop. My better judgment pleads to not go further, but I can't stop this mechanism inside—pushing me on to its final mind-bending destination—the temple of doom. The sanctuary of thought where that part of human anatomy housed a life. Where things were discovered, created, explained and dealt with. No longer a home for the soul. The eyes now sockets that house the resident maggots. The lopsided jaw suspended by one remaining strand of tissue.

I attempt to speak, but my mouth is dry as sand. Whether it was a shove from Ed or another force, I find myself falling face down into the swamp and gasping for air while gagging on mud and clutching at the grass along the firmer sides of the area. A bony foot presses the top of my head into the muck and I go under. My eyes fill with dirt while my lungs squeeze out the last bit of reserve.

"Paul—Paul, it's after nine."

It's Grace. Like corn on a hot skillet my eyes pop open.

"You should get up and have a shower so we can be there for the lunch crowd."

"Grace, you don't know how grateful I am to you for waking me up."

"Well, I'm glad to see you so excited about the restaurant. I was a little apprehensive after our long day yesterday. You sure bounced back."

"That's me. Once I get going on something it's hard to hold me back." Sometimes all it takes is a terrifying nightmare to motivate the day.

There is nothing more invigorating than a hot shower followed by a run out into the bitter cold and sitting in an icebox waiting for the heater to eliminate the fogged-up windows and warm our extremities. We stop off at Rebecca's to see how things are, and just as we expected, it's quiet. With winter rearing its head, tourists are a hard find; and with Willow's End having such a small population, the local dining is meager, but they do like the breakfast menu—and that keeps the wolves from the door.

—

We head for Ben's Place with less conversation than we had the day before, but certainly thrilled with the outcome of our opening.

"I think after the lunch crowd we should leave and allow the staff to stretch their wings without us hanging over them. What about taking in some of the local shops to get more acquainted with the community and then return for dinner hour?"

"That's a great idea, Grace."

I can see her smile through the corner of my eye as I continue driving.

"I thought you would say that. You're still tired, aren't you?"

"Somewhat, but I also think it's a great idea because it shows we have confidence in them. Positive thinking is contagious."

"You're good, Paul. Ever consider politics?"

"Too smart for that. I like to grab my paycheck and rush home."

"You're not that smart. You just screwed that up."

"I meant with my previous job."

She laughs, "Too late, I win."

—

We knew the opening would bring the crowd, mainly out of curiosity and word of mouth. Now for the litmus test, and there it is, the place is packed. Not a table or seat to be had except for the one in the corner where we see Tor sitting alone having breakfast. He sees us and waves us over.

I can't help myself, "Eating all the profits, I see."

"Not me. I'm investing. This place will be a going concern, and the staff and food are top-notch. I think it was a wise move."

"That was your doing, Tor. You were the one to come up with the idea, and you were nice enough to take us along for the ride."

"Like they say," says Tor, "ideas are a dime a dozen, but it took the two of you to pull this off."

"Let's just say three heads are better than one and leave it at that."

Grace notices a small gash on Tor's right cheek. "Tor, what happened?" She points to the wound.

He places his finger up to his cheek as his eyes shift a quick glimpse to me.

She catches it and assumes collusion. "And don't tell me that's from shaving."

Oh, oh.

"Just a tree branch I caught while surveying a new area for development," then quickly changes the subject. "I saw that old blind man you were talking about."

Tor may not be as fast as Grace, but he sure has me beat.

"Where did you see him?"

"Right here, this morning, having breakfast."

"I've got to find out about that guy. He's like a ghost."

"That blind old man again, Paul?" says Grace.

"One and the same."

"But why are you so interested in some old blind fella? He isn't a threat to you."

"Because I'm not sure if he is blind. He seems to watch every move I make."

"An old blind man is watching you. Sounds like the blind leading the blind."

"I'm telling you, Grace, he could be trouble, and I'm going to find out what his game is. Tor, which waitress served him?"

Tor points her out. "That one over there. I think her name is Janet."

"I'll be right back."

"Janet?"

"Yes, sir."

"You served a blind man earlier. Can you tell me about him? I mean, did he talk to you?"

"He just said good morning and asked for a grilled cheese sandwich with four strips of bacon on the side and a hot chocolate."

"Nothing else?"

"Just, thank you."

And once again I have to ask—"How did he pay?"

"It was cash and a very nice tip. It was more than the bill—ten dollars. Nice old fella."

"I'm sure he was with a tip like that." I walk back to the table with not a sniff of new information.

"What did you find out?" asks Tor.

"He's a good tipper—too good."

"Now that's something," says Tor.

"What do you mean?"

"That tells you he has money."

"Hmm, that's true."

Grace weighs in. "I think you are both overreacting. Don't you think this could all just be a coincidence?"

Tor ignores that comment and states, "That could mean he has the funds to take taxis wherever he goes, and that would explain why he gets around so well."

"True." He may have a point there, but what? The old guy has money. Probably has a good pension—but how much of a pension could a blind person have? It could be a disability pension. Yeah, an injury at work and he sued and got two or three big ones. But that still doesn't answer the question, Why he is suddenly all around me? What if he was a co-worker of mine and I somehow caused his blindness—some sort of accident and he's out for revenge. *Easy, cowboy, you're stretching that rubber band to absurdity.*

—

Dinner hour arrives, and we decide it's time to go since the staff has it under control. All the way home, Grace goes on about the success we are having, the wonderful staff, and what a great, supportive town Bridgeburg is. Once in a while I respond from the passenger seat, but for most part I take a few two-minute catnaps with the odd thought about the old blind man mixed in for good measure.

—

Today, we're back at Rebecca's—a far cry from the hectic atmosphere at Ben's Place. This should be a relaxing day. We haul out all the Christmas decorations and the artificial tree from the basement and pipe in the sounds of the season that have for the last fifty years turned my Cratchit into Scrooge. But I must say, because of Grace's enthusiasm last year, she warmed my heart. I fell for it, and embraced the season as I do her. She turned me back to the Cratchit of my youth.

We decorate the tree in the lobby, and the spirit of the season descends upon us as snow begins to fall.

"Look, it's snowing. Let's stop for a minute and look at it."

The dining room is a 3D spectacle of huge snowflakes gently floating down outside each window. We park ourselves at a table by one of the windows facing the street and hold each other close. Some of the locals are wandering from store to store, all bundled in their winter scarves and hats like a scene from a Capra movie. Bing Crosby is singing "White Christmas" in the background. All I need is Barry Fitzgerald dressed like a priest.

Grace becomes teary-eyed. "It's magical—putting up the tree, the music, and the falling snow. It's the Christmas spirit ringing in the season."

Looking down on the street I see a taxi pull up and an old man with a cane exit. He heads up the front porch to Rebecca's.

"Grace, look! It's the old blind man. I'll meet him at the door."

"Well, that Christmas moment was short-lived," says Grace.

I make it in time to open the door for him.

"Thank you," he says.

"Can I help you to a table?"

"First you open the door for me, and now you want to insult me by helping me to a table. Do I look like I need help?"

"I just thought with your disability—"

"Disability! And what disability is that—old age?" he says as the snow melts from his wool coat, along with my Christmas spirit.

"Well, you know...your loss of sight."

"Loss of—are calling me blind?"

I suddenly realize—no sunglasses. "I'm so sorry. I mistook you for someone else."

By this time Grace is poking her head out from the dining room entrance with a slight smile on her face.

"And I mistook you for an employee of this establishment," says the old man.

Grace hops in to action to rescue me.

"I'm sorry, sir. Right this way. There are plenty of tables available. Sit wherever you like."

"Well, finally some respect." He follows her into the dining room.

"And I would like to apologize," says Grace. "He's a new boy and hasn't been totally trained yet." Then turns back to me with a smile.

Women sure know how to get you. She saved my ass, but in doing so took a bite out of it, too. I'll bet she comes back and gives me the line about what happens when you assume.

She seats the old man, hands him a menu then makes a beeline to guess who. There's a grin, or is it a smirk—either way this may hurt.

"There, no harm done," and walks into the kitchen.

Wow. That's it? No reprimand? No sarcasm? Grace is too kind. Her parents picked the right name for her—wait a minute. Why do I still feel there's a sword over my head? She's worked her magic—keeps me guessing. Men don't stand a chance with these women, but they make life interesting. Boy, do I love her.

—

After our easy day at Rebecca's, Grace and I walk the slow road home. The snow has stopped and left a four-inch blanket. The trees are dressed in white with moist snowflakes clinging to every branch and shrub. The sky is cleared and full moon casts a fairyland motif that I haven't noticed since my youth.

"I can't imagine a prettier night. Isn't this the most beautiful sight you've ever seen?"

I look at her and I'm filled with so much love. I stop and turn Grace to me. "This is most the beautiful sight I've ever seen."

"Oh, Paul, I love you more each day. Do you remember the first day I brought you to the house and you stopped me on the way just like you did now? We were talking about living in Willow's End, and you looked at me lovingly and said I was enough to make any man stay a millennium."

"I do remember. I have a long way to go, but I'm working on it."

She wraps her arms around me and kisses me with such passion that I'm sure the snow has melted from my boots.

"I could never have imagined all of this—you, the house, Rebecca's, and now Ben's Place. How blessed we are."

Needless to say, that romantic scene stretched into the wee hours.

—

I wake up to an almost sensual aroma of freshly brewed coffee made by the loving hands of the most wonderful woman this side of heaven. A simple wardrobe of a housecoat and slippers and I'm kitchen-bound.

"Your coffee's already poured, sweetheart," she says from the couch.

"Now how did you know I was up?"

Grace chuckles. "You're not the church mouse you think you are," as she scans the mysterious graveside photo laying on the coffee table with a magnifying glass.

I grab my coffee and head to the couch to take in some warmth from the fire and Grace's body.

"I thought you didn't want to see that picture."

"I know. I just feel like we've missed something."

"Any luck?"

"No, just remembering it was sent anonymously. I don't feel as traumatized as I did, just more perplexed. Why someone would send anyone a picture like that is beyond me."

"They didn't send it—remember, someone dropped it off."

"That's right. I forgot about that. That's eerie in itself."

"Perhaps that was their intent, to scare us."

"But why?"

"Do you see anything? A clue?"

She turns to me. "No, I don't see anything new."

"Can I see that for a minute, Grace?"

She hands me the photo and magnifying glass.

I begin with the faces—none look familiar and all seem expressionless. No suits, just short-sleeve shirts. Not even the area around them looks familiar. Oh, wait a minute. I can see what looks to be part of a church in the background. I bring the glass closer to my eyes.

"Uh huh!"

"What is it, Paul?"

"I think I know the location. It's the church here in Willow's End—the one at the top of the hill, where they held Alex prisoner."

"Now that's scary. Too close to home."

"This may sound crazy, but—do you think Tor might have had a hand in this? It would have been easy for him to drop the photo at our doorstep."

"Tor? Come on, Paul. Give those Hardy Boys a shake. There was a time when I thought he might be an agent, but look at all he's done for us. He's been with us all the way."

"That's true. And he sure had no problem with that Agent Ed."

"And don't forget relocating Adam multiple times."

"And that beating he took. No, I think—"

"Wait a minute. What beating?"

Oh boy.

"Does this have anything to do with that tree branch he ran into?"

"You could say that."

"I am saying that. So now you have Tor deceiving me, too?"

"Well, it wasn't exactly a beating. It was more of a heated conversation."

She gives me a look I know well, and right behind it—"Paul?"

"Okay. I didn't mention it because I didn't want to worry you."

"And what happened to honest and forthright?"

119

"I think I need some brandy in this coffee."

"You're not going to avoid the issue, are you?"

"No, of course not."

I get up and take my cup to the kitchen and pour brandy into my coffee.

"Did you want a shot in yours, sweetheart?"

"No thanks. Just bring the bottle."

This won't be pretty.

Grace fills her empty cup as I unravel the event while her face imitates the thousand faces of Lon Chaney. Just as I get to the part about finding the remains of the agents, she intervenes.

"All right—I get it. I can understand why you wouldn't want to give me those details, but you could have told me about them beating Tor. Don't you think that would have been something I would want to know? We could have postponed the opening of the restaurant until we found out the reason why."

I finish my coffee brandy and add, "That's exactly it, Grace. It had nothing to do with us or Ben's Place. I was concerned that if you knew, you might want to abandon the whole project because of it."

"Then why were they after Tor?"

"For one of two reasons: They either suspected he killed Ed, of which they had no proof, or they wanted to know where Adam was holed up."

"So who killed the agents in the farmhouse?"

"That's the million-dollar question. I don't know—but whoever did, used a Q4."

"A Q4?"

Another misstep—sometimes I need to put a sock in it. "All I can tell you is...you don't want to know."

"Wait a minute. Where did this Q4 idea come from? What happened to the Q3 and how do you arrive at that conclusion?"

"Well—" I wish I could think of answers as quick as Grace unleashes her Gatling-gun questions.

"Is this part of that—*I didn't want you to close down the restaurant* story?"

"I'll be right back."

"You're not switching drinks, are you?"

"If I did I could make it a lot worse for myself." I walk out to the car and grab the Q4 from the glove compartment to show Grace.

"After Ed and his car disappeared, I found this by the woodpile."

"That's the Q4?"

"That's it."

"Looks like the—"

"It's an upgrade."

"So the agents were here and probably used it to make Ed and the car vanish. That's why we didn't hear a sound during the night."

"That's partly right."

"Partly? Do you think you could spit it out all at once for me?"

"An agent wouldn't be careless enough to drop one of these in our woodpile."

"So you're back to thinking it was someone else?"

"I am, but I don't believe they would have dropped it by mistake either. I think it was a message for us."

Grace's eyebrows are now seamless. "Another message on top of the photo, or another warning?"

"It wasn't a random toss into the woodpile. A powerful weapon like that wouldn't be a warning. It's a message. I think it's the same person or group who exterminated the agents in the farmhouse to save Tor."

I look into Grace's eyes. "Possibly to let us know they have the same capabilities as the UWC, but they're on our side and thought I should have it as protection."

Her eyes quickly move from side to side. "So there *is* someone on our side."

"Exactly."

"And once again, you didn't mention this to me because—"

"Because I love you and have always tried to protect you and keep you out of harm's way." Sometimes when it's all in one breath it adds some credence. Plus—it's one of the few tools I have in my toolbox.

She puts hers arms around me. "And I love you so much, but please understand, the more I know, the better I feel about our relationship, and that you trust me to handle whatever comes our way—together."

Good move. I could also mention I saw the old blind man on the road near the farm—but I feel I can withhold it because Grace has already discredited him as a character in my closet of paranoia.

She picks up the photo. "I guess this must have also come from the person or group against the UWC."

"That I'm sure of."

"You know, it almost seems like Adam has become the fall guy in all of this."

"I'm stumped. From the minute I walked into Willow's End, my whole perception of reality has at times been so bent out of shape it's hard to make a right decision. It's just been one mystery—one nightmare after another, except for one."

"What's that?" says Grace.

I look into her beautiful dark, inviting eyes.

"There's that look again," she says. "Now watch what you say, I don't have the energy I had last night."

"For all that's gone on in this town, *you* are the only reason I'm still here. And I will stay here, love you, and protect you to my last breath."

"And you mean the world to me. I have never felt so loved in my life."

"Now just to show you how much I love you, I'll make breakfast."

"I'm all for that. And what did you have in mind?"

"The word romantic comes to mind."

"A romantic breakfast?"

"And what could be more romantic than French toast?"

—

I drive to Rebecca's to drop Grace for the lunch crowd, which will consist of the usual six to eight people. I pull to the sidewalk, and we sit for a moment to admire the Christmas tree in the middle window of the dining room.

"I would say it is more than enough to brighten anyone's day."

"It sure is. We did a wonderful job."

"*You* did a wonderful job, Grace. I was just Santa's little helper."

Grace heads to the front porch steps, and I leave with a smile that is short-lived. No matter how hard I try to keep that good spirit alive on the way to Ben's Place, there are no Sugar Plum Fairies fluttering in my head—only question marks.

Keeping Rebecca's and even Ben's Place afloat I can handle, but I feel like I'm being taunted from the bleachers. It has been a struggle to distinguish a black hat from a white one. I wouldn't mention this to Grace, but if I could snap my fingers and have us out of here, leaving all this baggage at the station—I would.

But I could never deny the fact Willow's End has been good for me, yet Grace has been the one who has changed me in ways I never thought possible. And as other wise men have said—she's made me a better man.

CHAPTER 14

The breakfast menu is well underway and three-quarters capacity at Ben's Place. Justine, our manager, is handling the cash register. She is good at holding down the fort. What a great find she was. Catching my eye, she gives me a huge smile. I respond a with thumbs-up and move past the patrons to the kitchen. Unless there's a problem, I never want to bother the kitchen staff, they have a momentum and I don't ever interfere with it. If the mechanics of it looks well-oiled, leave it alone.

Back in the dining room I stop a couple of times to mingle with the customers. I make it short. People are here to eat, not to socialize with the staff. I ask how everything is and wish them a pleasant day, and if a problem arises I eliminate it immediately.

I make myself comfortable at one of the few unoccupied tables and ask the waitress for a cup of coffee. I scan the room and she is back with my coffee and newspaper.

"Here you are, Paul, and the local paper if you wish to look through it."

We have free copies of the local paper by the front door—a nice touch Grace added to the menu. I thank the waitress and scan the front page for exciting features like John Brown bought a new tractor. As in most small publications, advertising is 90 percent of content—including our own. Sixty seconds is all that is needed to bring me up to date on the goings-on in Bridgeburg.

I sip my coffee and browse the patrons to get the feel of the room. Everyone seems to be enjoying their meal, and the conversations appear light and cheery. I pass on a second cup and decide to take a walk down the main street to look in on other local businesses.

A pizza shop with a sign indicating they don't open until three has me questioning if we are cutting into their business by serving pizza. I realize they only have takeout or delivery, so as long as we stay inside the restaurant, we aren't competing.

A voice with my name breaks my train of thought.

"Paul."

I turn to the street and there beside me is a large Lincoln with the back door open. I peer inside and I'm shocked; there sits the old blind man.

"Yes."

"Is it possible we might have a word?" Then he motions for me to get in.

Hearing him speak puzzles me. I expected a rough, gravelly voice, almost incoherent, but it was clear and articulate and younger. My throat is dry and my mind goes into overdrive—and he called me Paul like he's known me for years.

What do I do? Should I get in and trust this old man with my life? Isn't this what I've tried to do for weeks on end, to clear up some of the mystery that has engulfed me? Okay, I'll do it.

With some trepidation I enter the vehicle on the driver's side and we're off. My mind eases somewhat when I see the back of the driver's head and shoulders. He looks well-groomed and no dark suit—just a brown leather jacket. No reason to show my knuckles, yet.

"If you don't mind, we are on a short trip, about twenty minutes."

"Can you tell me where and why?"

"All in good time."

Uh, the old vague approach. I can't count the number of times I've heard that phrase, *all in good time*, and usually it means things will get complicated and not in a good way.

There's a humming sound, and where the middle armrest should be, a small bottle of cognac slides out on a tray followed by two brandy glasses already poured.

"I assume brandy to be a good choice."

My guard begins to wane. "Absolutely."

He picks up his glass and proposes a toast. "To Ben's Place, may it flourish for many years to come."

"I'll drink to that."

For being blind he seemed to know exactly where that drink was. Probably out of habit. Then comes one more thought: Does he want to buy us out and take me to some secluded area to gently motivate me with some waterboarding?

All right, calm down. Stop making up shit. If he wanted to he would have had some thugs put you in the trunk.

"Beautiful country up here; a far cry from the hustle and bustle of your city life, I'm sure."

Now I'm nervous again. What does he know about me?

"It must have been lonely for you in that house since your divorce and retirement."

I recall Wagner saying he didn't know a thing about me until I got to Willow's End, and he was UWC. So who is this guy? I down the rest of the brandy, but it still doesn't relieve the intense pounding I feel in my chest.

"Care for another, Paul?"

"Sure."

"I thought you would say that. We have the same hobby."

Kindred spirits? Maybe there is some light at the end of this tunnel—or bottle. I watch as he pours two more drinks.

"You made a good decision to stay in Willow's End. Grace is the perfect companion for you, but of course you knew it the minute you laid eyes on her."

It feels like a conversation with the Almighty. "You seem to know so much about me, now who the hell are you?"

"We're almost there," he says.

Shrugging it off doesn't help my anxiety, and how does he know we're almost there? Either he has traveled this road so often it is second nature, or this is one big charade like I thought.

The car turns right and we are now on a country road of thick forest on either side. It must be a seldom-used road. I can hear gravel shoot up and hit the underbelly of the car. We cross over a small bridge, and out the side window I see a narrow creek below us. We pull off the road and continue on two well-used tire track paths just wide enough for the vehicle. The car takes its time wobbling through the random potholes. The deeper into the forest we go, the less light. Finally—we stop.

He opens his door to get out. "Let's go, Paul."

I get out and all I see is an old dilapidated shack. My chest begins to pound once more. I pray that I won't be subjected to a beating similar to what Tor had.

"You look worried."

"So, you can see."

He smiles. "Let's go inside."

I look back at the driver and see he remained with the car. I ease up on my tightened fists.

Once inside the shack there is no surprise, with four walls struggling to hold up a deteriorated plywood roof. My James Bond sense of humor rises to surface.

"I think a new interior decorator is in the forecast."

"I like your sense of humor, Paul, but don't be so quick to judge."

He reaches into his pocket, and once again I clench. A small gadget similar to the Q4 is exposed.

"Don't move."

You don't have to tell me twice. He holds it out in front of him, and my rubbery legs feel the weight of my body. I know in the next few seconds I may not exist. He aims the gadget at the far wall. There's a quick beep followed by a small blue light from the gadget.

An area on the wall starts to vibrate. It begins to blur and fades away and opens to a very comfortable living room.

Now I'm in awe. "Just a minute." I walk outside to the back of the shack, and I'm stunned to see what you would expect, the back of the shack. I return inside and confront him with—"How is this possible?"

"After you, Paul."

Of course the words, *after you,* with those sunglasses still intact and that bird's-nest beard, I can't make an evaluation of his expression. Could this be my doom, more imprisonment, or possibly another drug-induced trip back to the sixties?

He gestures to a couch. "Have a seat, Paul." He takes off the long heavy coat and hangs it on a coatrack.

I feel unnaturally ridged until, to my surprise and delight, across from me is a coffee table adorned with two glasses and a bottle of fine scotch. If he was a woman I'd think he'd be trying to seduce me.

"Forgive me if I'm wrong, but I would think from your enjoyment of the cognac at this time of the morning, you have no restrictions."

"Breakfast of champions, I always say," with a nervous grin.

"Good." He parks himself in a wingback chair across from me.

"First, let's get rid of this disguise."

Uh huh, I was right. He pulls the hat from his head, the long gray wig, then slowly peels away the beard and mustache—but no rubber nose.

"That's better; this stuff is so damn itchy. Well, what do you think? A bit of an improvement, I hope?"

"Very much so."

A more handsome man now, possibly pushing over the edge of mid-seventies. I try to concentrate on where I might have seen him before.

"And you're wondering, where have I seen this face before?"

"Well, yes."

"Let me help you. It was at your house."

"My house? Refresh my memory."

"Not physically, but I did send you a picture."

"Picture?" The cemetery picture and the three gravediggers. "You sent that photo?"

"Yes, I was sure you would put a few clues together, but you missed the important one. I was one of the three men by the graveside."

"I see, and you are—"

"You might want to steady yourself, Paul." He reaches across the table to shake my hand, and speaks two terrifying words—

"I'm Alex Miller."

My first reaction is none. I'm completely speechless. Then, almost in a whisper, I say, "Alex Miller? But you're—"

"Dead? According to the United World Corporation, I am."

I'm stunned. I can't wrap my head around it. "But how—"

"To start with, I couldn't take a chance on the UWC finding out that I still exist. They would've used my son to get to me. I thought if I sent you that photo you would examine it carefully and see that I was alive and well. I'm the one with the shovel. But in hindsight I realized you could have mistaken it for a threat from the UWC, and by the expression on your face, I was right. So I decided this casual, non-threatening environment would be a better way to explain it all." He smiles and points to the bottle. "And of course this adds its own contribution."

He picks up the bottle and pours us three fingers. That would be the one I normally pour myself at either end of the spectrum, in triumph or defeat.

He raises his glass to me and I follow his lead.

"To my mysterious return from the grave." He takes a sip then leans back into his chair, and almost immediately the contentment on his face is discarded for an expression of a more serious nature.

"So your son was lying all that time."

"My son told you everything he *thought* he knew about me and the United World Corporation, so I will start where he left off."

"Before you start, I would like to ask you one question: Why are you telling *me* about this?"

He folds his hands in his lap. "You have more to do with this than you think."

Suddenly my throat dries up like the Sahara, and I reach for my crutch to mellow my anxiety with a full-measured gulp.

"The horrific car crash I was supposed to have perished in didn't happen. With the help of some very close and loyal friends, we staged the accident."

"But what about the absence of a charred body?"

"Before we let out the story of my death, we dug a false grave. That's the photograph you saw. Then a few days later released the story to the local newspaper. The trunk of the car was the only part we left intact. I placed my briefcase inside it to give the credibility needed for the UWC to think I was at the wheel. It didn't take them long to find the car and briefcase at the wrecker's. Fortunately for me, they bought it and the cemetery plot."

"So your son had no idea you were still alive?"

He pauses and his eyes narrow, then he seems to stare into space. He takes in a deep breath and continues. "It was the most agonizing part." He takes another sip. "It pained me so much to have to deceive my son, and then have him grieve over me, but my hands were tied. If I had let him know I was still alive it would have meant a death sentence for us both."

"So how am I involved in this?"

His eyes blink, then focus and lock on mine.

"You and Grace rescued my son from church where he would have certainly perished at their hands."

Immediately I see an image of the car explosion with young Alex inside and drop my head. "But in the end, I still couldn't save him."

"He meant the world to me." His eyes shift into reflection.

I reach for words. "I know he felt the same way about you. You were his hero."

His eyes return to mine. "But you did all you could to keep him safe, and in the end you put your own life on the line to pursue that son of a bitch Rigby."

He downs the rest of his drink. "And you put an end to him, and for that I am eternally grateful."

"But I was the only one on that country road. How could you possibly know that?"

"In a sense, I was there. We had a tracker on Adam's car, as well as Rigby's, and yours."

"Mine, too?"

"When I saw Rigby had parked along a country road, then Adam's car headed that way, I knew what was to follow, and I had no time to react. My only hope was you."

"If I had only left a minute sooner or gone a little faster."

"Don't put this on yourself, Paul. You had no idea Rigby was there. At the time I thought Adam was driving, which was bad enough, but when I found out that—" His eyes tear up and I'm at a loss, but I try.

"I had a lot of respect for your son. He was a good man doing what was right."

"He was, and there isn't a day goes by I don't curse my involvement with those corporate scums. I was smart enough for army intelligence, but when I hooked up with that outfit I was too naive. They dangled expectations of saving the world and the financial carrot in front of me. I moved up the ranks, and they buttered my toast with all kinds of promises, until one day a file came my way by accident and my whole world changed.

"When the realization of what they were really up to came to me, it was like I was on the streets of Europe seeing beautiful buildings, gardens, and cafes, and then look up to see a huge swastika waving from a flagpole. It becomes a different world." He begins to finger the glass in his hand.

"You also had the misfortune of Rigby's wrath with the bomb in the restaurant. Thank God you both survived with no more than a few scrapes and bruises. And in the process of it all you lost some good, solid people: community-minded people."

Whenever I hear the word *community*, I see Ben's face. He would weave the thought through my head every chance he got, like a tailor stitching a new suit.

"I want you to trust me, Paul. So, any questions you have should come out now."

Why would I need to trust him? Does his plan that will involve me? "Well, obviously, I understand the disguise. You can't be parading around as a ghost, but why were you following me?"

"I wanted to get to know you better. How you get along with people and how you handle yourself in different situations and the relationship you have with Grace."

"Sounds like a job interview."

"You could say that."

"And what about Tor? Were you observing him, too?"

"Absolutely."

"And the incident in the farmhouse?"

"That's not something we encourage. It was over the top. I'm afraid at times an extreme measure is the only thing they understand. Now they will have to think twice, and it may cause them to fumble the ball. Anything else?"

"And...Agent Ed?"

"Originally, it was Tor's doing. I knew you were in a panic over it. I had to take care of it before you both stumbled into more hot water."

"You sure take care of things in a hurry. Thanks for that, too. I'm still wondering, though, why I'm here."

He picks up the bottle. "Another?"

For some strange reason I answer, "No thanks, I'm good." I've never turned down a drink, but I think this whole event jars me to the point where I don't want to hear it in a fog.

He pours himself a drink and deposits the whole shot into his mouth and swallows. "I'm sure some of what I am about to say isn't news to you, so consider it a refresher course. Corporations have one main goal."

"World domination."

"That's certainly a large part of it. Their objective is to squeeze every dollar from us and every profitable thing nature has to offer. Using legal means they make changes that bring our interests in line with their value system. They want the free market in control of all aspects of society, tear apart regulations, and take away all fairness and community well-being. At the moment it may look like we are losing the battle on all fronts: water, fish, forests, animals, even bees." His eyebrows lower. "And that's only part of the story. *We* will be disappearing before our eyes if we allow it to go on. And what's ironic is that they, in their greed, will go down with us."

"How's that?"

"Think about it. And now another threat: If this AI stuff takes off like they believe it will, what would happen to most of the workforce, and who will be left to support those at the top? How will these consumers continue to purchase anything when they can't even feed themselves?"

"I've been walking around in a cloud. Like you said, I know some things, but looking at them together—it's terrifying."

"Now you may say, but what part does the community play in all of this? Think about it, Paul. What is all around you?'

"Country."

"That's right! Fresh water, fish, animals, and farming with good topsoil. It's the last hope we have, and each community owns it! If they take that, it's game over! That's why keeping communities thriving is our best defense. We can't let them put up one hamburger franchise or box store."

"I get it, but what purpose does it serve them to be hiding underground with a roomful of computers?"

"You think they should rent some office space on main street of town and put up a sign, *We are keeping track of all your activities and have a nice day?* It's like a game of Monopoly. Strategically planning their next move. You saw it at the library."

"That's right, I did."

"And did you see any protesting about it?"

"Nothing, only me in my thoughts."

"Exactly. They give you what you want: coffee, donuts, and you have no idea you have just lost some rights."

"It seems like such a daunting task to slow it down, let alone stop them."

"That's what they want you to believe. Look what just you and Grace have done. You gave Willow's End back to the people, to the community. You showed them they have a fight on their hands. You were the catalyst in all of that."

"I never thought of it that way."

"Well, you should. And what happened after that? You both took over Rebecca's. You brought back the internet, cell phones, reconnected the road to town so the cars could return. Mike regained control of his garage. All this brought in more businesses and tourists, making the town more prosperous and self-sufficient—and, *you* gave Rebecca's back to the people, to the community."

"I guess in a way I did, but I'm no hero, that's for sure. I just reacted to whatever came up. You know, a knee-jerk."

"That's the sign of a true hero. If you had given it a second thought, like most people, you might not have reacted at all."

I have a flashback of that day. I was about to wimp out and leave town, but came back because of Grace. No matter the initial reason or how scared I was, I came back and faced the demons. Suddenly, for the first time in my life I feel like I have worth. Someone actually sees me as having value.

"I'll take you up on that drink now."

He pours me another drink and tops off his own.

"This time I think this toast should be in your honor, Paul." He smiles. "Cheers, to a community hero."

"Well, thanks Alex, but I certainly didn't do it on my own. The real heroes are the ones we lost: those who gave their lives, like your son, Doc Bradley, the turncoat agent Carl, Percy, and, of course, Ben."

"That's all true. But you don't have to be dead to be a hero."

He sure is praising me a lot, and in the dark corner of my mind, on the top shelf, I see a loaf of bread and a pound of butter being spread for me, like I'm being set up for something. *Can't you, for one second, appreciate what is being said about you without throwing a wrench into it?*

"You now have a basic knowledge of what we want—no, need to achieve."

I have to ask: "I don't mean to sound pessimistic, but how will you be able to put a dent in this whole global crisis? They hold all the cards—the money, and the politicians."

"Not quite. We also have people in high places with power and financial wealth, with no shut-off valve—brilliant and innovative minds with a tremendous understanding as to how this world should proceed."

"And eliminate the UWC?"

"In our crosshairs."

"I'm on board, but now with two restaurants, I don't think I can be of any help or value."

"But you already have and are, Paul. Just keep doing what you're doing, and we will be your guardian angels by overseeing any problems arising from the UWC that would hamper your businesses or any other community endeavors. We have the opportunity of a lifetime to make this planet a healthy place for all."

"Sounds a bit like Jacque Fresco, only he wanted to eliminate money altogether."

"And who knows, we may see the Venus Project become a reality if we can get rid of the corporate vampire. Let me give you something to think about. Have you ever read the novel by Fyodor Dostoevsky—*Crime and Punishment?*"

Avid reader, I'm not. "That does sound familiar."

"If you had, you would have remembered it."

My intellectual credibility was snuffed out in one sentence.

"In it he mentions that if you live in poverty, you may still preserve your nobility. You can still hold your head up. But destitution—it would be like living without a soul. Exactly what the Nazis did to the Jews in their camps. They stripped away their humanity, and in doing so, they were perceived as having no worth. This was the only way they could discard and eliminate those poor souls without any thought of guilt or compassion. Treating them like animals, they became animals themselves."

There's a slight pause. Whether he is reflecting or putting together his next thought, I'm not sure. He takes in air and gradually expels it.

"There was a woman named Hanna, who was in a concentration camp. She described it best when she wrote in her diary, *'We have not died, but we are dead.'* You don't need a crystal ball to see where all this is headed. If we don't fight back, we could all be the walking dead. They don't want us dead, Paul. They want us to conform. We aren't called consumers for nothing. We will consume every bit of bullshit they throw at us; and we'll do it with a smile. We did sort of wake up in the sixties. I guess we thought we had them on the ropes. Then we grew up, dropped the ball and conformed. Come with me."

We walk to another wall. Once again the Q4 is displayed and a function is executed. Immediately, as in the first entrance, the wall disappears and reveals another room.

"Boy, those Q4's are amazing."

"They're not bad."

"Not bad? Look what it can do." I scan the room with my outstretched arm.

"This isn't a Q4. It's one of our own. We call it TED."

I have to chuckle. "Ted? What the hell is that all about?"

"We saw this inventor on TED talk and thought he had such a brilliant mind, so we snapped him up; and the first thing he created was this gadget that rivals the Q4 to the point it surpasses it in its capabilities and speed."

"It just boggles my mind."

"Like I said, we have top-notch people, and they are just as ambitious and passionate about this cause as we are. Go ahead, Paul," he says as we enter the room.

First thing that I notice is the enormity of the room. It makes the facility in Rebecca's basement look like a bedroom next to a ballroom.

"I can't believe the size of this place! Humor me—give me a second." Once again, in disbelief, I leave the shack and head around back. All I see is what you would expect—forest. I walk back into the room. "How is this possible?"

"I'll quickly explain it this way. Have you ever seen a hologram?"

"I've seen them on TV."

"That's what you're seeing, but we've taken it a step further. The building is obviously here and there is forest all around it, but we have it hidden with a huge hologram. Your eyes are tricked into seeing the illusion of a forest blending in with the real one."

"That's incredible. Like a magician's smoke and mirrors."

"Every inch of this facility is utilized."

Next, I notice the amount of computers and people manning them. "You must have about fifty people working in here."

"Good guess, fifty-three. Come with me."

We pass cubicle after cubicle of people manning computers until he stops at one. "Bruce here," he motions toward him, "is only concerned with Willow's End."

As I look at the large monitor, it is split up into a number of smaller screens of different buildings and street scenes in Willow's End. "There's Rebecca's."

"Now watch this," says Alex.

Bruce taps Rebecca's small screen, and it opens to a large screen filled with multiple scenes in and outside of Rebecca's.

"Now, I'm not showing you this because we are spying on you. I'm showing you how protected you are. And yes, we watch your house, but not every room, of course. We know at a moment's notice where you are and what is going on at that location."

"But I've never noticed any cameras."

"Because there aren't any."

"What? Then how the hell can you—"

"That's another innovation we came up with. We don't need them. It's non-invasive and completely undetectable."

"Sure beats the pants off the UWC."

"We try."

"I'll say, but it does make me feel a little vulnerable. How long have you been...*observing* our home?" I meant to say invading.

"Rest easy, Paul. We had only added your house just before Tor arrived. Our system is so well secured the only way it could be exposed would be a breach from within, and everyone here has gone through exhausting background checks and their personal history. When they leave here each day their memories are scanned, and anything pertaining to the job is erased before they leave.

"You can do that? That's sci-fi stuff. So how does it all work?"

"I just told you, it is well secured, and already you want me to jeopardize it by telling you?"

"No, of course not." *You're close to losing your hero status. I'll bet he wouldn't even let you deliver his newspaper now.*

He puts a hand on Bruce's shoulder. "Bruce here is our best man, and even *he* has limited access to information."

"This facility is only one in a number of them spread out all over the country," says Bruce. "When things need a little tweaking—that's when I intervene."

"So it was you I saw on the snowmobile in the snowstorm?"

"Not me, but one of our men."

"So, that's how I made it out of that snowstorm."

"And how you got your ring back."

"Holy shit!" I turn to Alex. "You're better than God!"

"I wouldn't say that out loud."

"So, when the UWC starts a fire, you put it out."

"It's more than that. It's an ongoing War of the Worlds, and they are the aliens."

One thought suddenly occurred to me. What about the book coming out? "The book your son was going to publish to expose the UWC is now in Adam's hands, and they want him as a terrorist."

"Yes, the manuscript. When you see him again, tell him to ditch it. That will not change anything, but we can."

He escorts me back to the waiting Lincoln and leaves me with one sentence right out of the Godfather's handbook—

"Don't forget, Paul. We've got your back, but there may be a time when I will need *your* help."

"Absolutely, you've got it."

I get into the Lincoln and those words echo in my head. *I will need your help.* There were no pricking fingers and rubbing them together or spitting in our palms for a tight handshake, but nevertheless the contract has been signed.

No sooner than I have those thoughts, when there's a flash like the one in the snowstorm and I'm back in Bridgeburg, sitting in front of Ben's Place. I wonder if I could find my way there on my own. Then another thought surfaces: If this place is such a secret, which it is, why wasn't I blindfolded? Wait a minute. What if it was deliberate, like the Mafia would do to test someone's loyalty?

That's enough of that. He gave you so much praise for taking care of his son and doing everything to save him and avenging his death. This is a man who owes you. He's watching your back 24/7, saved your ass on a number of occasions, and that's the thanks he gets, and you question his loyalty?"

That's true. Don't look a gift horse in the mouth...or it could end up in your bed.

CHAPTER 15

Large, white flakes of snow begin to fall. I exhale with a sigh of relief as I enter my car, and for a moment I just sit there replaying the mind-bending experience with a supposedly dead man. As shocking as it was, I now feel more comfortable knowing Alex senior has my back, and no more sinister old blind man.

I start the car and wheel around into the opposite lane to head home. I look around at all the little shops and streetlights and feel my community enveloped by the spirit of the season. Let's try some vintage Christmas music on an FM.

"Hey brother, what's happenin'? Christmas is on its way. Grab your woman as fast as you can before Santa puts her in his sleigh."

CLICK! Sometimes—just the slow, and the swooshing back and forth of the wiper blades is enough.

—

Back at Rebecca's and I have to admit, all in all, my meeting with the Ghost of Christmas Past was, even with all the negatives Alex threw at me that are mind-blowing, the positives are flying high. I check the clock on the dash and I didn't make it for lunch. The snowfall has intensified. I hope she's still here. I don't want her to walk home in this.

I find the dining room almost empty with no Grace. "Oh, oh. I'm in trouble now."

"Oh, you're finally here," says Grace, coming out of the kitchen with her coat in hand.

"I was just about to put on my coat and head for home."

"Sorry, sweetheart, it was quite the afternoon."

"Is everything all right at Ben's?"

"Running like a Swiss. I have some surprising news, mixed in with shocking, exciting, and possibly stress-free."

"Well, this was worth the wait then. Bring it on."

"First, what's the special tonight?"

"Roast beef."

Out the window, I can hardly make out my car. "Looks like a roast beef night out there."

"That makes it easy for me," she says. "I'm starting to feel that Christmas spirit all over again."

We park ourselves at our favorite table by the window looking down the street with all the Christmas lights from the shops.

"Shall we start with a little bubbly?"

"Ooh, romantic, too."

Since today's adventure may take some time to tell, I open with, "I know who the old blind man is."

"Oh, we're back to him, are we?"

That's not the opening I should have used. She's already building that brick wall of resistance.

"After I checked on Ben's Place, I stepped outside and was confronted by the old blind man. He was in the back seat of a car with a chauffeur at the wheel."

"So he wasn't the poor, pathetic old blind man you thought he was."

"He called out to me by name and waved me to go with him."

"So he wasn't blind, either. Don't tell me you got in, and please don't tell me he was an agent."

"Grace, I need you to just hear me out without any extra commentary."

"All right, I can do that. Would you mind pouring me another glass first?"

I add one for myself and then continue with the ride and the cognac, and how the old man seemed to know so much about me and her.

Grace begins nibbling on her bottom lip. Now, I have her attention. Next is explaining the illusion of the shack and the large room behind it. Here it comes—her signature, singular eyebrow. Now to the part of the unveiling of the old blind man's Halloween costume.

"What? Alex's father!"

And then she hits me with a tsunami of rapid-fire, semi-automatic questions. "How is that possible? Was it all a joke? Nothing but lies? And what about the book? Was it all just bullshit?"

I lower my tone. "Grace, calm down and let me finish before you pass judgment."

She looks around the room and sees that she has caught a few eyes.

"Sorry—you're right. I'm jumping the gun."

"I want to remind you of what you had said on a number of occasions about me not being up-front with you. Well, here I am."

I never try to put Grace in an awkward or embarrassing position, but I think this minuscule, bitter pill I have handed her will actually help our line of communication. She reaches across the table and covers my hand with hers. "I'm sorry, Paul. I will never question your intentions again. I know you are doing your best to protect us."

"Let's make it easy. Just replace the word intention with the word love—and I love you with every breath."

Her eyes water and one unpretentious tear edges down the side of her cheek.

"I promise you by the time I'm finished, you'll feel a lot better about our situation."

Our meal arrives and we combine the wine and the dinner with the rest of conversation of my day's events.

"Okay, Grace, this is what I found out." I unravel the story in the order the events unfolded. Grace interprets every word with an assortment of facial expressions. "And his last words were, *we've got your back, but there may be a time when I will need your help.*"

"Hm, I wonder what that will entail."

"I don't know, but I'm sure it would never amount to the protection we've had from him. The one thing we have to keep in mind is we are on the same page. Communities are the last stronghold of our society and freedom."

"You sound like a politician."

"Please, Grace, no insults at the supper table."

—

One week before Christmas and the countdown begins. Grace and I find ourselves at Ben's Place having coffee while we discuss whether or not we should open on Christmas Day.

"Well, Rebecca's will be open, Grace. That's because we will have weekend skiers."

"I've got an idea. Why don't we open Ben's Place Christmas Eve day? We can serve an early Christmas dinner for lunch, for those who may not get one. Then close at three and invite the staff and their families back at seven for an employee Christmas party."

"That's a great idea, and what about Christmas Day?"

"We close, that way everyone can have that time with their families."

"Perfect."

Just as she says that, I notice two men at a table in the corner eating breakfast. Why have I noticed them? I'm trying to figure it out. Even though they're wearing toques and sweaters, one with a deer on it and the other with snowflakes, they just don't seem like they fit in, or maybe they are trying too hard to fit in. I glance down and there it is—dress pants and galoshes. If they were up here for any length of time they'd be wearing boots and jeans. So they must be businessmen, but what kind? They could be agents.

One of them looks my way. I lift my coffee cup to my lips and he turns back to his accomplice. I don't think he recognizes me, so that's a relief.

"So what's your thought on that?" asks Grace.

Oh, oh. What's the question? "My thought? Well—"

"Paul, it's not a brainteaser. Should we buy each of the staff a little gift?"

"Uh, well—what do we do at Rebecca's? Don't we give *them* a gift?"

"Thank you, question answered."

The two men get up from the table and walk past us to the cashier without even a blink my way. They pay their bill, but one says something to the cashier. She shrugs her shoulders, says something back, and they walk out.

"I'll be right back."

"Well, what about—"

"Those two men who just walked out, what did they ask you?"

"Oh, they just wanted to know if Tor drops in on a regular basis, and I said, I don't know about regular, but from time to time."

"Did he ask anything else?"

"Yes, he asked me what time of the day he would drop in and I said most times breakfast. Did I say something wrong?"

I smile. "No, that was exactly what you should say."

I know Grace will ask me what that was all about, and I had promised to be honest with her, so I have to find a positive in this or she may want a drink stronger than coffee.

"So what was that all about?"

I sit down and lean across the table to her. "Those two men that just left—I think they're agents."

She rolls her bottom lip into the top one and inhales enough oxygen through her nose to suck the hair from my head.

"Agents?"

"But the good news is they didn't seem to know who I was."

"Agents, just before Christmas, isn't that just wonderful."

She stops a waitress in her tracks. "Emily, could you come by with a shot of rye for my coffee please?"

"Certainly," then casts her eyes at me. "Did you want me to top off your coffee, too?"

"Oh no, mine is just fine the way it is."

"And you know this because—"

"The way they were dressed. They made a poor attempt to blend in as locals. The tip-off was their suit pants and galoshes to hide their Guccis."

"And what was the talk with the cashier?"

"One of them said something to her and I wanted to know what it was."

Emily drops by with her shot.

"Just pour it in the cup, please."

She stirs it slowly then takes a sip. "So what did he say?"

"He asked about Tor. Wanted to know when he ate here and how often."

Her eyes shift from side-to-side. So far she seems to be taking it well.

"So it boils down to, you're safe but Tor isn't."

"I guess they not only want him so they can locate Adam, but probably revenge for the farmhouse murders."

"That's about the size of it." I think.

"All we need is for Tor to be here when we have a full house and they come in like it's the Wild West to nab him."

"I don't think we have to worry about that, Grace."

"And why not?"

"I told you, Alex has our backs."

"If he does, how did those two get in here?"

She's got me there. "I don't know."

A fella at the next table, who could be in earshot, stands and walks over to us and opens his jacket, exposing an object clipped to his belt. Shit! It's a Q4—I mean a TED. Without a word he leaves us and walks out the door.

"What was that all about?" asks Grace.

"That, Grace, is why we don't have to worry. He is one of Alex's people."

"And how do you know that?"

"He's carrying a TED."

"Who's Ted, one of his buddies?"

"It's like a Q4, only more powerful and higher tech. Like I told you, Grace, these people are just as committed to straighten out this world as the UWC is to destroy it."

"That's incredible. They're big league."

"Exactly, no worries." Perhaps some concerns once in a while, but no worries.

"But what about Tor?"

"The same."

"And Adam?"

I reach across the table and hold her hand and with a smile, I say, "Yes, him, too."

"They really do have our backs, don't they?"

"They sure do. As a matter of fact, I'm so confident about it, I was going to drop in to see Adam and invite him to the staff party. He hasn't even seen the place yet."

"That's a great idea. It must get awfully lonely for him out there, and with Alex watching over us, I don't think he would have a problem with that if you explain the whole story to him."

"Grace, no one can know about Alex. We can't tell anyone —not even Tor."

"But you told me—"

"I told you we have to be up-front with each other. Do you think Alex has been wearing that old blind man getup because he's fixated with Halloween? As long as Alex is alive, the rest of us are, too. We are getting married and when we do that, we become one. Everything we do will be together, for each other. If we are going to be joined at the hip, there isn't a better time to be up-front. So for better or worse, you will know everything I know, and that's as far as it goes."

"Thank you, honey, I love you so much." She puts her other hand on top of mine.

"And I've loved you from that first cup of coffee you served me. What do you say we drive up to see Adam and give him the invite in person? I'm sure he'd be glad to see us."

"That's a great idea."

—

The highway we drive to get to Adam's place is the road less traveled at this time of year. Only the locals and the odd transport are found on it. The skiers are on the main highway and can't afford to waste their weekend and money on a leisurely drive for the scenery. For us it's the best part. Everywhere we look is a wonderland postcard of thousands of white-covered cedars, pine, and spruce.

Grace is captivated with the landscape, and I think how precious she is to me. I've never had such deep love for anyone. Even the friendships I've had were superficial except for my teenage friend Jim, who I had to watch waste away in a home. But here, I have made true friends. Another is discovering I could leave the insanity of a large city and adapt to a small community out in the country. Finally, after my raising-the-dead experience with Alex, I can't escape the evolving digital age. No matter how hard I try, it's in our lives to stay—like Amazon or Netflix. Maybe not the best examples, but I know what I mean.

"Paul? I just had a thought."

"What's that, Grace?"

"When we see Adam, why don't we invite him for Christmas dinner? It can't be much of a Christmas for him out there by himself."

"That's perfect. And I think Tor is in the same state, we could invite him, too, if that's okay with you."

"I think it would enhance our Christmas by sharing the day with others."

Sharing the day—my thoughts reflect back to the Christmas we invited Ben to share in our festivities, and finding him dead in his chair. It was, by far, the saddest day of my life.

I look at Grace and she puts the smile back on my face.

We pull up to the cottage, but can't make it into the driveway. It hasn't been plowed, and Adam's vehicle sits covered with about five inches of snow.

"Do you think he's all right?" asks Grace with concern.

I point to the smoke from the chimney. "I'm sure he's fine. He's just tucked in."

We walk up to the door which he did manage to clear, and just before I knock, it opens and there's Adam.

"Well, what a surprise. Come on in. I was just about to make breakfast, would you be interested?"

Grace looks at me for the answer.

"That sounds great. We just had coffee at Ben's Place."

He takes our coats and lays them over an armchair.

It's nice to see him sober for a change. He guides us into the living room with the huge windows looking out over the white landscape. We sit on a cozy plaid-covered sofa, which for some odd reason seems to fit with the room.

"Tor told me things are going very well over there," says Adam.

"They sure are," says Grace. "We just hope the enthusiasm from the community doesn't wane."

"I think it has the potential of becoming a stable fixture for years to come. A nice community is wonderful, made even better with a special place for people to gather in friendship and good food. Well, you can't get much better than that."

Boy, what a difference when he's sober. "I couldn't have said it better myself."

"Adam, I think you should get into advertising," says Grace.

"I'll think about it. Right now I'm trying to figure out what to do with the book."

Oh yeah—the book. Grace looks at me with concern as her eyes go into her half-squint. How the hell do I tell him to ditch it after all he's gone through to protect it? And what reason do I give without mentioning anything about Alex's dad being alive?

"Adam, about the book, I don't see a need for it anymore."

"No need for it? What are you saying? If I can get it out there it could make a world of difference."

Like a tennis match, Grace's eyes go back to me.

"Adam, I know how important this is to you. It may not be evident from our standpoint, but believe me, a big shift is about to happen, and there is no need for you to jeopardize your life for the book any longer."

Adam has a bewildered look. "Shit, I was going to offer you coffee, but I think you need a real drink. Where did this come from, Fox News or some nutbar on Fakebook?"

Grace turns to me once more. "I can't really explain where it came from. You'll have to trust me, there's no fake news here."

Grace jumps in. "What Paul is telling you is the truth. If you pursue the book, it won't change a thing. It will only make it worse for you."

"This doesn't sound like you, Grace. You were always behind the book coming out. What changed? Did you two switch sides? Are you getting some kind of incentives or benefits thrown at you from those bastards?"

Now I'm pissed. "Okay! That's enough of this shit! We don't have to prove it to you. If you want to toss your life away, it's up to you. Ask yourself this, if we were bought by the UWC, why the hell haven't we turned you in or told them where you are? And why would we drive out all the way out here to invite you for Christmas dinner?"

Adam's look and tone dissipate. "Christmas dinner?"

"That's right. We thought you'd be here by yourself on Christmas and didn't want you to be alone."

Grace throws in the other shoe. "We're going to invite Tor."

"I'm sorry," he says, then lowers his head. "I guess I've been so dedicated to this cause and Alex that I lost focus on reality. I can't say I haven't been upset, even scared to continue with the book. I can't say I can put it to rest, just keep it under wraps for now, and maybe with that I can breathe easier."

"You can finally move on."

Grace rushes over to Adam and puts her arms around him for a huge, comforting hug. "Only a hero would have kept going in the face of danger."

"Thanks, Grace. Now, I only have one other question."

"What's that?"

"Will there be dressing?"

"What do you think? We own two restaurants."

We all laugh and the world is good again.

—

Christmas Eve. We made it and got through it in great fashion. Keeping two businesses going at the same time during the most hectic holiday is truly a feather in our caps. For Grace, it's an accomplishment she would have considered daunting two years ago. She's upped her game to the point where her self-confidence has soared, yet her demeanor has never wavered. She's still the beautiful, wonderful Grace I first met.

I watch in amazement how she treats the staff. The respect, understanding, and empathy she has when it's needed, which in turn elevates their self-worth. They aren't just happy to have a job, they're happy to be at Ben's Place.

I worked for a corporation. The only thing I received from them was a paycheck and the reluctant benefits the union fought tooth and nail to get. In those years I was a victim of the big wheel of progress. I was strapped into my seat from the first day, like being on a roller coaster. Only I never felt that exhilaration of having any high points on the ride.

Grace has also taught me self-worth. I do seem to have skills that were hidden from me. And for the first time in my life, I feel great satisfaction in the joy of working.

And right now I reap its benefits: Grace, a little wine, a roaring fire and watching, what else, *It's a Wonderful Life.*

—

Christmas with the Terrorists, at least that's how the government and the UWC would describe it. For Grace and me, it does feel a little unsettling or at the least strange to know we are being watched, even if it's for a good reason. But not letting Adam and Tor know anything more than someone is watching their backs allows us to have a great Christmas dinner...with lots of dressing. The night ended after many hands of cards, wine, and music. They both stayed over, with Adam in the extra bedroom and Tor on the couch, so he could have his long legs stretched out with his feet over the armrest.

—

New Years has come and gone, and January drags behind it the shortest, longest month of the year—February. Even though it's hard to notice, the days are becoming longer. Spring is right around the corner, and our thoughts are already past it. The anticipation of our wedding is the center of attention.

"Paul, I was thinking of going to the city to look for my wedding dress."

"What's the matter with what you're wearing? The bulky sweater and jeans look great on you."

"Typical male response."

I stand in front of Grace with a smile. "Sweetheart, you go out and get the most beautiful wedding dress you can find, but not too sexy. I don't want to be in line at the altar with a half a dozen other guys ready to take my place."

"That's true. I never thought of that. Maybe I *should* wear the jeans and sweater."

"You're good, Grace." I kiss her on the nose. "Very good."

"I do two shows a day and a matinee on Sundays."

—

March becomes April, and the snow disappears as fast as the Super Mite plague hits our border.

"All borders between the US and Mexico have been closed. All trucks and migrant workers are being turned back. There is no telling what the impact on the economy will be."

"How about our lives? Oh yes, the economy first. It's corporations against corpses."

"The Mexican and American governments are feverishly working on a drug that will stop this horrible disease. So far there have been—"

I shut the damn news off and wonder how much of this is corporate hype and how much of it should have us truly worrying? This could also mean a food shortage.

From the bedroom Grace pipes up, "Who are you talking to, Paul?"

"Just watching the news." I'm glad I shut it off. Grace doesn't need anything else on her mind except the wedding.

"You're not yelling at those Republicans again, are you?"

"I was, but I shut it off before they could answer me."

Grace comes out of the bedroom. "I think I'll spend the whole day at Rebecca's. It's spring and I feel alive again, and summer will be here soon," she smiles. "As well as our big day."

"What big day was that again?"

She throws her arms around me and looks into my eyes, "The day we become one."

"I thought we were one from the start."

"Paul, you're talking physical, I'm talking legal. You know, what's yours is mine and what's mine is mine."

"Oh, that one."

We have our last cup of coffee for the day, then I drop Grace at Rebecca's. I continue on to one of the local greenhouses to see what's in stock and possibly pick out some plants to get started in the front garden of the restaurant.

CHAPTER 16

I finish my chores, and as soon as I enter Rebecca's, a waitress rushes up in a panic to tell me something has happened to Grace.

"She's at the bar!"

I rush in —"Oh my god!" Grace is on the floor. I kneel down beside her.

"Grace, what's happened? Are you sick?"

No response—she's out cold.

"What happened? Did she have an accident?"

"No," says the waitress. "A parcel came for her and she seemed surprised. She said she didn't remember ordering anything. I walked away as she began to open it, then I heard her scream, *'Oh, my god!'* I turned around and she dropped to the floor."

I see the open parcel beside her and a couple of feet away, a small, opened, brown paper bag with chestnuts all over the floor.

"What the hell is this? She got upset over chestnuts?"

Grace moans and starts to come around. She mumbles a couple of words about chestnuts and some guy named Joe and then she's out again. The chestnuts I'm not concerned with, but Joe, that's a different matter.

I carry her to the car with concerned staff bunched up on the porch.

"I'm sure she'll be fine."

"Please call us with an update, Paul."

"I will."

—

Safely home, I position Grace on the couch and put a pillow behind her head. I sit on the edge of the coffee table, holding her hand. Her eyes begin to open. She stares straight out—probably to get her bearings, then feels my hand and turns to me.

"Hi sweetheart, how are you feeling?"

She lifts herself up and swings her legs to the floor. "I'm okay. What happened?"

"You passed out at Rebecca's."

"I did?" she says with a concerned look. "Why would I—"

"It sounds ridiculous, but it seems to have something to do with...chestnuts."

"Oh shit!" She throws her hands to her face. "No, no, no!"

I move to the couch and wrap my arms around her. "Grace, what is it? How bad could it be? And who's Joe?"

She puts her hands down and looks at me. "Oh, my god, I said that?"

"Do you want to talk about it?"

"I guess I have to now. I'll need a double of whatever you can find."

"Pretty bad, is it?"

"I would consider a death threat pretty bad."

"Death threat?" I think I'll join her. If it's bad for her, it must be bad for me.

She downs half the glass and stares off into space.

"Everything has been picture-perfect, yet it seems that I can never truly let go and enjoy life because I always have a guilty feeling for thinking that I have all these wonderful things in my life, but I'm never sure if I deserve them."

"I don't understand how a bag of chestnuts becomes a death threat?"

"You will."

I take one good gulp and wait a few seconds for it to spread the warmth through my system, and then add a second.

"You remember I had mentioned I once worked at a bank?"

"Yes, that's when we compared our knowledge of computers with Ben."

"A few years ago when I was still in the city and working at the bank, I would always use my afternoon breaks to go outside for a walk. I was lonely and at times depressed about my life. I had the odd relationship that never panned out, mainly because what they were looking for was far less than what I wanted." She stops and looks into my eyes. "I wanted what we have.

"The only friend I had was Joyce. Actually, I used to babysit her when she was just starting school. She was a great source of support. Even though we had an age gap, I felt like her older sister. She has been my best friend, and when I think about her now, I realize how much I miss her.

"Anyway, on this one particular walk I noticed a vendor. He was a handsome man, and I couldn't understand why his lot in life would be selling chestnuts. He stopped me and charmed me into buying a candy apple. The more we talked, the more I became intrigued. I went back the next day and—"

She finishes her drink and shows me the empty glass. I refill it, as well as mine.

"There he was, busy with a customer who looked like a homeless man. He handed him a bag of chestnuts and I thought, how can someone dressed like that afford chestnuts? The man reached into his pocket and handed the vendor a small roll of bills, but the vendor didn't give him any change, and he didn't ask for any. Then he ran off. It seemed very odd to me."

"That does seem strange." I sip from my glass.

"Then he looked at me and said, 'Uh, there she is. The most beautiful woman in all of Venice!' Venice? I said. Then he added, 'Of course, if we were there that's what I would say.' How could I not fall for that?"

"Sounds like a true Casanova."

"Oh, yes. He certainly was that—and more. He gave me a free bag of chestnuts, which in turn had me asking if he made much money with that job. He smiled and said that they come from all over the city to buy from him."

"I guess the chestnuts were the clincher, and you were head-over-heels."

"Paul—keep in mind, this was way before you came along."

"Right."

"He invited me for dinner and said the restaurant was only a block away. He would meet me at that same spot at seven. As

I walked away with the bag of chestnuts, he hollered for me to wait. He rushed over in a panic and said the craziest thing. He said he gave me the wrong bag. I looked inside and told him that it looked like chestnuts to me. He said, no, that he must have that one back and he'd give me another one. I don't know what his problem was, but I was becoming irritated. I told him it was fine, and I had to get back to work. He tried to grab it from me and it ripped open, and the chestnuts fell to the sidewalk just as a police officer walked by and said, 'Okay, okay. That's enough. Here, let me help you, miss.' Then Joe jumped in. 'That's okay, officer, I'll get that.'

"The officer raised his hand to Joe and told him to stay where he was. Then he got down on one knee and started to pick up the chestnuts and noticed a small, clear package on the ground, and picked it up. He turned to me and asked me if it was in the bag. I told him it must have been. He said he gave me the wrong bag. The officer said he could understand why and pulled out his gun. He told Joe to turn around and put his hands behind his back. Then he asked me if I knew him. I told him I just met him yesterday. I got an apple from him and those chestnuts now. The officer said he was sure he'd find more goodies in Joe's cart."

"So you caught a drug dealer. That's pretty exciting, Grace."

"I'm not finished yet." She holds out her glass and I pour her another.

"Joe started swearing at me, saying he was going to kill me."

"I don't think you have to worry about that. He's probably still behind bars."

"And that brings me to the parcel I got today."

I glance at the bottle that is now half-spent, along with Grace.

"So you think he may be out of prison now and sent you the chestnuts to shake you up?"

"Oh, I think it's more than to shake me up. If it weren't for me, he wouldn't have been behind bars in the first place. He hasn't spent all this time trying to locate me to tell me I forgot my chestnuts."

I don't know what to say, but I better come up with something positive—and here it is. "In a way the timing couldn't be better, Grace."

"Shit," she laughs. "I think I should slow down. For a minute there I thought you said the timing couldn't be better."

"Grace, what I mean is—"

"No, no. Wait a minute. I think you're right, Paul. We have two businesses to run—a wedding coming up—which, if the timing is right, like you said, *you,* my friend, will have to marry yourself, and why is that? Because your beautiful, lovely bride" throwing her arms in the air "won't be available. She will be too (belch) busy being assas...assassinated—even murdered."

Like the end of a storm when a sliver of light peers through, I can feel a slight smile coming on. "No, Grace. Please, hear me out."

"You mean before I knock you out."

"Listen, Grace, what I'm saying is, we have Alex taking care of us, and all I have to do is let him know about the situation and he will take care of it."

"Oh, well that sounds simple enough. Do you think we can trust a ghost that comes back from the dead? He didn't keep his—what's the word? Word, that's it. He didn't keep his word about being dead, did he?"

I want to laugh because I know most of what she's saying is coming from the bottle, but it would only enrage her further.

"Look, just let me talk to him, and I'm sure he will ease your mind."

"Okay, call him."

"I—I don't have a number."

"Well, isn't that just *feachy*—it's times like this I *fish* Ben were here."

"Ben? What could he do?"

"What could he do? He'd r-o-l-l us a fat one, and then we could toast him with a mud—" she giggles—"a mug of Charlie boy's Supremes—which I could really use right now."

"Grace?"

"Hmm."

"I think I know what you need."

I pick her up and carry her into the bedroom.

"That's right, Pollywog. Carry me over the *freshold* now cause I won't be around later to..."

I give her a soft landing on the bed and she's out.

—

Grace hasn't moved a muscle all night. It's almost nine and she's still out, and I might say it's a blessing. I open a box of pancake mix and follow the simple instructions—water, an egg, then beat the hell out of it. I haven't tried them yet, but they do look like pancakes. I pop them into the warm oven until Grace comes out of her coma. She'll either have an appetite or won't even want to smell them.

I'm sure between the alcohol and her state of mind, she won't be going in to work today, and by some miracle I'll be able to get hold of Alex.

I pour another coffee and I hear a gentle knock on the front door. At least they're polite. At this time of the morning it's anybody's guess as to who it could be. After Grace's story I don't want to take anything for granted. I make sure I have Grace's revolver. I keep the door latch on, allow a small opening.

"Who's there?"

"Paul, my name is Eric. Mr. Miller asked me to see you. I have some information to pass along to you."

I look through the opening and see a man about my age—no suit, no sunglasses. I keep the gun at my side and unlatch the door, opening it with caution.

"You say Alex sent you?"

"That's right. I have some information about the death threat."

Death threat—but how would they—oh yes, the surveillance. Like the Catholics would always say, *You can't see him, but he's everywhere.*

"Come in."

He sees the gun at my side and I open my mouth to explain.

"It's all right, that's understandable."

Then, a voice from the dark side. "What's going on, Paul?"

It's Grace, all wrapped up in her robe, looking like she did a couple of rounds with George Foreman.

"This is Eric, Grace. He works for Alex."

"Nice to meet you, Grace. I have some information for you about the man who threatened you."

"Oh." Grace perks up. "Would you like to sit down?"

"Thank you."

"Can I get you a coffee, Eric?" I ask.

"That would be nice, thank you. Just black, please."

We make ourselves comfortable in the living room and I ask Grace if she wants coffee.

"Not right now. I'll wait until I hear what Eric has to say."

Eric takes a sip of coffee, clears his throat, which leads me to believe it will be noteworthy in substance and length.

"That fella that threatened you, Joseph Battaglia, when he was arrested there were several other crimes added to the list, which gave him a much lengthier sentence. Unfortunately for him, he decided to squeal on his distributors to knock some time off his sentence, and the plea deal ended up being his downfall. He was later transferred to another prison where he encountered a couple of inmates he had fingered, and last month one of them settled the score."

"He's dead? That's horrible," says Grace.

"Betrayal is a death sentence. He almost made it out, too. He would have been up for parole five days ago."

"So Grace doesn't have to worry, then?"

"Wait a minute, Paul," says Grace. "Then who sent me the chestnuts?"

"He did," says Eric.

"What? I don't—"

"From what we understand, Joe told someone in his family that if he didn't make it out of prison he wanted to have a bag of chestnuts sent to you."

That seems a little puzzling. "Why on earth would he do something like that?"

"Being in prison can leave a person with a lot of time for reflection and changes. Perhaps he realized his downfall was his own, and in his way the chestnuts might have been his way of saying he was sorry. So, as Paul said, you won't have to worry about it any longer."

He quickly finishes his coffee. "Well, I've got to go. Thanks for the coffee."

"Thank you so much for coming over and explaining everything. I do feel much safer now," says Grace.

"Good, I thought you would." He gives her a hug then shakes my hand. "I hear you two are getting married."

"Yes, we are," says Grace with a smile.

"I couldn't think of a nicer couple."

I put my arm around Grace and smile, "We couldn't either."

"Here," he says. "If you have any further questions or concerns, you can reach me here."

I take the card and see him out. When I return I'm relieved to see Grace pouring coffee.

"Coffee, I guess you are feeling better."

"That sure takes the stress off. But it still seems strange he would do that."

"What, send you chestnuts?"

"I may be overthinking this, but—he didn't know he was going to die, but did know he was up for parole, which means he could still have been thinking of revenge when he got out."

She is overthinking this. "Grace, it's over. He's gone. You can put this behind you."

"If he was feeling bad about his revenge on me, wouldn't he have put a note in the parcel to state that?"

She's making too much sense. I have to steer her away. "That is a possibility, I guess. He might not have been able to get a note to the person who sent them, but that is something we'll never know, sweetheart."

"No, we won't, will we?" She says it with a look I've never seen before, almost foreboding and creepy-like.

"Say, how's that reception menu coming?"

"What? Oh, the menu, it's all done, and it's going to be great!"

"Now we just have to figure out the invitations. Do you have an idea of how many?"

"It's a rough list," she says. "I think we should sit down and discuss this soon."

Good, she's back on track.

—

May flowers appear, and we are prepared for the wedding. We've even whittled down those wedding invitations to a cozy twenty-nine, with Mrs. Parson being the odd number. Charlie will be my best man, standing in for Ben, of course. Grace found an old address book to look up her old friend Joyce to be her maid of honor, and to Grace's delight, she accepted.

Both restaurants are doing well. We've stopped looking over our shoulders, and life is sweet all the way around. Getting outdoors in summer clothes sure feels good. Even Adam is upbeat when we drop by to see him, and as sad as it is, Tor told us there was no longer any sign of Ed in the woods. Speaking of Tor, prospective buyers are coming out to see his cottages —another sign of summer.

I haven't had any contact with Alex and that's fine. The feeling of having to reciprocate a favor still weighs on me.

—

Two and a half weeks before our big day and we finally get a chance to sit down and discuss the cherry on top—the honeymoon.

"I know Mexico with that disease they've got there isn't in the cards?" says Grace.

"And the islands are way too hot."

"You know, Paul, I've always dreamed about going to Europe, especially Paris and Tuscany. I know it can be warm there, too, but not with the same humidity like the islands."

"I like it, Grace. I had relatives in Italy on my mother's side. They're all gone now, but she showed me pictures, and it sure would be nice to visit. And Paris would be so romantic. I'm sold."

"Then that's the ticket for us."

"How's two weeks sound?"

"Two weeks is perfect. I'm sure the businesses will survive. Can you book that today?"

"Absolutely."

"I'm so glad you're on board with this. I think it will be so nice for us—the scenery, the art, the food, the culture."

"—and the wine."

Grace smiles, "And the wine."

Grace is so excited. This will bring us even closer—if that's possible. It will be like falling in love all over again.

CHAPTER 17

Our wedding day—I can't believe it's here. We want to do this right, so I spent the night at the house and Grace stayed at Rebecca's so I don't get to see her beforehand.

I was hoping for a great sleep to have enough energy to last into the night, and I got it. I owe it to those two slices of cold pizza before bed.

All right, let's see. The tux hangs over the bedroom door, the shoes directly underneath on the floor and nicely polished, I may add. I glance at the bedroom clock—7:15, excellent, lots of time.

A shower, a shave and a light breakfast.

Now, I guess I'll just hang around in my housecoat until noon. With the ceremony at two, I should be there at 1:15 to make sure all is in order. I think I'll check the latest news.

I can't wait to see Grace make her entrance down the stairs. She'll be breathtaking. I haven't had anything this well planned since my divorce papers. Oops, wrong time to bring that up.

—

I check myself out in the full-length mirror. "Well, how do I look? You look fantastic. Can I have your autograph? Not now, kid, I've got a wedding to attend—mine."

I begin to feel a little shaky. I stick out my hand and notice a slight tremor. "We don't need that." I pour a shot and wait a few seconds before I check my hand again. "That's better. Okay, on with the show." I lock the door and turn to the road.

"Oh, shit," I say under my breath. In the middle of the road is Alex's chauffeured car with Alex back in his old man disguise, next to an open rear door. All I can think of is, NOT NOW!

"Paul, you're the cat's meow."

"Yes, well, when you're about to get married this seems to be the attire. Your timing is impeccable. What do you want, Alex?"

"Don't be so defensive. I thought it would be improper for you to drive yourself to your own wedding."

"It's just down the road. I think I could manage that."

"Nonsense, allow me the honor."

I don't have the time or patience to argue. I get in and hope this won't be some long, drawn-out conversation about agents and corporations.

He holds out his hand.

"Congratulations, Paul. You've got a wonderful woman there, and I wish you both all the best."

He reaches down to the floor and pulls up a blue-and-pink wrapped gift. "Just a little something to show my appreciation for all you did for my son. I guess you could say a gift from both of us."

If I was double-jointed I'd kick my own ass right now. "That's very nice of you, Alex. I feel bad not inviting you to the wedding."

"Don't be. You know I couldn't be there anyway. I'm dead, remember."

We pull up to Rebecca's and I get out with gift in hand.

"Remember, Paul, having your back isn't a one-shot deal. As long as I'm alive, you'll never have to worry about any threats. I hope sending Eric to see you was beneficial."

Eric! "Yes, yes, it was. It certainly calmed Grace down. I can't thank you enough."

Chalk up another one for his side. If these favors keep up, I may have to work for him full-time.

He smiles. "Now get in there and seal the deal."

Now where have I heard that before?

—

It almost feels like an out-of-body experience being here to exchange the vows of our lifetime commitment to each other. I just can't take my eyes off her. She has never been one for makeup, and that's one thing I've always loved about her, her natural beauty, but whatever subtle changes with makeup she has made just amplifies that beauty. She is all smiles as she looks to her side to see Joyce. She looks beautiful as well.

I look to my best man, Charlie. He seems more emotional and nervous than I do. If I passed him on the street, I wouldn't recognize him. With his beard and hair trimmed and that pinstriped suit—slightly dated, yet he looks quite stately. This will be one hell of a great day.

When I look into Grace's eyes to deliver the most important words I will ever say, a calm comes over me. All the eyes that are focused on us seem to fade away, along with all our troubles. I feel like we are the only two in the room. I take her hand and hold it to my chest and announce in a soft voice how beautiful she looks and what she has meant to me—that my love for her grows stronger every moment we are together. My feelings cross over into the words flowing from my heart, words I'm sure I could never repeat as eloquently as I do now.

Her eyes fill and a tear and slowly trickles down the sides of each cheek. Her words sing to me like notes from a songbird, each one entering my heart and settling deep into my soul.

We seal our love with a kiss, and for all of those in attendance it must have moved them, too, for there was a moment of silence as though they were all trying to collect themselves.

—

Grace and I are just amazed how great our day turned out. All these people who two years ago I had no idea existed are now our friends—wonderful friends and great people.

Ben would drill it into me every chance he got—community is everything. He would have loved this.

—

The day gradually turns into night, and we slip into our civvy attire and, as they say, *dance the night away*. Eventually the music lightens up on our ears until it is barely audible. It was a long day for us both, and it was time for Cinderella to put those glass slippers to rest. There are only three tables of die-hards that remain, and as we approach them to say goodnight they all rise, exchanging handshakes and hugs, and we are on our way back to our castle down the road.

"It's such a gorgeous night and the air smells so wonderful. I'm glad we decided to walk," says Grace.

"We had no choice. Alex drove me over. Look—the moon to lead our way."

"Not that we need it. How many times have we made this trip?"

"And many in the dead of winter."

"And so many gifts. Those people are so kind. I love them."

"I guess we should have put them away."

"I left instructions to have them left in my office and we'll pick them up tomorrow."

"Grace, I have to say, you sure make a great manager. I think this marriage might just last awhile."

"Oh, you do, do you?"

We get to the house, and I'm so tired I can barely focus my eyes on the keyhole.

"I hope the great manager doesn't mean that *I* have to carry *you* over the threshold," says Grace.

"Never." I pick Grace up in my arms and push the door open with my foot.

"Oh, Rhett."

"Frankly, my dear, I do give a damn."

—

I guess I wasn't as tired as I thought. We are still in bed at ten in the morning. Me with my hands behind my head and a smile on my face—if this was an old movie I would have a Marlboro hanging from my lips. Grace has the sheets over her head to block the sun from the window. Then Grace's muffled voice from under the sheets, "Are you awake, Paul?"

"If I wasn't, I am now." I roll over to cuddle her.

"Paul, I don't even have my eyes open."

"Grace, you married *me*, remember—not a comic book hero."

"Thank goodness for that."

"It's a good thing we don't smoke."

She pulls the covers from her face. "What are you talking about?"

"We might have gone through a whole pack last night."

"What do you mean...oh, you're bad," she laughs. "Since you're so spunky this morning, how about you making the coffee?"

"Are you sure you want to trust me with all that caffeine?"

"I'll take my chances."

"I'm on my way."

Minutes later I hear her laugh, then she hollers, "How's that coffee coming!"

"I didn't know you were into fast food! Give me two minutes!"

Here she comes in her robe.

"Hey, I said a couple of minutes."

"I had a thought. Why don't we have that coffee then go to Rebecca's for breakfast and open our gifts? I'd like to say goodbye to Joyce."

"I think it was very nice of you to give her a room."

"That's the least I could do for driving all the way up here."

"Another reason I love you, you take care of your friends like family. So, breakfast and gifts. I'm all for that. Here's your coffee, Mrs. Fenton."

"I like the sound of that."

—

No sooner do we look at the menu, and Joyce enters the dining room.

"Joyce, over here," says Grace waving her hand.

"And how are the newlyweds this morning?"

"Wonderful. Would you like to join us?"

"Well, I don't want to im—"

"Impose, never. It will be a chance for me to get to know you," I say.

"Thank you."

"And order whatever your heart desires. We have a great breakfast menu. It's all on us."

"Thank you again. This is such a wonderful place," she says as she looks around. "The room is lovely, and I love the town. When you called me and said you lived in Willow's End, I was expecting it to be some little out-of-the-way fishing village."

We laugh.

"My god, Joyce, you must have been terrified driving up here with that image in your head."

"I was born and raised in the city. I had no idea of country life or small towns. When I arrived and saw the town and met some of the people, I began to realize why you came here and stayed. And, of course, I'm sure Paul played a large role in that."

"Well, maybe a little," I say with a smile.

"Paul was all of it and still is."

"You sure make a wonderful couple. You know, I was thinking, why don't I move up here? Why am I banging my head against the wall in the city? It's too big and I feel like I can't breathe."

I look at Grace. "That's exactly how we felt."

"Joyce, why don't you do it?" says Grace. "Move up here."

"But what would I do for a job?"

"You can work here. I would love to have you."

"Really, you mean that?"

"Of course."

"I'd need a place to stay. I have enough money for a down payment on a small house, and I heard it's a lot cheaper up here."

I jump in. "We can help you with that. We have a friend in the real estate business."

"That's right. I'm sure Tor would be happy to help you."

"You two drive a hard bargain. I'm sold."

"Good," says Grace. "You'll love it here."

Grace is painting such a beautiful picture and what she's saying is true, but I can't help thinking of the horrors we have unearthed.

After breakfast we say goodbye to Joyce with her commitment to be back as soon as she settles up with her rent and ties up her loose ends.

"It will be so nice to have Joyce living and working here. She needs the change as much as I did."

"And won't it be nice to have an old friend become a new friend again."

"That's true, Paul. It will be nice for me, too. I know we've gone through a lot, but that's on our plate. All Joyce has to do is enjoy work, nature, and this great community."

"Well, how about those gifts?"

"You're like a little kid at Christmas. Beat you there!"

We rush to Grace's office.

The gifts are piled up on the desk, and we each take one and begin unwrapping them.

We finally arrive at the last two gifts.

I open a gift from Charlie. "Well, that's Charlie, all right."

"What is it?"

"Two coffee mugs with our names on them and a jar of Emporium Supreme."

Grace laughs. "He's so sweet," then picks up the last gift. "Oh, this is pretty."

"That came from Alex."

"That was awfully nice of him."

She gently tears off the paper from the box. "It's almost a shame to rip this beautiful paper." She lifts the lid and reaches in, pulling away the inside layer of tissue paper. Her eyes widen. "Oh my god!"

"What is it?"

She just stands there frozen.

I gently take the box out from her hands and peer inside. "What the hell is this—chestnuts? Alex gives us chestnuts. What was he thinking—that this would be funny? I'll kill that son of a bitch!"

Grace is starting to teeter. I pull up a chair and have her sit.

"Obviously he's not the humanitarian I thought he was! And here he is watching every move we make, for what? To protect us! And who's protecting us from him?"

"Paul," says Grace in a calm, soft voice. "Call Eric, please."

"Eric. Yes, I'll call Eric." I look down at Grace and her face has the look of defeat. "Now, how do I get ahold of him?"

"He gave you his card, remember."

"That's right. I put it on the fridge door."

I don't know what else is going on in Grace's mind, but she seems more rational than I am. Self-control and judgment has left me. I feel like I'm possessed.

Grace doesn't want to move. "Are you all right if I go back to the house to call Eric?"

She nods.

"I won't be long, sweetheart." I tell one of the waitresses she's not feeling well and to keep an eye on her until I get back.

Pulling partially into the driveway, I'm so distraught that I run over a bush. I rush in and make the call. I know it's his job, but I find him exceptionally calm about it.

"I'll get back to you," he says.

That's not very helpful. Of course, if he works for Alex, there would be some bias there.

Back in the car, I reach into the glove compartment for the Magnum. Why? What the hell am I doing—leave it. I must calm down, and not just for Grace's sake, but my own.

I get back to Grace and she's not there. I ask one of the staff, and they say she went out and got into a car with some old man.

Old man—Alex, that was fast. Now why the hell does Alex want to see Grace, to apologize?

Walking out to the road, I see Alex's vehicle parked across the street about five stores up. Now it's time for the Magnum. I grab the gun, put it in my belt and head for Alex's car. I don't know what to expect or how to handle the situation. I'm five feet away and the rear door opens and out pops Grace, and I hear her say, "Thank you, Alex."

He says something back that is inaudible.

"I will," says Grace.

The car pulls away. Grace turns around to see me. "Paul. You just missed—"

"Yeah, I can see that. What's going on?" I'm fuming now. I want answers.

"Let's go back to Rebecca's and I'll tell you." She's a lot calmer than when I left her.

"All right, I could use a drink."

She notices the gun. "What are you doing with that?"

"I—I don't know."

"Do you really want to bring it into Rebecca's?"

I look down at the gun. "I'll leave it in the car."

The dining room is always empty between breakfast and lunch. We sit at our table looking out to the street. This will be a serious conversation. I decide to volley first.

"So, you talked to Alex." A gentle lob over the net.

"I did—very interesting, but strange. He said that gift didn't come from him."

"But that's the one he gave me. I put that in your office myself. What's he trying to pull?"

"Take it easy, Paul. Why would he do something like that, especially to us? Someone switched it."

"But they've got surveillance all through this place. I was there, I saw what they have and nothing could get by."

"Alex said they analyzed every move that went on in Rebecca's right from the moment you walked in with the gift."

"And—"

"They looked at my office, and for a three-second flash, that gift was absent and then reappeared. I asked him how it was possible. He said, think about it. What could make an object disappear?"

"A Q4."

"That's what I thought. But he said, why would they even have that information about the chestnuts and what would be their motive? What value or purpose would that serve them?"

"He's right, Grace. Did he have any other thoughts on who it might be?"

"He did. He said whoever did this was linked to Joe—possibly a relative—out to make things right with Joe."

"But this is ridiculous! You had no part in any of that!"

"I know."

"And how would a guy like that have a Q4 unless he—"

"Exactly—he killed an agent."

"Now this is becoming complicated. Why would he have killed an agent?"

"Alex said the UWC will use gangsters or motorcycle gangs to do a dirty job so it doesn't get traced back to them, and perhaps something went wrong. Maybe an agent was killed and his Q4 got into the wrong hands."

"So what does Alex intend to do?"

"He sounded very confident the problem would be resolved in the next few days."

"That's a relief."

"Oh, one more item—the amount we put on our credit card for our honeymoon."

"It was declined?"

"No, it was reversed."

"What do you mean, reversed?"

"This should change any concerns you had about Alex—he paid for our trip."

"You mean the whole package, flight and all?"

"He felt so bad about it, this was his way of making it right. I guess your original assessment of him was the one you need to remember; he has the power, and he sure cares about us."

"What a jerk I've been."

"I don't think so. I think you are just a loving husband protecting his wife."

I lean over the table and kiss her. "Thank you, sweetheart."

Now how many people will I have to put into my trunk to balance this out?

—

Alex was right. It only took a few days. There was a small hiccup about it in the city paper. All it said was local gangster disappears along with his car, and foul play was suspected. I would check the wreckers, but not for a car—just a cube of metal.

CHAPTER 18

The first day of our honeymoon has arrived. As the plane rests on the tarmac waiting for takeoff Grace says, "We must look like a couple high school kids on their first date."

"I haven't felt this giddy since Charlie gave me my first Emporium Supreme."

"For a romantic guy you can sure miss the mark at times."

"Grace, that's just coffee; in my book you reign supreme."

"That's my man. For a minute there I thought I lost you."

Finally, it's liftoff, and as the tires leave the ground and fold away, I remember one small item—I'm afraid of flying.

Grace smiles at me and grabs my hand. "Here we go."

I remember those words coming from my best friend as we reached the top of that steep roller-coaster track when I was ten. My breathing is compromised to the point I respond to her with a forced smile and possibly a look that could be misinterpreted as constipation. She's so excited it passes her by.

"I think I'll rest my eyes for a bit. We did have an early start."

I mange to squeak out, "Me, too." With my eyes now closed I search for some nice moment to deflect my paranoid state, but for some reason I'm forced to recall only one. Years ago I took a train trip to Toronto to visit an old friend. He told me he had just received his pilot's license and wanted to take me up for a spin around the city. *Why me?* I thought. He was so proud of his accomplishment. After a couple of drinks I felt the courage to overcome this childhood fear. It was one of those two-seaters, and once inside I shut the door to a very airtight sound like being in a Volkswagen Beetle. Then I really panicked. I'm going to be flying in a car with wings.

He was all smiles. "You're going to love it. You've never seen the city like this."

About five minutes in I started to relax. He circled the CN Tower. "Spectacular," I said. I was almost to the point of enjoying myself, until—

"I'll show you one of the tests you have to pass to get your license."

Trying to sound interested, "Oh, what's that?"

Right then. With no warning. He shut down the engine! We were floating like a kite without the string! We were going to go down! I was in the hands of a maniac! I was going to DIE! To say I panicked was an understatement. I was yelling every obscenity I had ever heard and just two words away from—*Mummy!*

He turned the engine back on and began to laugh and said, "You'd never get your license."

I hear Grace's voice calling me and open my eyes.

"Paul, it's time to eat. Here's a list of the options." She hands me a small sheet of paper.

"Those are options?"

"We aren't in Paris yet, sweetheart."

"No kidding."

Similar to my first flight experience, I begin to relax. Of course, after three and a half hours in, what else is there to do.

—

Ah, Paris—filled with art, outdoor cafés, and fantastic food. At night, a lovers' paradise. Grace fits in so well. She looks absolutely stunning—capturing the eyes of waiters, artists and patrons. They really appreciate women here. There's a respect for beauty that you don't find back home, and Grace loves every minute of it—and I love every minute with her.

As we stroll down one of the main streets a fashionable clothing store catches Grace's attention. "Paul, I'd like to go in and have a look, would you mind?"

"Actually, I was hoping you would say that. Enjoy yourself, that's why we're here. I'll make myself comfortable at that outdoor bar across the way."

Since we've been together she's never gone out and bought anything for herself. But then that's Grace—the work comes first.

There is a difference sitting outside at a Paris bar. What it is I can't say for sure, but I like it a lot. I order a beer and entertain myself watching the other patrons as well as those passing by. Life here seems to be at a pace that suits me. If I had to describe it, I would compare it to a car. In the US we would get one mile of pleasure for every ten gallons, and here it's the opposite.

Here we are, our last night in Paris. Just for fun we decide to pick up a baguette, some cheeses, a bottle of red, and walk down the street like true Parisians to our hotel. We take the tiny elevator up to our room, sit out on the balcony, crack open the bottle of wine, pull apart some bread and cheese and enjoy the magic of this city. We raise our glasses and make a toast to us, this wonderful honeymoon and our further journey in life together.

—

"Ahhhhh!"

I wake up to Grace thrashing and talking in her sleep. "Grace. Grace, wake up."

Her eyes pop open and she's panting.

"Are you all right? You've been dreaming."

"Oh, my god! Not a dream, a terrible nightmare. That guy Joe and chestnuts."

"That's still with you, huh?"

"It was awful, Paul. We were at the airport. I had a craving for a snack. I looked around and noticed a row of vending machines. I told you that I'd be right back. I saw a bag of corn chips and shoved a Euro into the coin slot, then watched the transition from top shelf to the bottom door. Just as I reached down to open the door, a familiar voice rings out, 'How about these?'

"I turned around to see a brown paper bag hurtling toward my face. I tried to block it. The bag broke and chestnuts flew in the air—then a hideous laugh—it was Joe! Oh, my god, Paul—it was terrifying. His face was gray-blue. His throat was cut open so wide and deep, I could see his spinal cord. Blood spewed from his mouth as he told me I still owed him a dinner. I would never have had a thought like that, let alone a nightmare."

I hold her in my arms. "Funny how our subconscious picks up on those things, like a knee-jerk reaction to reality, distorting it into something out of a Stephen King novel." I wonder if he gets his ideas the same way.

"Anyway, we have so much to look forward to. It's all good now, sweetheart."

She smiles, "Yes, it is."

—

Italy—we start in Florence. I looked up the word, and it was no surprise to find out it means blossoming, flourishing, and prosperous. It's mesmerizing—the buildings, the art, the gardens, and always the food, wine, and people. I never thought I would ever have an opportunity to see any part of the Old World. My only glimpse has been watching Rick Steves on PBS.

I pull out a couple of pictures from my travel bag that I had picked out from one my grandmother's old photo albums. "Look, Grace. My mother when she was about ten years old with my grandmother standing right here at this very pillar. Isn't that amazing?"

"That is amazing. Feels like you should be able to reach out and touch them."

"It does," I say, wiping a tear from my eye. This is a wonderful experience, especially for me. The only way to describe it is to use that one word, surreal.

Before we leave a waiter suggests we go to Piazzale Michelangelo to really capture and appreciate the city. I don't think I could appreciate it any more than I do now, but Grace is all for it.

It takes us about ten minutes to walk a fairly steep hill, but the effort sure pays off.

"Oh my gosh, Paul! Have you ever in your life?"

"And probably never again. It's magnificent!"

A 360-degree view of the Tuscan capital and the surrounding area. Our tour of the city couldn't end on a higher note, literally.

—

Our next stop is Rome. Grace suggests that I pick the first sight on this tour, and I choose theColosseum. This is the real one, not a movie set. In those Roman days there would have be 65,000 bloodthirsty spectators watching battles between gladiators to the death—similar to watching political news on TV.

Grace understands a man's fascination with this time period, but she is not at all interested in the gore and madness it holds. Possibly a few planters of flowers would make a difference.

Our next stop is the beautiful Trevi Fountain. Now we're talking Grace's language.

"What a magnificent work of art," says Grace.

"It boggles my mind how anyone could create work of this magnitude and elegance, truly the centerpiece of the city."

"It is, Paul. Pictures are one thing, but to be here and take in its scale is more than breathtaking."

"You know, Grace, when I think about it, it seems like we have lost our ability to create beautiful cities anymore."

"Oh, I'm sure we have the ability, we just don't have the time or interest in doing that. I think the architects of today might consider it a step backwards."

"I guess cutting-edge means exactly that. Cold, sharp angles and lines is what they call creative."

—

During the next two days we take in the Pantheon, St. Peter's Basilica, and we both agreed, our favorite is Michelangelo's Sistine Chapel. Neither one of us has any religious ties, but I have to say, the second we walked in, we felt something spiritual, even mystical. How that genius accomplished such an amazing work is beyond me. The height of scaffolding alone would be scary enough.

Our day meals are spent at little cafés and the evenings at restaurants. A local suggests that we go to the opposite bank of the River Tiber to the old working-class neighborhood called Trastevere.

"What do you think, Grace? Should we give it a go?"

"Nothing ventured."

"Getting lost in this part of the city would be easy. A maze of narrow streets with medieval houses and—"

"Restaurants," says Grace.

We find one with lively music, and the people make us feel like family.

We are enjoying every moment of our honeymoon. Roaming the towns and villages makes me realize that this country is more than wine and good food. A lot more. It's the people, their history and the closeness of their families. There is a respect for the older generation that permeates right down to the children. Ben was on the right track about community, but this is like a higher order. I notice two other components to their lifestyle, they do a lot of walking and talking, and are never short of an opinion. They could argue about anything. Waving their arms in the air with great animation, but no one pulled a knife or a gun. They just have another glass of wine.

We rent a small car and leave all the glamour and historical sights of the cities and head to a humble little town, the place where my ancestors lived. Even the drive is breathtaking. Tuscany is incredible. Huge homes dot the landscape amongst the quaint little farmhouses and the hillsides covered with rows upon rows of grapes, which also make wine, by the way.

"Wouldn't it be nice to have a place here where we could retreat to every year?" says Grace.

"You wouldn't have to ask me twice."

Grace starts singing. "Fairy tales can come true, it can happen to you, when you're young at heart."

"And have deep pockets."

"Can't you think out of the box?"

"Isn't that how we got Ben's Place?"

"There you go."

"What about, don't bite off more than you can chew"?

"That's only for people with dentures."

—

We are in the small town of Borgo a Mozzano—the Devil's Bridge. A spectacular stone bridge over the Serchio River that was built in the fourteenth century.

"This is the town where my grandmother lived." My voice has a slight quiver as I talk about it.

"Come on, Paul. Let's walk it to the middle."

We stand in the middle of the bridge, and what a nice view. "What's the story behind the Devil's Bridge? It sounds eerie," says Grace.

"From what I understand, the master builder for the bridge was having a hard time trying to finish it because at the time the strong currents of the river wouldn't allow him to continue. One day this stranger came into town and told him that he could help him build it in one day. The only stipulation was that he could take the soul of the first person who crossed it. He knew then it was the devil. He went to the priest to ask for help, and he told him to have a dog be the first to walk the bridge. So he did and the devil left in a huff and never returned."

"That's quite a story, I like it."

I point to a building on the other side of the river. "You see that apartment building? That second-floor window is where my great-grandmother lived, along with my grandmother and my mother, when she was a little girl."

Grace grabs my arm and pushes up against me. "It's wonderful, Paul. I'm so glad we got to do this."

"Me too. I guess that's the second item off my bucket list."

"What was the first?"

"Marrying you."

We spend our last two days walking the streets, taking in the local cuisine and a limited amount of hillsides. I think I'll be sleeping the whole trip home.

—

Like Dorothy said, *"There's no place like home."* I finally understand that line, *going back to the future.*

We have one B-grade meal on the plane, but pass on the nuts.

CHAPTER 19

Charlie wanted to pick us up at the airport and he does, with an ear-to-ear smile detectable under his whiskers. We laugh as he holds up a sign that reads—*Paul and Grace, Welcome home.*

"Charlie, we're so glad to see you," says Grace.

"By the way, there was no need for the sign, that's only used if you don't know who you're picking up."

"Oh well. I saw it in a movie once, seemed like a good thing. Adds a little drama, don't you think?"

"Of course, we are always short of that. How's everything at home?"

Charlie brings us up to date during our ride home. "I've been thinking of starting another business. Have you got your seat belts on?"

"Of course," says Grace.

"Okay. I'm going to sell cans of coffee, Supremes."

"But that would be illegal. You could be put in jail."

"Not anymore, Paul. They finally legalized it last week."

"I'd like to get in on that venture."

"Sure thing—I'll give you 30 percent off each can."

"That's not quite what I had in mind. I was thinking more of a partnership."

"Oh, I see. I'll have to talk that over with my other investor, Bo."

"Bo?" asks Grace.

"Yep. I picked him up at the pound three days ago. Now that I'll be dealing drugs, so to speak, I'll need top security, and he's almost as smart as I am."

It's hard to keep a straight face, but somehow I manage.

"So how strong will this coffee be?" asks Grace.

"Well, you don't want it too strong, people still have to function. I tested it on myself and finally made a recipe of coffee beans and the leafy lettuce that are in perfect balance. I would say it's smooth and mellow."

"Have you had a chance to drop in at Willow's End or Bridgeburg?" I ask.

"You asked me to and I did it to the best of my ability—I went to both in one day. Had an early breakfast at Ben's Place, then a late lunch at Rebecca's. It was all good and everything seemed to be running well at both establishments."

"That was quite the sacrifice, Charlie—you didn't have indigestion, I hope."

"Me? No. Everything I'm asked to do, I do with a smile." He smiles. "I'll send you the meal receipts."

"I'm sure you will," I say with a grin.

—

We're home. As we move along the main street of town, we round the bend at Rebecca's and glance up at the windows of the dining room, and it looks like things are in full swing for lunch.

"Looks like the place is still in one piece."

"And doing well, like you said," says Grace.

"See," says Charlie, "just like I said, everything is going well—nothing to worry about."

Charlie pulls up to our house and it looks so inviting. Our house—I never would have imagined any of it on the day I took that drive in the country. We say goodbye to Charlie and enter the house.

"Oh, it's so nice to be home," says Grace, then plops herself on the sofa. "Even this couch with the slight bulge from that one spring doesn't bother me."

I laugh. "Give it a week."

—

We're back at work. Grace at Rebecca's where she runs the show, and I grab the reins at Ben's Place. I have an easier job of it. Justine is our day manager, and you might say I'm more of an observer. When she smiles, I smile. If she doesn't, that's when I spring into action.

"Paul, we're getting a little low on eggs," she says.

"I'm on it." See what I mean?

Walking into the kitchen, I look on the bulletin board where Grace had conveniently placed a sheet of all the companies and farmers we deal with. *Eggs—Andrew's Family Farm.*

Under that is the telephone number—I sure have it rough.

Since everything is under control here, I think I'll leave early and head to Rebecca's to see if I can be of any use to Grace. Perhaps *she* needs eggs.

No sooner do I arrive, there rests Alex's vehicle with the back door open, but no Alex. I peer inside and the driver announces, "Mr. Fenton, Mr. Miller would appreciate your company."

I'm not sure I would appreciate his. *Don't be so negative. He may just want to know how your honeymoon went. After all, he did pay for it.* That's right. If *I* had put out that kind of dough for someone, I would sure like to know if they had a good time. I climb in.

"Onward, Jeeves."

"Jeeves is a butler."

"Oh, well what should I call you then?"

He turns back to me. "Anas?"

Boy, he's leaving himself wide open with that one. "Right."

"It means popularity."

In some circles I'm sure. "Very nice. Fine day isn't it—Anus?"

"It's pronounced A*nas*."

That's a hard call. If you say it fast it pretty much sounds the same. I won't make that mistake again. I know enough that a name in other countries can have a lot more thought put into them. A name would have honor and respect. Far more than picking a name out of a hat or giving the kid a name that the poor bugger will have to change when they grow up all because their parents decided on, *ET,* when they were going through a pound of mushrooms a week to get them to a fifth dimension. This might be a good one for a sitcom—just saying.

I guess that's the end of the conversation, then there's a blinding flash of white light. I close my eyes for a moment then open them to find the vehicle parked in front of Alex's shack.

"We're here," says Anas.

I won't bother to ask, I'm sure it was a TED. I walk inside and stand in the same area as the first time. With Alex not here to open it, I don't know how long I will be standing here befo—The wall opens up to the other room and I can see Alex standing there with two glasses of refreshment.

"Well, you look pretty relaxed for a married man." He extends one of the glasses toward me.

"I think you would be very disappointed if I wasn't, after paying for our honeymoon. I can't thank you enough." Oh-oh. I'm setting myself up.

"It was my pleasure. Come and sit down."

Try to look comfortable and relaxed with my honeymoon face. It isn't as easy as I thought it would be when I have that Godfather feeling looming over me.

"So, how did Grace enjoy the trip?"

"I've never seen her so happy. We were in awe of it all."

"And has she eliminated that threat from her mind?"

I won't mention the nightmare. "I think it was Paris that nipped that in the bud."

"Good. I know she's a hard worker and dedicated to Rebecca's and ready to get back."

"And, of course, it's not that she didn't love it there."

"Like they say, there's no place like home."

Hmm, was he eavesdropping, and why so many questions about Grace? I take a sip of scotch and experience a brief moment of uneasy silence, at least on my part.

"Paul, I've also asked you here for another reason."

Here it comes.

"With your permission, I would like to place some cameras in and around Ben's Place."

"You're expecting some kind of trouble there?"

"I hope not, but something in my gut tells me it would be a good idea."

"So, why ask me? Why don't you just have one of your computer guys, like Bruce, keep an eye on the place?"

"I can't afford to tie up a man on a feeling when simple cameras will do the job. That's why, as a courtesy, I'm asking you to allow me to put them in place. I want to be as up-front with you as best I can on anything that may concern you or have any repercussions that could interfere with you and Grace's well-being. Besides, every business should have at least the minimum security in place."

Boy, talk about watching my back. "We've never had them in Rebecca's."

"That's because the UWC was running the show before you inherited it, and there was no reason for them to watch themselves."

"Alex—after all you've done for us, I'll do whatever it takes to help you to keep our towns safe."

"Good," he says, then picks up something from a side table. "This is for you." He reaches out and hands me a TED.

"For me? But I have that Q4."

"I can't have you walking around with outdated equipment. Besides, you don't have that Q4 anymore."

"What do you mean?"

"I confiscated it."

"But how did you do that without—you used a TED."

"All I ask is that you go home and study it. Get familiar with it."

He reaches into his shirt pocket and pulls out a business-sized card and hands it to me. It has a code on it.

"Put that code into your cell phone, and it will bring up everything you need to know about the TED."

"This is very nice of you, Alex."

"It has nothing to do with nice. It's the best weapon you could have—use it with the utmost respect and always think twice before you do. If you make a mistake with that, they stay mistakes. Now go home and do your homework."

In a matter of seconds after getting back into the vehicle, I find myself getting out at Rebecca's. I say thanks to *Anas* and keep a straight face.

—

The dining room is still very busy even though lunch hour is coming to an end. Grace is sitting at a table sipping coffee and looking through the local paper.

"Well, you look busy."

Grace looks up. "Actually, it has been a busy day. I've been training."

"Training, training who?"

"Joyce."

"I thought that was left up to one of the waitresses."

"But she won't be waitressing."

"Then what?"

"Sit down, Paul. I got to thinking that I would be wasting Joyce as a waitress. Not only does she have a lot of banking knowledge, but she has taken courses in accounting."

"Oh, I see. You want her to take over the office."

"Exactly."

"So, you want to concentrate on more important things, like I'm doing."

"And what, pray tell, are you doing?"

She has a sparkle in her eyes and I know what's coming. This is one of those great things I love about her, when she follows my lead of sarcasm.

"Take this morning for instance. We were running out of eggs and I had to jump into action. I rushed into the kitchen, searched the corkboard and honed in on the right business card that corresponded to the problem at hand. Then, with great skill I placed the order over the phone. I used calm and eloquent speech. *I need eggs,* I said. You see how that rolls off the tongue. Not one word wasted—straight to the point. Amazing what you can do under pressure."

"That's so true, and you did all that on your own. Perhaps I should stay in my boring position of just doing *everything.* I'm sure it would be much less stressful than the complicated act of ordering eggs. The prospect of opening a carton and finding that you're one short of a dozen could be devastating."

I smile and watch her lips curl up at the ends. "You know, Grace, when we finally retire from this business I think we should take this show on the road—the improvisational team of Paul and Grace."

"I'm for that, with one minor adjustment: Grace and Paul."

"I think I could handle that—as long as I'm paid the same."

We've put ourselves in a good place right now, which means I can tell her about my conversation with Alex.

"I also saw Alex this morning."

"Alex? He dropped into Ben's Place?"

"No. His chauffeur An—" I pretend to clear my throat. "His chauffeur picked me up."

"I guess he was interested to know how our trip was."

"He was and I thanked him once again."

"Good. He's been so nice to us. I hope we can remain friends."

"He seemed to be very interested in you."

"Me? How's that?"

"He asked how much you enjoyed yourself and that he knows you are a hard worker and dedicated to Rebecca's."

"That seems like normal conversation to me, Paul. This isn't one of your detective personalities coming out, is it?"

"No, you're right. He was also asking if you were over the chestnut ordeal."

"That was very nice of him to ask. You didn't mention my crazy nightmare?"

"No."

I take a short commercial break. I call the waitress over for a grilled cheese sandwich and a beer. "Did you want anything, Grace?"

"I do feel a little peckish. I'll have a grilled cheese, too."

"There was something else."

"I just had a feeling it couldn't all be roses. What's the underbelly?"

"I wouldn't say underbelly. He wants to put cameras in Ben's Place."

"Okay, why?"

"He just has a feeling."

"A feeling? What kind of feeling, like someone wants to do some damage to the place?"

"I'm not sure. I guess that's part of his commitment to protecting us."

Her eyes drift from side to side, as though she were watching a slow tennis match. "Why can't he do the less-intrusive spying, like what he does to Rebecca's and our private home, where they could look in anytime while we're walking around naked?"

"He said that wouldn't happen. They would only check in if something looked suspicious. Now the reason he gave me for using cameras was, there was no point in tying up a man on a feeling when simple cameras will do the job."

"That makes sense, but this business about a feeling makes me nervous. What kind of feeling are we talking about? Is it fear? Is it indigestion? What's he worried about?"

"It may be the UWC. It's just precautionary."

"I feel like we have to do whatever he says."

"He asked me first, Grace. He wants to be up-front with as much as possible with anything that concerns us. He wants us to be as protected as possible. Look—" I pull the TED from my pocket. "He gave me a TED. You see, everything he does is for our benefit."

"It is, isn't it? I guess my only concern is that our customers may think we are watching them as if they are thieves."

"We tell them the same thing that Alex told us, protection."

"Protection from what? We can't say the UWC."

"Protection from...unruly customers. And besides, Grace, they won't be those honkin' commercial cameras. They'll be like, little pinholes or something. No one will even know they're there."

—

"I see you got some cameras installed," says Gus as I refill his coffee cup.

That didn't last long. "How do you know that?"

"Had to get up last night to drain a vein and noticed a van out front and they were bringing in some wiring and cables."

"So you assumed it was for cameras."

"I think the giveaway was on the side of the van. It had a picture of a lens with an eye in it."

"You wouldn't mind keeping that to yourself, would you Gus?"

"Sure thing, we wouldn't want the town to think you don't trust them."

"Exactly," I say with a smile. "It's just for our customers' protection in case we get some disgruntled guests."

"I'll tell you one thing: I won't be one of them. Ben's Place will be a fixture in Bridgeburg for years to come."

"Thanks, Gus. I appreciate that."

"Some places you can tell right off the bat they won't make it. Like a sub shop opening across the street from another sub shop. How could it possibly survive?"

"I think it would if it was kosher."

"Kosher?"

I leave Gus with his puzzled look to examine the dining room for cameras, and to my surprise, I can't detect any. Those guys are good, mind you. I've never had a James Bond mentality. My interest stopped with The Hardy Boys, and even then, the storylines got confusing. Okay, so I wasn't an avid reader.

CHAPTER 20

The end of another day of fraternizing with the public and I'm tired. Doing practically nothing all day is a lot harder than it seems. Learning that lesson came early in my life when I got a job sweeping floors in a factory. After pushing a broom around for an hour, I asked a co-worker what I should do now, and he said, look busy. It was one of the hardest jobs I ever had. Between that and trying to hide from our boss for eight hours took a special talent. It finally wore me down and I quit.

Grace won't be home for another hour. I'll have one more coffee for the road and take the time to read everything I need to know about TED. I put the code that Alex gave me into my cell. The more I read, the more uncomfortable I feel. One tap of the wrong selection and it could be another catastrophe like Wagner. Turning another human being into burnt toast is not something I want to repeat, even though he deserved some bad karma.

On my way home I decide the best way to get over any fear would be to test the TED out. There's an old country road just up ahead. I turn down it and it veers sharply to the left. Perfect, I can't be seen from the road. Getting out of the car I look around for a target. I'd like to use it on the person who dumped his garbage here, what a mess. I'll focus on that old sofa and see if I can move it. I would set it to T1, but I think in its water-logged condition, I'll go for T2, aim and PRESS. Without any hesitation it takes off like a rocket over the treetops and explodes into snowflake-like particles that fill the sky and slowly drift down, showering the forest.

"Holee shit!" I turn TED off. Wow! I look at the powerhouse of technology and feel a god-like, superhero status permeating from the darkest place in my soul. This is way beyond a Q3. I notice that the T's go up to 5. My imagination can't go to what that last number would do. And look at that, the battery is still at 90 percent charge. I think that's enough practice for one day. It's too dangerous to keep in my pocket—I might trigger it without even knowing. I'll leave it in the glove box, where I keep the Magnum, which seems a little obsolete now.

I hear an engine and the sound of gravel being crushed under tires. The engine shuts down just before the bend. The sound of a car door opens and closes. There's commotion and a struggling, muffled voice.

"Let's walk him around the bend."

"Who's it going to be?"

"I'll let you do the honors."

"I think that honor was mine last time."

Last time? Cold-blooded killers.

Their voices become louder.

Think! Think! I race over to the passenger door and gently, but quickly, open the door and grab the gun and TED. I can't point TED at them and expect them to shake in their boots, but may need it as insurance in case things go awry. If I'm quiet enough I can slip through the trees and get behind them.

They spot my car. "Somebody's here."

"That's unfortunate, for them."

Through the leaves I make out three men. One with a gun and the second one holding the third man with his hands tied behind him and duct tape across his mouth. The one thing that sticks out is the second man's hair, flaming red.

A breeze in their faces rustles the nearby poplars, making it easier to creep up behind them.

"Anyone here?" asks the one toting the gun.

I have the Magnum in my right hand and TED in my left.

For a span of about eight seconds, I don't move or speak. That seems to throw a cloak of nervous uncertainty over them.

"What do you think, Pete?"

"Maybe they went for a piss or a walk in the woods."

Hoping to sound confident and with some authority I call out, "I'm right behind you."

Their bodies jerk at the sound of my voice. They sharply pivot around to see me.

"You've got some business here, asshole?"

"I do now. Let that guy go." Did I just say that?

The bound man squirms. The second man pulls a revolver from his coat. "I think you're overpowered, boot licker."

Boot licker? It's strange how humor can creep into these dire situations. I guess the ball's in my court. I'll stall for a moment to think.

"Whatever he's done, I don't think it warrants the death penalty."

"And what the hell would you know? He's done plenty."

He continues, as I plot my next move, rambling off a list of offenses that seem to be fabricated as he stumbles and stutters.

"Now, throw that gun into the bushes," says the first man.

I think this is the opening I've been waiting for. I throw the gun away. They could shoot me where I stand or, as I'm hoping for, more conversation. They have no idea that this cell phone-looking piece of equipment is what they should have asked me to throw away.

While the first man continues to talk, I try to aim TED at him without lifting my arm. I think I have him in my crosshairs. Without looking down I try to finger the correct button and PRESS.

He immediately spots the red light from TED, but it's too late. During that split-hair of a second I realize I had forgotten to turn TED down to 1. SHIT!

My aim was perfect but the result was, to say the least, devastating. With the speed of a bullet the bead strikes him. His body glows a bloody red, then explodes in all directions into a million fragmented particles of flesh, bone, and blood.

I step back to avoid the shower of grotesque particles, but some manage to paint a speckled pattern on my shoes. I swallow to keep my stomach down. Pelted with his remains, the two figures stand frozen. The second man screams with a pitch I haven't heard since Daniel Stern was attacked by the pigeons in *Home Alone 2*. Out of his mind with terror, he pushes the enslaved man aside and races in three directions like a chicken after losing his head and with his red hair blazing like a human candle. He finally rounds the bend toward his car wearing his freshly painted attire. I hear a door slam and the engine rev up to a squeal, then the sound of gravel spitting from the high velocity of the tires.

Their prisoner stands strangely silent. Perhaps he is more concerned about his fate and the power I'm wielding.

I, too, stand silent as though the whole world took in a breath and held it. I stare down at my shoes. Slowly reality eases its way back in, I can hear the birds singing again and the rustling leaves of the poplars.

Walking over to free the man it strikes me this is the second person I have killed using this type of device, both accidents. If I take into account Rigby's ending, that makes three. Whether by error or not, in the eyes of the world, or at least the courts, I would be considered a murderer. Then, I recall a few words from Alex, "If you make a mistake with that, they stay mistakes." That doesn't help.

I begin to untie the man's hands and try to justify the guilt I feel for the killing, but then add the fact that I just saved this man's life. Is it like a point system, where I get some marks or validation on my side? Justice does show a scale of balance. But what does that mean? It all equals out or something, like, tit for tat.

His hands are free now and he rips the tape from his mouth, then turns to face me and I recognize him as Indian, Native Indian, or American Indigenous—how about a human being. Did I miss a label? Why can't we just be people? I think this is just white guilt.

At that moment, something strikes me deep inside. I feel a strange but familiar feeling about him, even though I have never seen him before.

"Thanks. I owe you one," he says, then looks over his Jackson Pollack-designed clothes and says, "What the hell happened? One second that bastard is there, next second I'm wearing him. If it wasn't for the tape over my mouth, I would have puked. I thought *my* ending was going to be bad." He looks down at my hand holding the TED.

"What kind of a cell phone is that? I know it didn't come from Amazon. Is it Elon?"

"No to both. It would take some explaining. I'm Paul."

"Dakota, but for some reason white people want to call me Dan."

"I like Dakota. I call most of *them* assholes. It's a label I like to use from time to time."

"I know that tribe very well," he says with a smile.

"So what was that all about?"

"That would also take some explaining."

"Can I offer you a ride?"

"Sounds good."

I can't have him sitting in the car like that.

"You can't walk around in those clothes. I have a sweat suit in the trunk. You're welcome to it."

"Thanks, Paul. I'd appreciate that."

I sit in the car and wait for him to change. I can see him from the waist up and realize that if those two didn't have guns, Dakota would show them his and they'd be toast. I would say he's in his early thirties with a sculptured physique. He throws his clothes into the bushes and hops in. He doesn't bother with his seat belt and that leaves me concerned—not for his safety, but mine. I'm trusting that he *is* the victim and not the perpetrator. Keeping in mind his state of fitness, he could overtake me and throw me out and take the car.

I pull out to the main road. "So where can I drop you?"

"If you're going left, that's where I'm headed, about five miles down the road."

"That makes it easy."

He turns to face me and puts his back against the door. There's a moment of silence. I know where I want to take the conversation and I think he does, too.

"I guess you'd like to know what that was all about back there," he says.

"That's totally up to you, but since I saved your ass and killed a man, it would seem only fair."

"And you're right. They were drug dealers, dealing in fentanyl."

"Shit, that's the worst."

His face becomes a mixture of hate and grief. His eyes become watery, and the white around his dark pupils redden.

"The cops should know about this."

"Cops? Not when it comes to us. We don't exist. Our women disappear, raped and murdered. Not to mention our children that were abused, killed and buried in the name of religion—and they called us savages."

I am at a loss as to what to say, but I do have an opinion about religion. "Religion certainly has an evil side." And then I think about the world in general, but don't we all.

"And now our young ones are committing suicide, and these bastards are helping them. I caught those two handing one of the kids that shit just outside the schoolyard. I told the boy to go home. When he was out of sight, I started to lay a beating on one of them until the other one pulled a gun and they hustled me away in their car. That's when you showed up."

"My being there was just a fluke, but I'm glad I was. Assholes like that have no place in this world."

His face changes from anger to curiosity. "So what's with that little box of lightning? I've never seen anything more dangerous."

"It's very dangerous. All I can tell you is—it was given to me for my protection. I can't expose the source or why I need it except to fight some of that evil. If I did tell you, I might be putting you in danger, and I wouldn't want that. You seem to be someone who wants to protect his people. This sounds a bit cliché, but you don't need any more white man's bullshit. You have enough on your plate without crossing that line into my world."

"I get it."

"So, where can I drop you off?"

"Actually, we're here. Just by that large oak tree up ahead."

I pull over and he reaches across and shakes my hand with a very strong grip. "Thanks, Paul. You're one of the good ones."

"All we can do is try, and hopefully it catches on."

"Oh, how can I get your clothes back to you?"

"Don't worry about it. I caused the mess."

Dakota chuckles as he gets out of the car.

I look around and see nothing but thick forest on both sides of the road. "So, where do you go from here?"

He points. "Right through there." I see a small path leading into the thicket. "I follow it right to my doorstep. Fifteen minutes and I'm home."

"Is that where your Reservation is?"

"We call it the Rez."

"Is that like Black people calling their place, the Hood?"

"I guess you could say that. It's just short form. My family is on the Rez. I live in a cabin with my grandfather."

"That used to be the case years ago."

"How do you mean?"

"The old folk would stay with the family. Now they shuffle them off to a home to die, like the elephants' graveyard."

"Now I think you're talking about your side of the fence. That's a lack of respect. Elders are leaders, full of wisdom. Through their life experiences they teach and show us the way to live a good life. My grandfather is valuable to me."

"I wish I could say the same of my father. He didn't have the wisdom, he had the whiskey."

"Another disease I know well. Perhaps we'll meet again, Paul."

"I'd like that. Take care of yourself, Dakota."

He waits for me to leave, and through the rearview he quickly vanishes into the trees. As I drive away, I have that strange but familiar feeling resurface. I'm trying hard to search for the source in my memory. It had something to do with my dad back in my teenage years. I had to do a school project about family history —genealogy.

I remember my father sitting in his recliner doing what he does best, bending his elbow and yelling at a football game that his team was obviously losing. I was sitting on the couch beside him doing some research on the subject. I was looking through an old family album and was struck by a yellowish photo of an old woman sitting in a chair in the middle of an open field. There was no name, no location or date under it like all the others photos. In between his gulps and his rants over the game I leaned over, showed him the photo and asked him who it was.

The anger in his eyes over the game immediately transferred over to the photo.

"Why are you looking at that?" he scowled. "It's nothing! Nobody!"

"If it's nobody, why is it here?"

He reached out and snatched the album from me. "That's enough of that bullshit." He dropped it on the floor on the opposite side of his chair and went back to yelling at the TV.

When he finally passed out, as he always did, I retrieved the album and took out the photo and checked the back, and there it was: her name, the location and the year—1843. A folded sheet of paper fell out of the album as I placed it back on the floor. When I opened it, it was my family tree.

I found her name close to the top and discovered why she was nobody. She was an Indian of the Micmac tribe. My dad never had a good word to say about Indians. I guess he considered that a mark on his family.

That's why it was familiar. I have Native blood. I feel that meeting up with Dakota was meant to be. It fleshed out this forgotten memory. I don't feel the anger that my father had. I feel complete. More connected to this land and my ancestors than I ever did. I feel a sense of pride and wholeness.

—

Grace should be home by now. Pulling into the driveway my first thought is, should I tell her about Dakota? I can't bring him up without talking about the two men and the demise of one by my own hand. Okay, I've got it. I'll just say I saw him on the side of the road and gave him a lift. That way if we ever bump into him she'll remember it as a nothing encounter. *What about your disclosure policy?* Well...this doesn't have anything to do with Grace, so...why worry her. *But don't you think*—I'm trying not to.

The house seems suspiciously quiet. I peer into the living room and there is Grace sleeping peacefully on the couch. My eyes move to the coffee table where my detective side comes into play. The only item on the table is her ring of keys for the house and Rebecca's. So, this tells me she was exhausted from work to the point where she put the keys on the table just before she collapsed on the couch. If she had done this through stress from work there would have been a bottle or at least a glass. I rest my case.

In the kitchen I check out the contents of the fridge. Great, enough items for a cold platter of cheeses and cold cuts. A box of crackers from the cupboard and a bottle of red would be a delight for anyone recovering from a hard day's work. A few stuffed olives added to the platter and the entire buffet laid out on the coffee table awaiting for the Princess to wake from her slumber and receive a kiss from the Prince.

Once in Ben's chair I, too, begin to drift...then dream.

A country landscape appears. In the distance I see my great-grandmother from the photo sitting in the chair in the field. She smiles and motions me to come closer. As I do, she reaches out with both arms to embrace me.

I feel a kiss on my lips and open my eyes, staring straight into Grace's.

She smiles and in a soft tone, "Did I wake you too soon? Were you dreaming? I hope it was pleasant."

"It was."

"Thank you, sweetheart."

"For what?"

"For the snack and wine. I assume it's for us. Would you care to join me now?"

I have to smile. "More than ever."

—

Another day and another death rests uncomfortably over my head like a block of concrete. How do I shake this? If I didn't have a conscience like those two killers, I could do that, but I'm a regular guy with empathy and all that shit. If it didn't bother me I would have to reassess my place in the world. *So this is a good thing?* I guess. What doesn't kill you makes you stronger. *Or, what kills them makes you stronger.* My overthinking is overthinking.

I tell Grace I'll drive her to Rebecca's then continue on to Ben's Place. When I open the car door for Grace I see a wallet on the floor behind her feet—Dakota. I don't say a word and hopefully she doesn't spot it when she gets out. Not that I can't easily explain picking up a hitchhiker, but it's best I don't. Grace is very good at spotting any sliver of anxiety or paranoia from me, which seems to be my trademark.

All is well. I tell her that I will see her for lunch and head out.

—

I drive past the spot of yesterday's scene and try to block out the details, trying to focus on my possible new friendship with Dakota. On the next road, I approach an accident scene. A burned-out car and the front end halfway up a tree. A tow truck driver is giving it the hook.

I stop and lower my passenger window. "That doesn't look good."

He glances at me. "Not for the car, but amazingly the driver survived."

"When did this happen?"

"Yesterday, around four."

That coincides with the time of my encounter.

"I just happened by when they were pulling him out. They told me to come back today once the thing cooled down."

"Did you see what he looked like?"

"Looked like? His face was black as tar from the smoke, but believe it or not his red hair wasn't even singed."

Oh, oh. "So he was alive?"

"He was alive all right—yelling crazy things like he was out of his mind. He must have been in shock."

Shock, that's an understatement. "That's too bad. At least he survived. Thanks."

I start to think that though you hate to see that happen, even to that lowlife, it may be to my benefit. He'll be out of circulation for some time and, possibly, his recollection of yesterday will only be a vague memory. If he started talking about his buddy's Fourth of July demise, people would chalk it up to the accident —a head injury.

The chances of meeting up with him again would be practically nil. And if I did, he wouldn't have any idea who I am. I'm sure I can rest easy now. Any retaliation would now be null and void.

CHAPTER 21

My focus is on locating the entrance to Dakota's cabin. I should have paid more attention when I dropped him off. I think that tree ahead is the marker. I pull off to the side and spot the narrow opening in the brush. I get out of the car, open the passenger door, and grab the wallet.

The TED was still in my pocket, and for one quick second I thought of leaving it in the glove compartment, but thought better of it. All I needed was for someone to steal it and assume it was a cell phone and—I can't even go there.

I begin my walk and hopefully this path continues to his cabin. Getting lost in a forest isn't something I want to do.

The deeper in I go, the more the forest floor is exposed. It's a pleasant walk with cooler air and the intoxicating scent of wood. The feeling is wonderful as well, like Mother Nature is wrapping her arms around me. I feel a sense of comfort and security. It's not hard to understand why Dakota lives out here.

I approach a large stream with a small, man-made wooden bridge. For a simple cross-over it appears very well constructed. It must have taken some time to build. In the water, I see a few fish, looks like perch. Between that and the wildlife, it certainly would be enough food to sustain a person.

Beyond the bridge I stop, close my eyes and my nostrils suck in the classic sweet smell of burning cedar. I see a light haze of smoke beginning to surround me. Dakota can't be far off.

I take a few steps and something hard presses into my back, then two pokes, and if I read this right, I should start walking. If I stay on the path I think I'll be fine, but if I'm nudged to leave it, I could be in for trouble.

I clear my throat. "I'm looking for Dakota."

The only response is another poke.

Down the pathway, above the trees I see what I'm hoping is my destination—a wooden peak at the top of a hill. The closer we get the more substantial this cabin is.

By the roofline it's a type of A-frame. A vaulted ceiling that resembles a teepee with huge picture windows. There are offshoots on either side of the main building, each with a different tone of wood, which tells me they were added at different times. I thought the wooden bridge was a work of craftsmanship, but this is really spectacular. A large front deck with a railing surrounds the face of the main building. As I'm nudged closer, I see the front door open and out steps Dakota.

"Paul!" he says with a huge smile. "I see you've met my grandfather."

"Actually, I can't say I have."

The poke in my back is gone, and his grandfather walks to my front holding what I didn't expect, a walking stick. Ben would be rolling on the ground laughing.

His grandfather stares at me with such intensity that I feel like I'm standing naked.

"I'm surprised to see you here," says Dakota.

I pull his wallet from my pocket and raise it into the air. "I found your wallet in my car."

His grandfather's white-knuckled expression softens, allowing the blood to surge back into his face. A gentle smile. His hand reaches for mine and I grasp it. For whatever reason I could conjure up in my crazy little mind, I feel an energy I can't deny, a yearning for a place and time that I have no reference point other than the photo of my great-grandmother.

My hand is released and what remains is not only the warmth I see in his eyes, but recognition.

Dakota notices and hollers down, "Are you all right?"

"Yeah, I'm fine."

"Most people take others at their word. Grandfather's different. He uses a handshake, and the smile on his face means you have his stamp of approval. Come on up." Dakota motions with a full arm swing in the direction of the cabin.

Crossing the threshold is even more stunning. I know Tor's cottages are beautiful and the craftsmanship is excellent, but this is something beyond that. It's personal and creative.

As my eyes wander around the room, "This place is amazing. It must have cost you—and the man-hours. How many people did you have working on it?"

"Just me."

"Just you?"

"I started ten years ago when I was twenty-five. I wanted a safe place for Grandfather and me."

"Back to your roots."

"In some ways, but mainly to get far enough away from the crazies like the two we encountered."

"I get that. I was looking for the same thing. I left the insanity of the city to find a quiet peaceful life in the country."

"And did you find it?"

"I did. At least I thought I did until I found the disease had crept into the small communities."

"How so?"

I look at my watch. "I'm afraid that's a longer story than I have time for."

"You are the only outsider that knows of this place."

"You mean white guy?"

"Not that there's anything wrong with that."

I have to laugh. "So, you watched *Seinfeld*, too."

"Reruns when the antenna picks it up."

"I have to tell you one thing about *this* white guy, I do have ancestors from the Micmac tribe."

His grandfather finally speaks. "I knew there was something good about you. I could feel your spirit."

"I'd like to know more about this community disease," says Dakota.

"Perhaps I can visit again. Do you have a number?"

"I have no outside communication other than that path. You're welcome to come by anytime."

"I'd like that. And I will."

Walking briskly along the path I recall the words of Chief Dan George in *Little Big Man*—"*my heart soars like an eagle.*"

Meeting up with Dakota and his grandfather seems even more relevant now, though the circumstances and outcome weren't something I would wish on anyone.

I definitely saved Dakota's life, and I may have saved others in the process. Can't sink any lower than dealing to kids.

In spite of my father's failure to accept his own heritage, I've rediscovered mine. Even though they are not my tribe, we are of the same lineage and I want to embrace it. I'm a mixed-race descendent of the originals of this continent.

Perhaps the reason I wanted to leave the city wasn't for peace and quiet, but a deep-seated longing. From the first day I arrived here, there was something that made sense. Grace for sure, but there was something more. Community has resonated with me ever since Ben started hammering that into my head, and tribe is also community. I may have the best of both worlds.

The brief visit with Dakota made it impossible to visit Ben's Place and still make it back to Rebecca's to meet Grace for lunch. It was only going to be a short visit anyway. The staff will be fine without me looking over their shoulders for one day. I'm sure if there were any problems they would have called me. There, guilt avoided. I've never considered myself a problem-solver, but I think this job is good for me. It brings out qualities I didn't know I had. Now off to meet with Grace.

CHAPTER 22

Stepping into the dining room of Rebecca's, the lunch crowd is at full capacity. I look around for a table and spot Grace. She sees me, smiles, and points. Our favorite spot by the window has a reserved sign on the table. I smile back and walk over and make myself comfortable. Gazing out the window, my thoughts return to Dakota and his grandfather living the peaceful, quiet life in the forest. I ask myself if that is something for me. The idea appeals to me, but in all honestly I can't see myself living so remotely. I'm just too white.

Across the room and seeing that smile on Grace's face as she interacts with the customers and staff, I know she wouldn't go for it, either. We both left the big city for a simple life, not a lonely one.

"Hi, sweetheart," she says and takes her seat.

"How is everything at Ben's?"

Oh, oh. "Ben's...well...I didn't quite get there."

"What happened? Did you have a flat tire? Did you call the insurance to send a tow truck driver over to fix it? That's what we're paying them for."

"No, no flat."

Her eyes widen. "Not an accident?"

"Nothing bad, Grace, but I should explain what happened yesterday."

"Yesterday?"

"It wasn't anything important." At least not the part I'm going to tell.

"On my way back from Ben's Place, I saw a fella walking along the side of the road and offered him a ride. He's an Indian."

"Indigenous—yes, go ahead."

"Anyway, I dropped him off a few miles down the road, and his cabin was in the forest with only a small path leading to it. We had a nice chat. I let him out and said goodbye.

"After I dropped you off this morning I found his wallet on the floor of the car and decided to take it to him. By the time I got to him and met his grandfather, it was too late to go to Ben's and still keep my lunch date with you. And, of course, I couldn't miss that." I smile. "So here I am."

"That sounds feasible. Now I have something to confess and I have mixed feelings about it. Or perhaps I should say confused feelings as to how I should feel."

"You met an Indian, too?"

"Indigenous."

"Right."

"No, smarty, I stopped working this morning, sat and had a chat with Alex."

"Alex was here? Was he in costume?"

"Very much so."

"Why was he here? Was it my payback mission? Is it something dangerous I have to do?"

"Boy, look at you go. It had nothing to do with you, so stop the flight of the paranoia plane. It was about me."

"Oh."

She's right. I hate when I do that.

"It seemed like a strange conversation. He was asking me all sorts of questions about my life; some general, some more personal."

"Personal, sounds like he crossed a line there. What kind of personal are we talking?"

"Not what you're thinking, just things about my school years and best friends: my high school prom and what my parents were like. Nothing interesting, but *he* seemed very interested."

"That was it?"

"He wanted to know more about our honeymoon trip and seemed thrilled that we had such a good time."

"Maybe he's a guy who can't get enough thank yous."

"Well I did thank him again, and again."

"It's like he's looking for reassurance, and from what I know of him from our meetings, he just hasn't presented himself as insecure in any way. It all seems a little...odd."

"I'm wondering, too, why he would want to know about my parents."

"Your parents?"

"I told him my parents were parents. They loved and cared for me, always supported me, and that I miss them very much."

"You know, Grace, this all started when we took that first trip to Bridgeburg and he was watching us in the park."

"That's right."

"Then taking me to his facility and showing me the ropes and telling me he had our backs and all the rest of it."

For a moment we fall silent. I replay the sequence of events in my head and a light bulb turns on. "These have all been stepping stones. Grace, I know what's going on, but the reason eludes me."

"What do you think it is?"

I look into her eyes. "It's you."

"What do you mean, it's me?"

"That I don't know, but it was all planned for this day. For some strange reason he needed that information."

"But what could I have said that would be of any importance to anyone?"

"That's what we have to find out."

—

While wracking our brains over the matter, we stayed up longer and drank more than we should have. Now at ten in the morning we're paying the price, wandering around in our housecoats.

"Paul, would you like a couple of eggs?"

"I think I could handle one soft-boiled, if you don't mind, Grace."

"Sounds good to me."

"I think I'll go check the car, I think I left it unlocked overnight." I pray the Magnum is still there.

It's a beautiful morning. The trees have a hint of color, and that means only a few weeks before we hit the beginning of short days and long, cold dark nights—a slight shiver passes through me.

The car doors are still locked, and before I walk back in I turn to the mailbox and see a manila envelope peeking out. The mail doesn't arrive for a couple more hours. If he's consistent, it would have to be Alex. The front of the envelope bears one word —GRACE.

Walking back into the house I hand it to her.

"Another special delivery. This one's for you."

She shows her squinted look of concern. "I'm afraid to open it. I don't like these special delivery packages."

"Did you want to eat your egg first?"

"No, depending on what's in it, it might come back up."

She grabs a knife and slices the top along the fold. Inside there is a photo. "I hope it's not another graveyard scene."

Her apprehension allows for the slow and dramatic reveal of its content—a slightly out-of-focus old photo of a young man and woman holding a baby.

"Now, who do you suppose they are?" I ask.

Grace doesn't say a word, remaining focused on the photo as she moves to the couch and lowers herself into her seat.

I can see her eyes shift from one person to the other. There is some recognition. "Paul...I need some coffee."

I don't know what to make of that. Usually if it is something that upsets her she wouldn't be asking for coffee. I pour two cups and sit down beside her and wait for her. I hand her a cup to hear her explain.

"This...this is a picture of my mother holding me in her arms."

"Well, isn't that a nice memory."

"Could you put some whiskey in this coffee, please?"

That sounds more like it. I deliver the goods and ask, "What is it? What's wrong?"

She looks into my eyes with confusion and fear. "I don't know who that man is. That's not my father. That's not my father."

"Are you sure that's—"

"I don't understand why he would send this picture to me without an explanation. Why didn't he show it to me yesterday? He reels me in with all this concerned talk as if he cares about me, then leaves this on my doorstep to figure it out like some kind of game."

"I don't know, Grace. It's not logical. But he didn't send any explanation for the first photo, either. He said he thought we would figure it out."

At this moment I realize a problem. I get up from the couch and head to the bedroom.

"Paul?"

From the bedroom I call out, "Grace, I have something I want to show you. Would you come in here for a minute?"

"What is it? What's so important?"

"We're being too open. Remember they have their security watching us, but not in here. There must be some link between your mother, that guy in the picture, and Alex. Do you have all of your family's photo albums?"

"I do. There was no room for them here, so I have them stored in the attic at Rebecca's."

"I think we should bring them here and go through them to see if that guy is in any of them. There might be one with a name attached."

"That's a good idea."

"Are they in a box?"

"Actually, three boxes."

"Good. We should bring them into the bedroom and go through them. We don't want Alex and his band of merry men to have any idea what we are doing."

"Did you want to do this now?"

"No. Let's walk out of here like all is good. We'll have lunch and then you ask me about picking up something at Rebecca's."

"I have to think of something that could be in three boxes. I know, tax files. I want to go through tax files."

—

We arrive home and place the boxes on the floor beside our bed to begin the task of *Finding Waldo*. Two of the boxes have albums and the third has loose photos with some in envelopes.

"I guess we should start with the oldest album," says Grace.

An hour in and nothing. We tackle the box of loose photos. This, too, becomes discouraging until Grace opens an envelope.

"Paul! I found one."

I move beside her and we study the picture. It's another hazy shot of Grace's mother alongside the same guy, wearing the same clothes with their arms around each other, but without baby Grace.

"It must have been the same day as the first photo."

"Check the back, Grace."

She turns the photo over to reveal writing. *Judith and Thomas–1967*

"Of course, 1967, the year I was born. The name Thomas doesn't ring a bell. I don't recall my mother mentioning that name, ever."

"Well, it's a start." I notice a larger envelope stuck at the bottom of the box. "What's this, Grace?" I hand it to her.

She opens it. "It's my parents' marriage license."

The paper begins to shake in her hands and she starts breathing heavily. "What is it, Grace?"

Her eyes leave the paper and stare straight out. "The date," she whispers.

"What about the date?"

I look at the date—Dec. 1968.

"I was born in January of '67 and they got married in December of '68. That's almost two years—and why wasn't my father in the picture with me?"

Think, think. "I know, because it was your father taking the picture. I'll bet he was a friend of your father's, that's why your mother never mentioned him."

"Wait a minute," she says. She rushes into the spare bedroom. I follow her and find her deep into her cedar chest. She pulls out a stack of bound letters and unties the ribbon. "My father was in Vietnam."

I'm not sure what she's getting at, so I keep quiet while she thumbs through the letters. "Here it is." With all speed she opens it and proceeds to read—"*I will be back next week and can't wait to put my arms around you once again.*"

"This was the last letter my father wrote to my mother before he returned from the war. It was one week before he came home. The date was March 19th, 1967."

"Okay."

"Don't you see? Nine months before that he was still fighting the war."

Oh boy. "So your father wasn't—"

"Oh, my god! So who is this Thomas guy? Is *he* my real father?"

Her eyes move quickly from side to side. "Why did Alex show me that picture! What's wrong with that man! He pays for our honeymoon and seems to take a genuine interest in me, then shatters my whole world!"

"Grace, the surveillance, they can hear you."

"I don't give a damn what they hear!" She runs into the living room. "You hear me! I don't give a damn what you hear!"

She free-falls on the couch face down and cries a river. When someone is in that state you don't want to be all over them trying to console that grief, so I sit on the coffee table and place my hand gently on her shoulder. I know what her first words will be when she levels out from this tailspin, so I'll head it off at the pass.

Some people are social drinkers, and that's why I always include myself. Two glasses, one bottle. I pour two drinks and rest them on the coffee table beside me and wait to be summoned into action.

My experience with women, which has been minimal, is the fact that they are well equipped with their toolbox overloaded with words. If those words were bullets, they could outgun any man. Grace won't be down on the mat for long before she replenishes that toolbox and has Alex in her crosshairs.

Shortly after I receive the signal. She extends her right arm with an open hand and I place the drink in it. She maintains that position momentarily then slowly turns over, not spilling a drop. Sitting up with her back resting on the arm of the couch and her knees bent she finally takes a sip, then a deep breath, and slowly lets it out.

All this time I don't speak, but I do indulge. In my own head I'm saying to myself, how would something like this affect me? It's more the apples and oranges. If I found out that my father wasn't my father, I might say, now that makes sense.

"I guess you know what I'm thinking," says Grace.

"Yes, I do." I think.

"And the only way to find out is to confront the one that started your history lesson." She stands and looks around the room, and I have an idea what's coming next. That toolbox will open any second now.

"I know you don't use cameras, so there's no place for me to focus on what I'm about to say. I want to speak to—no. I need to meet with Alex tomorrow morning at ten o'clock. Either here or wherever his little clubhouse is. In the meantime, tell him we don't want his protection anymore."

"Grace, don't you think that might be a little overactive?"

She's on a roll and doesn't hear me. "So, however you're doing this intrusion—stop right now."

Protection is a good thing, and with all we've been through it's been valid; but it has always had a flip side: our privacy, which is long gone. The truth of the matter, it's not just Alex. The very second you open up anything on your phone or computer they attack like vultures, looking for the tiniest bit of your life they can sell. Our private information means money. The more we open up, the more they know about us. I think Grace does have a valid point, but then you're leaving yourself open at both ends.

"I'm sorry, Paul, but I have to get to the bottom of this."

"I agree. That was a cruel thing to do. What I don't get is, what does he seek to gain?"

"I guess we'll find out in the morning."

—

The morning sun with its warmth and good vibes from vitamin D is nowhere to be seen—a dismal day for a dismal situation, and the anxiety and tension from the day before looms over our little house.

Neither one of us feels like making breakfast. A couple of day-old muffins with coffee will suffice. We sit at the island gazing through the patio doors at the gray gloom without a word between us. The kitchen clock reads 9:15. I pick up my cell and see that it's out of juice and decide to charge it up in case Alex tries to call.

"How's *your* phone, Grace?"

She grabs hers from the coffee table. "Mine's dead, too."

My cell buzzes. "Talk about timing."

"Is it him?" she asks nervously.

"It's the police."

"The police!"

"Mr. Fenton?"

"Yes."

"Officer Goodwill. You own a restaurant in Bridgeburg called Ben's Place?"

"Yes, why? What's wrong?"

"There was a break-in early this morning."

"A break-in!"

"Oh no!"

Another item to add to our plate. "How bad?"

"Bad enough. Looks like they trashed the place."

"What's your description of trashed?"

"Like a small tornado. The cash drawers were emptied."

"That wouldn't have amounted to much."

"Paul," says Grace.

"Hang on please." I turn to Grace. "Looks like some interior damage."

Grace doesn't say a word. She looks at the floor in defeat.

"Mr. Fenton."

"Sorry, go ahead."

"You'll have to come down to assess the damage."

"I'm leaving now."

"Oh, Mr. Fenton, I was told you have a partner. I think it would be a good idea if you have him meet us there as well."

"You're right, I'll call him now."

"Grace, they want to meet me at Ben's to assess the damage, and Tor should be there, too. Can you call him and tell him to meet me there?"

"Of course."

I put my arms around her. "We sure didn't need this. Are you going to be all right?"

"I hope so. It's Alex that should be worried. I'll need you there to throw a leash on me if I get out of hand."

"I'll be right beside you. Don't use all your tools in that box."

"Tools?"

"Nothing—okay, I'm off."

"Paul—"

I kiss her on the forehead. "I'll be back soon. This shouldn't take long."

There is nothing harder than leaving my wife to deal with a difficult problem on her own. I guess I always want to be her hero and show my worth in the relationship.

—

I keep a heavy foot to shorten my trip to make it back for Grace. I park on a bit of an angle on the street and walk briskly to the restaurant and up the steps. Opening the door causes more anxiety as I'm afraid to see what has been destroyed.

What the hell! Everything looks normal. The waitresses are serving customers—ambiance music in the background and everyone smiling.

"Paul, what a pleasant surprise," says the one of the waitresses. "Are you going to be joining us for breakfast?"

Okay, calm down. Let's not create something that doesn't seem to exist. "No, I was close by and thought I'd pop in to say hi. It looks like all is well here, so I'll head out."

"Are you sure you won't stay for a coffee?"

"No, I've got a few things to do at Rebecca's."

"That's funny."

"What is?"

"Tor was here about ten minutes ago and asked if everything was all right, then he left right away. Well, have a nice day."

"You, too."

Tor was here already? If I didn't know any better, I'd think I was on that pink acid-type trip they put me on when I was held prisoner. Tor must think I'm crazy, too. Having him drive out to a break-in that never happened. I have to get back to Grace. She's the only sanity I know.

I leave town and turn onto the highway and notice a car up ahead pulled off to the side. I slow down as I pass. It looks like Tor's rented SUV. "Damn it!"

I pull in front of it and walk back. The driver's side is unlocked. I climb in to find the keys still in the ignition and realize it's still running. Looking around for evidence that it belongs to Tor I find real estate papers with his name on them. My stomach begins to turn.

I search around the area and find no sign of anything that might look like a struggle. It quickly adds up that it must be the FBI, and not the police. It was a setup to nab Tor. They must have followed him out of town. I can't do anything about it. I wouldn't know where to start. I shut down his SUV, take the keys and lock it up.

Almost home and I check the time on the dash: 11:20 and time to switch gears. I just can't deal with this new event right now. Not knowing what may have transpired between Grace and Alex makes me very uneasy. Turning on our road I fail to see any vehicle by the house and that tells me what—nothing.

In the living room, Grace sits with her feet on the coffee table directing her attention into the fireplace.

In keeping with the atmosphere in the room, I compose myself and try to be as normal as possible.

"Grace."

Without any movement or emotion in her voice she states, "I'm here, Paul."

There isn't a bottle on the table, nor a glass in her hand. I've never known her to face any obstacle without some form of fortification, so I can't even speculate as to her frame of mind or what might have transpired with Alex. I sit down beside her. Her eyes still planted on the fire. I remain silent.

A moment later she turns her face to me and with a Mona Lisa smile, she reaches over and holds my hand, then turns back to the fire. Perhaps now would be a time to communicate.

"Is there anything I can get you, sweetheart?"

"Paul, if you found out that your father wasn't your real father, would that change anything in your life today or going forward?"

"I guess when you put it that way, I would have to say no."

"And what if you found out your real father was still alive?"

I have to pause on that one, but I know she wants some response. "Well, I guess I would want to know who he was and all about him and why he chose not to have me in his life. He's still alive then?"

"Alex says he is."

"And is it the man in that picture?"

"It is. Alex told me that I have never left his heart and that he loves me dearly."

"So Alex knows him?"

"Apparently, and he wants to see me."

"And how do you feel about that?"

She turns to me. "Scared. I thought I had this, but I need you beside me. I'm going to need your support."

"Whatever you need, I'm here, you know that."

"I know," she says as she holds my hand.

"Did Alex come here?"

"No, I had to go to him. His driver picked me up. I think his name was Amos."

"Close enough."

"All I did was get into the back of the car, I saw a flash and we were there."

"I had that happen the last time, but the first time I was driven there. Strange, I'll have to ask him about that. So what happened?"

"Actually, not much. He showed me around and we sat for a few minutes. He tried to reassure me that all was well, and that as soon as the time is right we would get together and everything would be disclosed to me."

"So when will that happen?"

"Tomorrow, and he'll have us picked up at three."

"Us?"

"He said this will involve you, too."

"That's strange. I don't know why."

In a way I'm glad she's totally entrenched in this. It gives me some time to figure out what and when to discuss our other obstacle.

"What about Ben's Place?"

The old sucker punch. "It's all good, Grace. No real damage. Just some mopping up and setting up the tables and chairs again." That sounded convincing.

"That's good. We don't need any more on our plate."

"That's for sure." It's not a plate, it's more a buffet.

CHAPTER 23

Another day of pins and needles arrives, as we await our shuttle. And I have to hand it to Grace, she hasn't asked for one drink. For me, Tor is right there, front and center in my mind.

"Paul, it's two-thirty."

"Yeah, I guess we should get ready to go."

Anas arrives and in a single flash we're there. I feel like we're in the middle of a David Copperfield illusion.

Alex greets us at the entrance to the shack. "Glad you decided to come, Paul."

"I'm here for Grace."

We enter the main room and are seated across from Alex. The coffee table is between us, but this time no bottle of cognac or glasses. I look up from the table. "I guess this will be quite a conversation."

His demeanor turns somber and his tone is rather chilling. "What I have to tell you will not be easy for either of us."

Grace doesn't blink, but the terror in her eyes bleeds down into her hands that rest in her lap. I detect a slight quiver. I reach down with my left hand and hold them. I hope the story comes out in a shorter time frame than this introduction. I feel like screaming out, *Just get on with it!*

"Years ago—"

Finally.

"February, 1966 to be exact, a man named Thomas Webster came into your mother's life. She was young and beautiful and took to Thomas the moment she laid eyes on him, as did he, and they began the most wonderful relationship. A few months had passed and Judith found herself pregnant. After the initial shock they were overjoyed and began making arrangements for their wedding. Two months before the scheduled birth she went into labor. The baby was born on the seventh of January, 1967."

"So I was right, Thomas Webster *is* my father."

Alex's Adam's apple rises then lowers. "Yes. I can tell you that they loved you more than life itself, and all was well for a few weeks."

"A few weeks?" says Grace.

"About six months prior, Thomas had just returned from his stint in 'Nam and began to feel disturbed, and then violent. He was suffering from PTSD. He was worried for the safety of Judith and especially the baby. He finally had to make the biggest decision of his life—he left."

"So what happened?" asks Grace.

"Your mother met an old beau that helped her through it all. He supported her financially, and eventually they got married."

"And my father?"

"He received therapy for a number of years and got married and had a son, but before he was able to shake the trauma completely, his marriage ended."

"So where is he now?"

I lean forward.

Alex looks nervously into her eyes—"You're looking at him."

What! If I wasn't sitting down I'd drop to the floor. I don't know whose eyes were popping more, mine or Grace's.

"What?" she says. "You're Thomas Webster?"

"When I finally got my PTSD under control, I thought it best to change my name to Alex Miller and start fresh. That's when I joined up with the UWC."

She shakes her head in disbelief as she repeats, "No, no."

"When your mother and stepfather passed on I wanted to watch over you, even if it had to be from afar. Things got more complicated when Paul entered the picture, and when I heard of your upcoming wedding, I decided I wanted to give you the best wedding gift I could. I was hoping that when this day came you would see how much I love you and that we could build some kind of relationship that would allow me to be part of your life."

"And your son Alex was... my half-brother? Oh my god!"

"You see, Grace, at that time the UWC wouldn't rest until they destroyed me."

His eyes begin to express the arrival of tears. "Everyone, including Alex, had to think I was dead. So here I was with a son who thought I was dead and a daughter who had no idea I existed," he says, then he drops his head.

Silence weighs heavily in the air as both Grace and I absorb this mind-blowing revelation.

Grace stares into the abyss. I know the wheels are turning, and her seesaws of emotions are struggling to come to grips with this life-altering information.

Finally, she pulls out of her trance and announces in a soft tone, "I wish to go home."

Alex raises his red, watery eyes to her. "I understand."

He grabs a small blank card and scribbles something on it then hands it to Grace. "I will always be available to you."

Grace takes the card.

We enter the car and FLASH—we are home.

Grace zones in on the kitchen cupboard and grabs two glasses and decides on a bottle of red wine. That means only one thing, she's calming down.

Once again I find myself short on words, which is probably a good thing. She will let me know when she is ready to talk.

If she asks me questions I want to be able to answer them. This could be a long one, so I place a log on the fire while she pours. We sink into the couch and place our feet on the coffee table. She sips her drink, which is a good sign, and while I wait for her to speak my concern is Tor. Where is he and in whose company? I'm sure it has to do with—

"I have so many mixed feelings," she says.

By her stare into the fire I can see that she's trying hard to arrange her thoughts and feelings into some palatable, digestive order.

"At first I felt some kind of betrayal by my parents for never disclosing it to me, but on the other hand, the circumstances may have led to some uneasiness in our relationship. Then, as I think back, there was no reason to disclose it. As far as I was concerned I had a great up-bringing, a good life—case closed."

214

I take my first sip of wine and follow her lead. "That makes a lot of sense, Grace. No regrets."

"No, no I don't." She empties her glass and takes a victory lap by pouring another. "Okay...now for the other half of my shock treatment. At the time I felt my rant was justified, but now that I know the truth—the whole story, I must see things from Alex's eyes. He lost the love of his life, his son, his daughter, and his identity because of a war, plus years of mental instability and anguish. His life has been all about loss. What have I lost? Nothing. Actually, I have gained a father, and from what I've seen so far, this man desperately wants to be in my life. How could I not embrace him with all my heart?"

"Grace, at times, I'm in awe of you. That was beautifully said." My cell rings out. Should I answer it in the middle of this beautiful experience? It rings again.

"Aren't you going to see who that is?" she says.

I pick up my cell and am shocked but relieved to see it's Tor. "Tor! Are you all right?"

"Mostly, but I did take a bullet to the shoulder."

"Something happen to Tor?"

"Hang on, Grace."

"What happened?"

"I'm not sure if it was UWC or the FBI. I guess they're still looking for their agent, Ed."

"How many?"

I can't allow this problem to bleed over to Grace just when she's getting a handle on it, so I try not to engage any dialogue over the phone.

"Four."

Grace starts pacing the room.

"I found your car on Woodland Road, are you near there?"

"Farther up the road in the same direction. I seem to have lost them when I turned down a narrow path. Good thing they weren't in better shape."

"Path?"

"I kept going until I came to a small bridge over some water."

What a stroke of luck this is. "Okay, I know where you are. I'm on my way."

"Paul! What happened?" says Grace.

Think fast. "He had some...car trouble."

"You seem pretty excited over some car trouble."

"He said his brakes failed and ended up in a ditch and hurt his shoulder, but he's fine."

"Thank goodness. It could have ended a lot worse."

"That's for sure. I'll pick him up and take him home."

"That's nice of you, Paul."

"I'll be back as soon as I can."

I feel some guilt hiding this from her, but I know it's the best thing right now. I give her a kiss, grab my coat and I'm out the door.

CHAPTER 24

There's the tree and the path. Okay, I've got my phone. I open the glove box, grab the Magnum and the TED. I open the trunk and snag the small red-colored first-aid kit and off I go.

Tor said there were four of them. Just in case I run into them, I don't want to have a reoccurrence of the exploding drug dealer. I adjust it to minimal and drop it into my coat pocket, then give Tor a call to let him know I'm here.

"Paul?"

"I'm just heading down the path. I'll be there shortly."

"I'm not going anywhere."

I run along the path and realize I have to slow down to a comfortable jog or I'll collapse before I get there. From my first trip I recognize a clump of birch trees just before the bridge. As soon as I round this bend—SHIT! There are the FOUR AGENTS surrounding Tor who rests on the ground with his right hand covering the left shoulder of his blood-soaked, white sleeve.

"Sorry, Paul, they just arrived."

There's always one spokesman, and usually the tallest or the shortest and usually dumpy. "If I were you, I'd turn around and go back where I came from."

Dumpy has it, and since Tor has an injury, they felt it unnecessary to expose their artillery. Depending on what I'm about to say, that could change.

"I'm not going anywhere."

I raise the first-aid kit. "I'm here to take care of my friend."

In unison, as I expected, four guns appear from their coats. I could pull out the Magnum, but to what avail. It would end in a very short version of the OK Corral.

It is possible if I bring out TED they may take it to be a cell, not knowing that I would have access to a sophisticated weapon, just a regular guy trying to help a friend.

"Who do you think you're going to call?"

He bought it. I raise it chest high so as not to pick up Tor in the head—here goes.

"You mean this?" I raise it and PRESS.

Before Dumpy has time to let out a squeaker, all four are thrown a hundred feet from where they stood. Two hit trees, one a boulder, and Dumpy lands in the stream face down, which is unfortunate. Not really, but they're all out for the count.

I rush to help Tor up and we begin to head back to my car, and I have a revelation: *take him to Dakota's.* That's right. It's a shorter distance, and when these bozos wake, up they'll assume we took the path back to the road.

One good thing is that his injury wasn't a leg. With his long stride it's *me* trying to keep up with him. We stop at midpoint so that I can give his wound some attention. Another stroke of luck, if you want to call it that, the bullet went right on through—less likely he'll need to see a doctor and be given the third degree.

We arrive at Dakota's place, and in true salesman's form Tor says, "Where did this come from? Is it for sale?"

"Dream on."

Reaching the top of the stairs I give it a gentle rap.

"So whose place is this?"

"A new friend of mine, Dakota."

The door opens and Dakota's grandfather stands solemn.

"—and his grandfather."

Grandfather's eyes narrow into two thin lines. "I recognize you now, Paul. Who's your friend?"

"This is Tor. He's been—"

"Shot, by the looks of it."

I sense a split-second of decision-making, and then with a tone of, *I should have stayed in bed*—"Come in." He motions us to sit on the couch facing the huge windows. "Who did it?"

"How do you know it wasn't an accident?"

"I know it firsthand, he's Black. Second, your emotions are too high for an accident, and more out of fear."

"Very perceptive," says Tor.

"I've had to be. As you can see, I'm not white either. It's the only reason I've lived so long, and I'm sure that's why you're still here."

"Well put," says Tor.

"Is Dakota around?"

"He went hunting about a half-hour ago. He should be back soon. He's a good hunter; never takes more than an hour for his catch."

"Fishing?" I ask.

"No, that will be tomorrow, deer today. If he's having a bad day it will be rabbit."

There's a pause as he looks us over. "So, how many men are we talking: three, four?"

"How did you know it was more than one?" asks Tor.

"Once again, perception. One or two would not be a problem for you. It would take three or four to overtake your size and strength."

"Why, you're a regular Sherlock Holmes," I add.

"I've read his bullshit stories. You can write anything into a story, then go back and change it to make it look like the hero is so damn smart. I call it elementary fiction."

We laugh and find ourselves at ease with his commentary on Holmes. At that precise moment Dakota walks through the door looking like he just stepped out of the 1800s with a quiver of arrows slung over his back, a bow in his grip and a large rabbit slung around his neck.

We stand to greet him.

"What do we have here, a little pow wow? Nice to see you again, Paul."

He turns to Tor and looks him up and down. He reaches out and shakes his hand. "Dakota."

"Tor."

Acknowledging the bandaged shoulder he says, "Looks like we're all having some conflict these days."

"Tor was ambushed. There were four of them."

"Yes, I can see it would take four."

"Elementary," says Grandfather.

"Sounds like Grandfather has been giving you his Sherlock Holmes lecture."

"He's very entertaining," says Tor.

"I'm eighty-three, you think I'm too old for stand-up?"

I can't resist. "Maybe Custer's Last Stand-up."

"Now there was a joker," says Grandfather.

"Don't get him started," says Dakota. "How's that shoulder, Tor?"

"A lot better now."

"Good, and would you fellas be interested in joining us for some rabbit stew?"

"You don't have to twist my arm," says Tor.

We laugh and even Grandfather chuckles. I better call Grace and let her know I won't be home for supper.

Talking to Grace eases my mind. She's feeling a lot better and is fine with me staying with Tor.

Grandfather does the butchering and Dakota, the cooking. This stew is delicious. I think it was that half-bottle of wine he added. Perhaps something we should add to our menu at Rebecca's, but I know Grace would nix that with, *Bunnies are so damn cute.*

With full bellies we drift out to the front porch, grab a chair and enjoy the last couple of hours of daylight. Grandfather entertains us with stories from his childhood—some good, some bad. Without any reason or apology he stops. His eyes close and his chin rests on his chest.

The sounds of the day creatures are less frequent now. The warmth of the sun begins to dissipate to make room for the cool night air, creating a soft but deliberate breeze, and the poplars to play their ocean-like waves as they rustle. Unless you live here this whole experience would elude you, and for that brief moment in time, all is right in the world.

Words seem irrelevant, as each of us descends into our own meditative state. It's an eye-opener with your eyes shut—a wonderful moment.

SUDDENLY—feeling like a bolt of lightning cracking through my skull, the sound of a rifle shot echoes through the forest! A large sliver of wood parts from the railing goes flying beside Tor.

Grandfather wakes with a jerk. "What the hell was—"

"INTO THE HOUSE!" yells Dakota.

We scramble for the door as another shot rings out, hitting the top of the doorframe. Inside, we all dive for the floor except for Dakota. He races to a large cabinet—opens it and I'm in awe. A large array of assault weapons is on display.

"That is quite the arsenal."

"Land disputes with burning tires got lost in the translation," says Dakota.

He pulls them out like weeds and slides them along the floor to us. "Choose one, they're all loaded," he says. "I guess these are your friends, Tor?"

"It appears to be. Sorry about that."

Through a megaphone we hear—"This is the FBI...that was a warning. I want all four of you to come out with hands raised behind your head."

I know we can't shoot it out, that would be insane—TED! I pull it out of my pocket.

"Now you're talking," says Dakota.

"What do you expect to do with that?" asks Grandfather. "Throw it at them?"

"You just watch, Grandfather," say Dakota. "It will blow your mind."

"Or they will," says Grandfather.

"Paul," says Tor, "what can you do from in here?"

"I haven't tried this but it should work." I turn on GPS and program it for body temperatures outside. Six spots show up and I put beads on all of them.

"Looks like they've added two more troops."

"The odds are getting better all the time," says Tor.

Once again the megaphone blasts out. "The one with the Q3, toss it outside first."

"He thinks you have a Q3," says Tor.

"I'll throw out my cell phone instead. From that distance they won't know any different."

I park myself by the edge of the door and open it enough to holler, "Okay, here it is." I throw it out on the front porch and turn back into the room.

"All right, I want to see those bodies filing out one at a time with arms in the air."

Tor looks to me. "What are you waiting for?" he says.

"He didn't use the megaphone and we can hear him. That means he's getting cocky, he's moving closer. I have to reset his position on TED." I make the proper adjustment. "Here we go." I set the distance and PRESS.

"I said, I want to see those—"

"What happened?" asks Grandfather.

"They're gone."

"Gone?"

"I sent them to Neverland."

"You killed them?"

"No. Just set them on a long trip."

"See, I told you it would blow your mind," says Dakota.

"Wish we had that in the 1800s," says Grandfather.

"Now that would have been scary."

"Not for us. We'd be pulling the strings today."

I have to throw in an apology here. "Sorry to bring this your way."

"Being outgunned had a far better ending than I thought," says Dakota.

"The only time minorities are in the majority is when they've been murdered or sent to prison," says Grandfather.

"Yep, these laws have to change," I say.

"Until then," says Grandfather, "you wouldn't have an extra one of those gadgets, would you? I can think of a few I'd like to send away."

At least we can chuckle over that.

—

I ask Tor if he's able to drive and he's fine, so I drop him off at his vehicle and hand him his keys.

"Hang on for a minute, Paul."

He gets out and kneels down and checks the underside of his SUV. He feels around and pulls out a tracking device. He waves it in the air and shouts, "I'm good now, Paul."

I wave back and head for home while enjoying a spectacular orange-red glow above the tree line. I turn on the headlights and think about Grace. I can't believe with all that has gone on I was able to keep it from her, and for the first time I have no regrets about it. She has enough to think about with Alex.

Sometime ago, I remember entertaining the thought of the UWC handing over the Willow's End case to the FBI, and now it's been verified. What I would like to know is, how long does it go on? I keep reminding myself there is nothing to worry about because my only connection to Ed was the fact that he worked for Tor briefly. The only thing these assholes know is that he's missing. Hopefully this will be a deterrent and not an escalation.

—

As I follow my headlights down the road to our house, I can just make out a glow from a fire in the back yard with two figures facing each other. We have company, and for a change I hope that's good news; but just in case, as I park in the driveway I keep TED with me and return the Magnum to the glove box.

Rounding the corner to the patio my anxiety level drops when I see Grace's glowing face laughing and waving her arms in conversation. The guest is a man and has his back to me. I casually make my presence known.

"I see we have company?"

"Paul, I'm glad you're back. We've been having some great conversations."

I move around to see who the other half of *we* is, and at the same time the guest turns his face to meet mine. To my surprise, or should I say, amazement, it's Alex, the man of many faces—a resurrected dead man, a blind man, a long-lost father, and last but not least, my father-in-law.

"Evening, Paul."

"Well, this is certainly a surprise, and no disguise."

"We've been having a wonderful time. Alex has so many interesting stories."

I guess things are moving along.

"The more I know, the more I realize how and why things happened the way they did. Alex says the only way to understand the past is to look at where you are in the present. If you are in a good place, that means that everything that happened to you, whether good or bad, has led you here."

"You mean, like the past has no future, but the present does?"

"Not quite." I glance at Grace. She looks absolutely stunning in the firelight. My anxiety from the day's events turns into higher levels of adrenaline and testosterone arousal. If I had to choose right now, Alex would be home sitting by his own fire.

Alex's cell begins to hum—have my prayers been answered?

"Yes, Anas."

Grace turns to me. "I thought his name was Amos?"

"One and the same, Grace." I think the jury's still out on that one, depending what comes out of his mouth.

"So, it's true then. Pick me up," says Alex, morphing from *Father Knows Best* back to *Commander-in-chief.* "I'm sorry, I have to leave. We've had a serious breach."

"Is it a turncoat situation? They seem to be in style."

"Here's a lesson for you—as soon as you get too smart, too comfortable, that's when you're the most vulnerable."

I wonder if I can squeeze him for more.

"I hope it isn't anything too severe?"

"I think having them find out that I'm still alive would be a big one."

"You mean...the UWC?" says Grace.

Before he answers there's flash and the Lincoln appears in the driveway.

"I'm afraid so," says Alex. "I'll see you both later."

"Please take care," says Grace, then adds, "Dad."

Getting into the vehicle he turns to her with a soft smile. "Thank you, Grace."

FLASH and gone.

"Paul, I'm so worried for him. I can't imagine what they would do to him if they got their hands on him. Look what they've done to us and this community, and we are of little importance compared to my dad."

"To be honest, Grace, from what I've seen, I don't think you have much to worry about, as he seems to be ahead of them in smarts and technology. He's not standing alone on top of that mountain waving the flag of freedom and democracy all by himself. He has top guns around the world that think in the same way and they're backing him. You know, Grace, with all these people working for him, he must go under a company name of some sort. It could be a name to disguise what they do—like Alex's Plumbing and Heating."

"Now you're being silly."

I wonder if that little conversation I had with him awhile back about being there when he calls might be closer than I think—I have a feeling this may lead to my *pay the piper* part.

—

It has been two days since Alex left us by the fire and no further contact, which has left Grace on edge.

"Do you think I should call him? He did give me his private number."

"If it were me, I wouldn't call. Since you are his daughter, his family, you should call. I just remembered, that makes me his son-in-law. It's all in the family, go ahead and make the call."

She finds the card with his number and nervously taps the numbers on her cell. "Hel—"

There's a pause and her eyebrows pull together. She puts down her cell.

"What's wrong, Grace?"

"It's no longer in service. What do we do now?"

"Too bad I don't have a number for Amos."

"You mean, Anas."

I give her a double take. "Right."

Could I possibly retrace that first drive to his hideout? "Give me a second."

"What are you thinking?"

I raise my hand to her as I map it out in my head. I think ...yes, I should be able to do it.

"I'm sure I can retrace my drive with him to the place."

"I'm supposed to be at Rebecca's at noon," says Grace. "I'll call Joyce and tell her to fill in for me."

"You do that and I'll pour us a couple of coffees to take with us."

—

My memory is a little foggier than I thought. I've had to double back twice, and now I come to that old fork in the road.

"Not sure?" says a concerned Grace.

"Uh...wait. I remember we started to turn slightly to the left and looking out the window and seeing another road appear on the right, so that must have been this fork."

"So we go left?"

"We go left."

"This is it, Grace. I remember the gravel road. We should be coming up to a small bridge...there it is."

"Good memory, Paul."

"Must have been that broccoli you forced me to eat."

"Mother knows best. How much farther?"

"Not much, but I know at some point we turned onto a sort of path. The grass was flat from previous tires. I should slow down, so I don't miss it."

I don't think it took this long and hope I haven't passed it.

"Stop!" says Grace.

"Could this be it on my side? The grass is so tall I almost missed it."

I get out and walk around to have a look. I push away some of the grass and I can see a tire track. "This is it."

I continue along and remember this rough part with plenty of potholes.

Grace points out the window. "There it is!"

I stop the car. We get out and walk quickly to the door of the shack. Walking in I realize that the other entrance had to be opened by Alex.

"Now what?" says Grace.

"I guess we could bang on the wall where the opening would be."

Banging and hollering seemed futile.

Suddenly—we are startled by the beep of a car horn. We exit the building and see the Lincoln. I open the back door and we climb in. I never thought I would ever say I was glad to see Anas.

"Hi folks," he says.

"Is everything all right? Where's Alex?" asks Grace in panic mode.

"Everything is fine," he says in a clam voice. "We've moved the facility."

With those words and tone Grace calms right down.

"I'm taking you there now."

"What do you mean, you moved the facility?"

We get the expected flash and we're there, wherever there is.

Getting out of the car and looking around, everything is the same. We haven't moved one inch from where we stood a moment ago. Looking back Anas is outside of the vehicle with his arms crossed over the roof of the car.

"What's going on?"

"Looks exactly the same, doesn't it?" says Anas.

"What is this, some kind of game?"

"In a way, but not a game you're involved in. It's the same place in another dimension. Cool, isn't it?"

Another? Too cool, if you ask me. My thoughts move faster than I can blink. What's he trying to pull? Is he working for the UWC? Is he here to intercept us from finding Alex? Is he the turncoat Alex was talking about?

Grace decides to weigh in. "So what are you saying?"

Why didn't I say that?

"I'll explain it to the best of my understanding. The facility was compromised."

"Okay, I get that."

"How it works, I have no idea, but everything has moved into, like I said, another dimension in the same place."

"Are we talking *Twilight Zone*, fifth-dimension?"

"That's the one. I loved that series. Remember the one when Burgess—"

"What do you think, Paul?"

"We don't have much choice."

"When you go in this time, Alex will be there to meet you."

I place my right hand over my pants pocket to make sure I still have TED, and we proceed to the shack.

Once inside, the door appears and Alex walks through. I feel some guilt that we had some apprehension in trusting Anas, but when he talks another dimension, it's not a stretch to doubt his credibility.

Alex smiles. "Come on in."

Right away I feel my anxiety level drop. I look at Grace and I can tell she also feels less tense.

As we enter the lounging area, everything looks exactly the same. We take our usual seating positions with Alex across the table. There is one difference, though, no bottle or glasses on the table. Now I'm nervous again. Either he's strapped financially, or what he has to say and what we will hear must be done with complete sobriety. That's not like him or me. Once again I turn to Grace to see if she is aware of that alteration, and it's obvious that she is as she stares down at the empty table, squints, and lo and behold she's back to one eyebrow.

"Is everything all right?" asks Grace.

Alex sees her eyes focused on the table. "Refreshments will arrive in due time. I want to make sure what I am about to reveal is clearly understood. At the moment everything is in good standing, as the problem has been eliminated."

Eliminated: That could only mean one thing around here.

"I must apologize for not contacting you sooner and for disconnecting that phone line. By the way, Paul, your memory for getting here is amazing."

"When I don't know where I'm going I try to remember where I've been. I still don't understand why you just didn't zap me here the first time."

"I wanted you to be relaxed and not feel threatened. I thought a nice leisurely ride in the country and a couple of drinks would do it. Now, before we engage in any other conversation, I must have this important one with you."

He focuses on Grace. "Grace, you are the only family I have left. Now that we have connected, I want to protect you both from any blowback that might occur from any decisions or commitments that I must adhere to. I feel an obligation to inform you of everything I possibly can, so that for the most part you will understand more clearly the things that I may have to do. Most importantly, that you know that whatever goes on is being done for the well-being of not just us, but every human on the planet."

I turn to Grace, and I think she's having the same thought as I am—*refreshments should have come first.*

He leans forward. "What are your thoughts about UFOs?"

We glance at each other and then back to Alex. "You mean, if we think they are real?" says Grace.

"Yes. Do you believe there are extraterrestrial beings out there?"

While she ponders that I throw in my two cents. "I know flying saucers are making a serious attempt to be front and center lately, with the government allowing some of that information that has been documented over the years to be declassified."

"But what are *your* thoughts?"

"I don't think I can answer that," says Grace. "I mean, if I have to go by proof, from my perspective, I haven't seen any. Even with all the photos and film, in this digital world, who knows anymore what's real or not?"

"That's very true, Grace. And what about you, Paul?"

"I think that with all the technology out there, especially what I have personally witnessed in Willow's End, from Q3 to TED, and now this fifth-dimension stuff, we could manufacture any fictional story that would be believable today."

"So from what I gather, you think the UFO world is man made."

"You're going to tell us different, aren't you?" says Grace, then bites her bottom lip.

"What would you think about us working in tandem?"

"What do you mean by that?"

"Do you think we have figured out this powerful technology on our own?"

"Dad, are you saying there are UFOs and aliens from other planets here?" I think I would rather this notion as a sign of dementia.

"I didn't believe it myself when it first came to light, but it's true. We have been given what I would call a gift from the heavens."

Please, Alex, don't get up on that pulpit and tell me to open up a scripture and say it's manna from heaven. I may scream. Of course, they could be feeding him those mushrooms.

"We have been working with these aliens for some time now. They didn't have to land here to see what damage was being done. They want to save this place, even if we wiped ourselves off the map. They weren't going to stand by and see this planet destroyed. They want us to continue to be the stewards of this world. They are giving us the tools to overcome—pardon the *Star Wars* reference—the *dark side*."

"I assume you mean the UWC."

"Exactly."

Grace is taken aback, but curious. "Have you...seen them?"

"Seen them, talked to them, and had meetings with them."

"How do you communicate?"

"Telepathically, thought transference."

Wish I could transfer somewhere else. I'm sure I know the answer, but I'll ask it anyway. "Does the UWC know about this?"

"Know about it? Who do you think captured that saucer at Roswell?"

"You mean the UWC has been around since then?"

"Longer than you could imagine."

No wonder we've been living in the dirt for a hundred years.

"I thought they changed that story and said they were spy balloons from Russia," says Grace. "I read that it went back to being a saucer with dead aliens on board."

Alex clears his throat, which I take as an indication for me to lean into the conversation. "The only thing you haven't asked is how would an alien ship with all its sophisticated technology crash on its own."

"You think the UWC brought it down?"

"They didn't want anyone else to have access to whatever technology could be had, and the only way to get it was to shoot it down."

"Shit! And the aliens haven't responded by attacking us?"

"They thought their craft might have been too close to Earth and that we found it threatening, so they racked it up to being their fault. The UWC was busy trying to piece together any technology that might be of value from the wreckage. Their problem is that they think they can reverse engineer what the aliens can do with only our form of technology. The key is working with the aliens to obtain the level of knowledge needed to understand, and use these special gifts their knowledge of the fifth dimension for the benefit of mankind. We knew from the air force tapes there was a fifth dimension. The saucers would be there one second, then disappear the next, like slipping through a veil. That was the only way it could be done."

"So, in not so many words, what is this fifth dimension?"

"The fifth dimension is a micro-dimension. It's between gravity and electromagnetism. We can't see it because it exists on a level that we can't perceive. These beings had observed our interest in this phenomenon and decided to come down to help us achieve that goal."

"Well, that was very nice of them," says Grace.

Alex is on a roll now. His excitement is somewhat contagious. "They have shown us that we can change the world for the better in so many ways to cut down on using our natural resources, free energy, food for everyone, and so much more."

"Free energy! That sounds like Tesla."

"You're absolutely right, Paul. Only this time the UWC won't be there to destroy those dreams."

For the first time Grace has a smile on her face. "If all this is true...it would be incredible."

"When the leak of me being alive came out, I couldn't risk the UWC finding out. I'm sure you can see that now. We have to take every precaution to keep everything under wraps by hiding it in plain sight using fifth-dimension technology and keeping it all safe from those bastards. The only way to get you here was to use it."

I don't think my mind can handle any more. This is reading like a Marvel comic. I know of just *one* cure. "Is it time for those refreshments yet?"

Alex grins. "I think you're right. I've said enough to keep you in refreshments for a while."

No kidding.

After a few drinks and more about saucers and aliens, I hear some unwelcome news.

"Paul, I want you to know the war between us and the UWC is escalating. At some point I may need your help."

Back to the Mafia. Funny how *need your help* always crops up, as if my subconscious was being programmed so when the time comes I will do my master's work like some kind of robot...or alien. I can see it playing out now—permanent residence in the fifth dimension with Spock.

"I would never put you in any danger."

Are you kidding me? You eat danger for breakfast. The only help I would want to give is...maybe handing out flyers. Then again, I wasn't very good at that when I was a kid. I got two cents a flyer and decided to take a shortcut and dumped the hundred down a sewer. I would never repeat that to anyone: a dark time in my adolescent days. I just realized something, too, the pendulum swings both ways. "I'm sure that would also mean that you would be there for me if I needed your help."

"Of course, and I have been doing that, and it will never change."

Good, now I have my side of the contract met.

"Before you leave—" He hands us each a card and says, "Just in case it's needed, my new number."

We depart and go in one car door and come out the same one a split-second after the flash. Back in our car we have lots to think about and discuss on the drive home. The first thing that comes out of Grace's mouth is, "You think he's crazy, don't you?"

"Right now, I'm the crazy one."

"Why would you say that?"

"Because I believe him. What choice do we have? We can't deny we stepped into a fifth dimension. If we did we'd have to doubt our sanity, which I am doubting already."

"What about the aliens and their ships?"

"We know the fifth dimension is real because we witnessed it, but we haven't seen any firsthand evidence of aliens, so that could still be up for debate, but I think we would need therapy if he introduced us to one."

"I don't think he would lie to us. In some ways I wish he would have held back that information. The whole thought about aliens from another planet or dimension scares the hell out of me. All I want to do, Paul, is live my life. You, me, Rebecca's, and Ben's Place."

Since the first day I stepped foot in Willow's End I had to deal with all kinds of crazy things that I didn't understand at first, but eventually, for the most part, every event that has happened has begun to make sense at some point and I was able to handle them, but aliens—if this is real, I'm with Grace, this is scary shit.

We plop ourselves down on the couch with question marks still looming over our heads. The one hanging over my head is, why did he tell us that? I would think it to be top-secret stuff. Just look what happened to the turncoat that was going to expose him—eliminated.

"What are we supposed to take away from that, and what are we to do with it?"

"I don't know, Paul."

"I hope that's all it is. I realize you are his daughter, and when you throw me into the mix, we are his only family. I guess the more he tells us the less he'll have to explain if—"

"If what?"

"If things get a little dicey."

"But he said he wouldn't let anything happen to us."

"You're right, Grace, nothing to worry about"—yet.

"It could also be that the more we know the easier it would be to spot any foreshadowing events that may occur."

"That makes sense, Grace. And you know what else makes sense?"

"That we love each other?"

"Close—that bottle up in the cupboard."

"Oh, you are a little bugger, aren't you?"

—

Finally night is over and I wake up more exhausted than when I went to bed. My sleeping hours were not filled with fairies and sugarplums or even saucers and aliens. It consisted of an all-nighter of me and Richard Dreyfuss building models of Devil's Tower from clay and Jell-O. The dream ended when he went wild on me after I had eaten all the Jell-O.

We ask each other if we had actually traveled into a fifth dimension or—or what? I guess we didn't drink enough to obliterate yesterday from our memory.

Two glazed donuts and coffee is all we care to deal with. Somehow we have to go back to just being normal citizens, thinking normal things, important things like, what's the latest movie on Netflix, or are we running out of Teflon toilet paper.

Anyway, Grace is off to work and I will head back out to Ben's Place. It should be an easy day, but how many times have I left with that thought?

CHAPTER 25

The coffee only wakes me to the point where I am imagining a flow of alien creatures roaming around in my head. I lower my car window to suck in the fresh air to drive away those images. That brought up another unrelated thought: How are Dakota and his grandfather doing? I can't even call him. I think I'll go out and buy him one, then drop it off to him and see how they're doing.

Almost there, I see the bridge. Funny how the more times you travel to the same destination the less time it seems to take. Reaching the house it doesn't look like Dakota is coming to the door to greet me. He's probably gone hunting. I'll leave it with Grandfather.

I knock and wait in silence. Then, to my surprise, the door opens a crack and the barrel of a shotgun slides through the opening.

"Grandfather, is that you?"

"Who is it?"

"It's Paul. Dakota's friend, remember?"

The barrel pulls back inside. "Oh, Paul. Come in."

I step in and he turns away from me with the words, "The one guy I don't want to see."

"What's wrong?"

"They took my grandson."

"Who did?"

"Those bastards you invited over last time you were here."

"Oh shit!"

"Shit is right. What the hell would they want with him?" then he sits in a chair. "This is all your fault. Bringing your problems to our doorstep."

"You're right, and I'm sorry for that. Did they say where they were going to take him?"

"Oh sure, even left me a map and a coupon for a Happy Meal."

I sit on the couch across from him. "I don't know where to begin."

"I'm sure you don't, but I can tell you where it will end, and I'm not liking what I see."

"When did this happen?"

"Yesterday—rushed right in. Took us completely by surprise. We didn't have a chance."

"Did they hurt you?"

"All they had to do is stick a gun to my forehead and I got the message. Can you tell me why the hell they would take Dakota?"

"I assume Dakota would be a good bet to give them information about Tor's whereabouts or mine." Wish I was in that other dimension right now.

"So, what happens now? In the old days we would send out a war party."

My two-way verbal contract with Alex comes to mind. I pull out his card from my jacket pocket. "I have a friend—"

"Just one?"

I noticed that in myself. The older I get, the more smart-ass I become. "I think you would consider him somewhat of a chief. I'll call him."

The phone is ringing, but he's not picking up.

"Can't get him, huh, some chief."

My cell buzzes.

"That should be him." I feel like turning to Grandfather and sticking out my tongue.

"Alex? That's okay, I understand...I have a problem...the FBI." I go on to explain the whole story while Grandfather walks over to the fridge, pulls out two beers and drops one on the table in front of me.

"Okay. All right. No, I won't say a word to Grace. Thanks." Even Alex thinks it's a good idea not to tell Grace. Having heard that, I feel somewhat vindicated when I've concealed things from her.

Grandfather chugs half his beer then says, "Well, what did your chief say?"

"He said he'll get right on it."

"He must have a lot of pull with the government. The only pull I ever got from them was a finger saying, *pull this*."

—

I'm off to Ben's Place, leaving Grandfather with the new cell with my number already programmed and with the assurance that Dakota would be back within twenty-four hours. I think that's a tall order, even for Alex, but choices are limited, I mean zilch.

Grace's timing couldn't be better as she calls the very second I walk through the front door of Ben's Place.

"Hi sweetheart. I was missing you so I thought I'd call to see how things were going over there."

I glance around at the near-capacity lunch crowd. "Everything is good here. Packed for lunch."

"That's great. Okay, you must be busy, I'll let you go."

Yes, very busy. What should I do? It is lunchtime so I'll grab a table. I might check the inventory after I eat. If I was my own boss I would have fired me by now.

Finishing my toasted western, I decide to lead by example and show the staff how the boss works. With a determined look I head for the kitchen. Connor is the man that handles the stock, and being the lunch hour, he's as busy as a streetwalker on New Year's Eve.

Between the overhead fans, sizzling meat, rattling of plates and cutlery, the voice of a stage actor is required. "Looking pretty busy there, Connor!"

"Yes, sir!"

"Anything needing attention?"

"I would say ground beef! About forty pounds should do it!"

"I'll get right on it."

I call it in then spend a few minutes with Justine, and that's my work for the day. Exhausting, for the staff, I mean.

—

Only five minutes into the drive home and I'm getting a call, it's Grandfather. I pull off the road.

"Paul."

I'm shocked. "Dakota?"

"It's me."

"Are you hurt?"

"No."

"And they let you go."

"I wouldn't say that. They took me to this shack, sat me in a chair, and before they said one word to me they disappeared."

"Disappeared?"

"Here's the strangest part. Out of nowhere this old blind man appears and tells me to follow him back outside where there's a car waiting with some chauffeur guy behind the wheel. Paul, he didn't move that car an inch. There was a flash and I was back at the path leading home."

I have to laugh. Now he's *good old* Alex.

"That's wonderful."

"Wonderful? Did you or your magical cell phone have anything to do with this?"

"I would have to say, indirectly." I just had a thought. "Listen, I am so sorry that I brought you into my world and caused you so much bullshit. I want to at least invite you and Grandfather to dinner at our restaurant."

"You have a restaurant?"

"Two, as a matter of fact."

"Is one of them that new one in Bridgeburg?"

"Yes, but I'd like to take you to the one in Willow's End. It's a little more upscale."

"That's sounds good to me, and a nice change from rabbit."

"Great. Could you be at the roadside at five-thirty? I'll pick you up."

"We'll be there."

"Oh, don't mention any of this to my wife, Grace. I always like to explain things in my own way."

"Got it."

Good, the lunchies have left the building, and there's Grace at one of the tables talking with Joyce.

"Well, all done for the day, sir?"

"It's a rough place, that Bridgeburg. Everyone smiles at you, and my face is sore."

Joyce laughs.

"Don't encourage him, Joyce."

"I guess I'll get back to the office. Can't stop smiling every time I see all of that paperwork," says Joyce.

"See, Joyce understands."

"You know, Paul...never mind."

I give her my biggest grin and she can't resist and smiles back, then grabs my nose and tweaks it. "You are such a smart-ass."

"I think those words are contradictory."

Grace sits back and folds her arms with her smile still locked in, which is something she does a lot when I pull out the, *I got you* card.

"Okay, go on. Throw it out there, Shakespeare."

"Smart-ass...now let me see...smart is what it is."

"I'm loving it so far."

"I thought you would."

"And ass is more or less not smart. So there you have it —contradiction."

"Why, that is so true. You are such an inspiration. So much so that I realize it means that you are a contradiction. So in order to rectify my statement I would have to leave out the villain in this sentence. I hereby remove the improper word and leave the word with its true intent—ASS."

"Anyway...you own the first part."

"Thank you, sweetheart."

"Oh, I almost forgot." Not really. "You remember Dakota and his grandfather?"

"Of course, that was a nice connection for you. If you'd like, we could have them over for dinner sometime."

"Great. I invited them tonight."

"Tonight! I haven't got time to make dinner on this short a notice."

"No, no. I mean here, Grace."

"Oh, here. That means I don't have to cook tonight."

"No, you just relax and enjoy the evening. I think you'll like Dakota and his grandfather."

"If you like them, then what's not to like?"

"Good, I will be picking them up and should be back just before six."

"Gives me enough time to go home and freshen up."

—

Ten more minutes and I'll be picking them up. Two more friends added to my life that I thought I would never have. Friends are good, and in a way, they're like vitamins—gotta have 'em.

Pondering that, Alex enters my mind, and more and more I realize how much of a friend he is, and that I shouldn't entertain or be consumed in that Mafia mentality. For all the things he has done for me, I should embrace any help I can give to him, because, after all—it's all in the family.

That's quite a turnaround. What's happening to me? Am I getting soft in my later years? No, I think that makes me stronger. All these people who have entered my life have added to it. It's like they are reshaping me into becoming a better version of myself, and that's especially true of Grace and Ben.

All right, just coming up to the tree and they aren't there.

"Paul!"

I spin my head around. Across the street I see Grandfather standing under an apple tree as Dakota climbs down.

"We got here a little early so I thought a couple of apples wouldn't spoil supper."

"That's the way I would see it."

They walk to the car and I take note of their attire. Dakota is wearing a tanned buckskin jacket over a nice white shirt and jeans. Grandfather has gone all out, decked in beautiful buckskin from head to toe. Dakota hands me an apple through my open window and says, "If one's guilty, we might as well all be guilty."

"That seems to be the case for all races except one," says Grandfather.

I want this to be a nice evening, so I try to dim that light a little. "I must say, I love the buckskin, looks magnificent. The amount of work that goes into that must be staggering."

There's a slight smile on Grandfather's face and pride in his voice. "My mother made it for me a year before she entered the spirit world."

240

I think that got him on another track.

"Once in a while I like to wear it in public." Then smiles, "Pisses some people off."

I understand where he's coming from. I'm sure he's witnessed firsthand and heard the atrocities of his people through the generations, but I have to go back to that old saying, you can't paint everyone with the same brush. Then again, there's the one about walking a mile in his shoes.

—

Grace is already seated at a table and stands the moment she sees us. Right away her hand reaches out and she has her irresistible smile.

"I'm so glad to meet you both, I'm Grace."

"Dakota," he says with a beaming smile. Then motions to grandfather, "And this is Grandfather."

"Pleased to meet you," says Grace, still smiling.

Grandfather takes Grace's hand and covers it with the other. "As Chief Dan George would have said, *My heart soars like an eagle*."

He may have his prejudicial moments, but he sure knows how to charm the ladies.

"That's so beautiful. Thank you so much. And so does mine," says Grace.

"She's just saying that because it's true." They all seem to laugh at my humor, which may be the opening to a good evening or a night of my over-the-top stand-up, which I hope I can handcuff.

We make ourselves comfortable as the waitress hands out the menus and states, "Our special tonight is prime rib."

"That's sounds very tempting to me. Does that appeal to your palates, gentlemen?"

"I won't even open the menu," say Dakota.

"I'll make it three," says Grandfather.

"And, Grace?"

"How can I go against three handsome gentlemen."

Grace notices Joyce at the entrance and waves her over.

"Joyce, I'd like you to meet our new friends, Dakota and Grandfather."

Dakota and Grandfather stand. Now I could be wrong on this, but past experience tells me I'm on the money. When Joyce and Dakota greet each other, the light that shines in their eyes is blinding. If Joyce had a smile any larger, it would have to reach around the back of her head.

"Nice to meet you...both," she says.

I shouldn't be doing a play-by-play, but look at the sparkle in her eyes and that slight blush in her face. And Dakota is no slouch either. It looks like he's just finished a round of peyote, and from what I can recall from my early days, the word means "to glisten."

I get up and take a chair from another table and place it between Grace and Dakota.

"Joyce, would you care to join us?"

"Well, I don't—"

"You're not, is she, Grace?"

"Absolutely not."

You could strike all the lights in the room and call it a candlelight dinner just from the glow those two emanate. Now that we have eliminated two from our conversation, we direct our attention to Grandfather, and he doesn't let us down. We are captivated by his stories from his younger days that catapult us back centuries.

I order two bottles of red, even though we all seem pretty relaxed and comfortable.

The prime rib is as we expect—primo, and there seems to be a connection, a cohesiveness within this group. The last two events of the dinner are dessert and coffee.

Our new friends respectfully decline, even with Grace's nudge toward the cherry cheesecake.

"I'm sure it's delicious, Grace," says Dakota. "But we discovered a long time ago that most white food means diabetes in our culture."

"In all cultures if you look at the state of the world," says Grandfather.

"I think I'll just have coffee," says Grace.

"Please, Grace, that's not necessary. We are more prone to that disease, that's all," says Dakota.

"Well, perhaps a thin slice," she says.

"And for Joyce?"

"I'm fine," she says, staring into Dakota's eyes.

"I'll have a regular slice. I'm prone to dessert."

—

The evening comes to a close, but apparently not for our young couple, who seem to be oblivious to their surroundings until Grandfather steps in with some soft chant that seems to alert Dakota.

"Well," says Dakota, "I guess we should be heading home," he says to Joyce without taking his eyes from hers.

I'm sure I had that same puppy-like look the first time I met Grace, and at times I still do as I watch her beautiful smile appear while observing the young couple. She reaches over and holds my hand.

"Guess I'll go out and start the car."

"Oh, you need a ride?" says Joyce. "I'd be happy to drive you home."

Dakota looks to me. "That suites me fine. I think I might have over indulged in the wine, slightly."

I didn't think Joyce's face could beam any brighter.

Grace and I are now alone at the table. She gazes out the window to see the sun about fifteen minutes away from closing shop.

"Paul, let's walk home. It's a beautiful evening."

"I could walk off some of that prime rib."

"I think it has more to do with that cheese cake."

"That I'm saving for my marathon run."

CHAPTER 26

It's a nice, easygoing walk that certainly won't have any effect on our dinner, but does soothe the mind.

"Paul, I must be more tired than I thought."

"Well, you did have some wine."

"Yes, but not enough for me to go blind. Where's our house?"

"Our house? You are tired. It's right—"

It's gone! Completely gone, even the patio and firepit!

"Do you think Alex had something to do with it? Remember the broken-down shack trick?"

"You mean, it's still there, but hidden? That's possible, but we have no shack to go into. There's no entrance. And why would he do that?"

"I'll call him," says Grace.

She pulls her cell from her handbag. "Dad, did you do this to our house?"

There's a pause, then she disconnects.

"What did he say?"

"He said that he'd be right here, and in the meantime walk to where the patio should be."

"All right, let's go. It's a little late in the day for games."

"Okay, here we are."

"Paul, turn around."

"Okay, I see nothing but trees."

"You don't see the patio doors surrounded by vines?"

"Clever."

"Let's go in. I've got to sit down."

Once inside Grace plops herself on the couch, and since we'll be having company, I grab a couple of bottles of wine and three glasses. Staying with wine is a good thing, unless, of course, the last of our evening tanks if Alex hits us with his usual gamut of surprises.

I place the wine and glasses on the coffee table. My timing is impeccable, or is it his? He walks through the patio doors and begins to apologize before he even enters the living room.

"I'm so sorry. I thought I would have a little more time before you left your dinner party."

How did he know that? Oh, yes, I almost forgot, he's all knowing, all seeing.

"I thought I could explain things better in person."

"Yes, we can't wait to hear the reason for leaving us in the dark about our house being turned into a rendition of your mystical cabin in the woods."

"Paul, I'm sure Dad has a good explanation for what he did."

I better pull in the reins a bit. This is no longer Alex and Grace, it's father and daughter.

"Remember when you wanted me to stop giving you high security because you felt it was an invasion of your privacy?"

"Can't forget that. Grace was furious."

"I apologized for that, and now I find myself having to apologize once again, but once again with the best of intentions. I was trying to figure out a way to protect you without invading your privacy, and this is what I came up with. Anytime you feel threatened, you use the TED."

"So our house would be as safe as your facility."

"Exactly." He takes out a TED and presses it a couple of times.

"There, your house is back. All I need is to place that code on your TED to put that change in motion."

I reach for the TED in my pocket. It's not there! "I don't have it."

"What do you mean, you don't have it! It should be with you at all times! That's your lifeline! Your survival kit!"

"Paul, where did you leave it?" says Grace.

"In my car."

"Did you lock the car?"

Did I lock the car? "I'm not sure."

"Paul, I'm telling you right now, that item stays with you, no matter where you go. You better go get it right now."

Since I've been in Willow's End I've never heard of one incident of someone stealing anything. But coming from Alex and in that tone, I have no choice but to retrieve it now. If it were up to me, I would leave it until morning.

"Hurry back, Paul. Don't let me worry," says Grace.

I open the front door to a now pitch-black scene. I grab a flashlight from the front closet and head out. The only other source of light is the last lamppost at the corner of Rebecca's, and from here, only a tiny star that flickers in and out of the tree branches.

—

After closing, Rebecca's is lit up with the usual minimal lighting inside and out. The car sits right out front with just enough light from Rebecca's and the street lamp to discourage any vandalism, which, like I said, never happens. I open the passenger door then the glove box.

What did I just say?

"Shit!" It's not here, neither is the Magnum! How the hell can I go back without it? I've really done it to myself this time. Who could have taken it? Only the locals know the car is mine.

"Shit! Shit! Shit!"

The longer I stand here wondering, the more frantic Grace will be, and then Alex's wrath—whatever that may look like. He may just consider me a liability now and remove the protections that are in place for our benefit. And what will Grace have to say about it? I'm already writing the first lines of dialogue and they're not very constructive. I know one thing for certain; I'll be catching up on those drinks. I get in the car and drive back to the house.

—

Standing at the front door with shaky hands, dried mouth, and sweaty palms is only making the inevitable worse. I feel like a fireman rushing into a burning building.

To my surprise they're joking and laughing and expecting to hear nothing but the most positive news from me.

Their heads turn to me and see the defeated look on my face. It's game over.

"You did get it, didn't you?" says Alex with suspicion.

"No, it's gone."

"Gone!" they say in unison.

Grace's calm indulgence has now become a tsunami. "Oh no!" She passes the ball to Alex.

"That's just," His teeth clench. "Wonderful!"

He takes out his cell and makes a call.

I lower my head and can see through the corner of my eye Grace staring at me. I know she has a look of disappointment, but I can't turn my head to look at her. I would feel worse.

"Check surveillance on Rebecca's in Willow's End for the last two hours. Get back to me right away."

Without another word he looks at me with disdain, contempt, and any other tasteless description that can be had.

Grace doesn't know how to respond, so she doesn't. She sits almost in a prim and proper state, but her deflated spirit shows on her face. Is it an indication of how she feels about me, or the circumstances?

"This may be a long evening," says Alex.

And as we hit the five-minute mark of excruciating silence, I find myself desperately praying for the sound of his cell phone, if nothing else, just to fill that void in the air.

Moments later, Alex's cell releases a soft buzz that still amplifies through the room and startles Grace.

"Go ahead," says Alex. He listens intently with one eyebrow slowly lifting and crinkling his forehead. "Send it and stay on that area for the rest of the night."

Our eyes are focused on him as though we were watching the last scene in a murder mystery to find out who the killer is.

There's a bleep from his cell. He opens the screen and tells me to turn the TV on. He taps the cell twice—a picture shows up on the TV screen.

I can't believe it. "That's my car."

"Keep watching and pay attention. A man will come into the shot, and you tell me if you can identify him."

We are glued to the screen.

Suddenly a tall man wearing a baseball cap and totally in silhouette enters the picture. He stares at the car as he walks by then stops, bends down as if he notices something. He walks over to the passenger side, tries the door and opens it. He seems to reach in and grabs something out of the glove box. It looks like my ownership papers. He begins to read it, then puts it back, but takes two items that must be the gun and TED. Quickly puts them inside his jacket and drops out of camera range, then promptly returns to the driver's side with some kind of box-shaped object. He bends down out of sight, then reappears about a minute later and leaves soon after with the box.

"Well," says Alex, "that was of little help, other than the fact that he was tall and wears a baseball cap."

"My Magnum's missing, too." Why did I have to add that?

"You sure know how to make it harder on yourself."

"I've heard that." Mainly from me.

"I know it's almost impossible, but do you see anything recognizable other than his hat?"

"There are a number of tall people around that might fit that look, but not one of them would ever be considered a threat or a thief. And as far as the baseball hat goes, I don't know anyone in town who has one or wears one," says Grace.

"All right. Let's call it a night. If we're extremely lucky he may show up again. He may even show up for breakfast at Rebecca's. Grace, I would suggest you be there first thing in the morning."

"I will."

"And Paul, from now on, if we get that back—"

"I know, keep it with me at all times."

"I shouldn't have to tell you how dangerous it is in the wrong hands...and sometimes...in the right hands. In the meantime, I will have my people working on it."

CHAPTER 27

Grace seems to be sleeping soundly. After all, she had done nothing wrong.

As for me, it was a night of guilt and reflection. It wasn't that I didn't know it was my fault or that I didn't deserve that tongue-lashing, but I feel embarrassed that he had raked me over the coals in front of Grace. To Grace, I have been her hero, her knight in shining armor. Now, probably not so much.

For me, I dig a little deeper and begin to regurgitate those horrific days in grade school, where I would be chastised by the teacher for some insignificant matter like not paying attention. There would be two sets of punishment. Standing in a corner facing the wall or, as one sadistic teacher would have it, removing myself from my desk and spend the rest of the period on my haunches—something I'm sure he picked up from watching *Bridge on the River Kwai*. The only other kid to have it worse was Bailey; Big Boy Bailey they called him. He was shorter than I was, but twice as wide, and when he was told to get down, you could hear the boys moan and the girls sniffle. His face would turn as red as Rudolf's nose in a matter of seconds, and the sweat poured from the boy's brow or worse, and would leave a puddle on the floor. It was inhumane.

At the end of the school year, by the skin of my teeth, I passed and would be heading to high school. I had heard that Bailey didn't make it. He would have to repeat. I couldn't imagine him going though another year of brutality. They said the teacher had a smile on his face when he announced it to Bailey—sadistic bastard. A week later they found Bailey floating downriver, and he wasn't swimming.

The most punishing blow would be to have the ridicule spill out into the schoolyard at recess, where I would be further pounded with words, gestures, and the occasional fist. You can't beat those fond memories of youth—no matter how big a stick you use.

—

My sleep, of course, was lacking in depth, but the aroma of coffee that seeps under the bedroom door and into my nose brings me to full alertness. Most would say it's the addiction of the caffeine that you're craving. What's the problem with just saying, it tastes good? What the hell is wrong with people? Why does there have to be this undertone—underbelly? Who are these people to determine my thoughts, my motives?

It's too early to bring the world into my head. I need that coffee to calm down. Entering the kitchen I expect to see a somber-looking Grace, but instead I see the coffee pot with a subtle rise of steam and two blueberry muffins on the island and a note. I wonder if I should eat the muffins first. No—don't need the drama.

> *Sweetheart,*
> *I'm out early as Dad suggested.*
> *Everything will work out. You*
> *are still my hero, the best part of*
> *my life. See you when you get*
> *back from Ben's.*
> *Love you. XOXO*

Isn't she something—and now for those muffins.

While soothing my appetite I can hear the sound of a vehicle coming up the road. Sounds like it's stopped in front of the house. I put the second muffin down and listen.

Seconds later there's a knock at the door. I think about the scare that Alex left me with and can't take anything for granted. Gently placing the chain on the door I revert back to my foot ajar method and open to a crack.

"Hi, Paul."

It's Mike. I unchain the door.

"Mike. It's been awhile. Come in. Can I get you a coffee?"

"Coffee sounds good."

He sits in Ben's chair while I pour him a cup then join him on the couch.

"So, what brings you here so early in the morning? Usually you'd already be in full swing at the garage."

"I thought it was more important that I bring you these." He partially opens his jacket and pulls out the Magnum and the TED.

I'm speechless, and then realize something that I hadn't focused on—he's wearing the baseball cap.

"So it was you that took them, but why?" I say in a somewhat hostile way.

"Hold on now, Paul. Let me tell you what happened."

I take a sip of coffee and lean forward.

"I was on my way home last night, and as I passed Rebecca's I saw your car parked out front. I noticed you had a flat rear tire, and seeing Rebecca's was closed, I thought you had left it there because of it. I didn't want to start to change it without knowing for sure it was yours. People get a little concerned if they see you mucking around with their car, so I tried the door and it was open. Checked the glove box for the ownership, and I was right. I knew you had that gun and what looked to be a newer version of a Q3, and I didn't think that was something I should leave around. So I plugged your flat, and since I see that the car's here, I guess I did a pretty good job. So, here I am.

"Oh, by the way—" He takes off the cap and points to the words on it. "Mike's Garage, nice, huh? It's a birthday present from my cousin."

I am speechless. My mouth hangs open like a dead carp. "Mike, you just saved my life."

"Your life. Geez, Paul, it was just a flat. I wouldn't want to see what a response I would get if I had to rebuild your transmission."

This has got to be the high point of the week for me. I just can't take the smile from my face as I drive over to Ben's. Good old, down-to-earth—sometimes semiconscious, Mike. Who would have guessed it?

Entering Ben's Place I receive another surprise. It's Tor sitting at a table having breakfast with none other than Adam.

"How's that shoulder, Tor?"

He lifts his arm up, "Almost perfect."

"And how's our Gypsy Boy?"

"You got the title right. I'll be on the move again shortly."

"Why is that?"

"I sold that cottage he's staying in," says Tor with a smile.

"Any plans, Adam?"

"The family that's renting my place has bought their own home and will be moving out, so I'm thinking of moving back in."

"Do you think that's wise? I mean, safe?"

"Tor and I were talking it over, and we've come to the conclusion that since the book was never published, that I'm no longer a threat, and hopefully the whole thing has fizzled out. Besides, there isn't a publisher this side of the universe that would touch that book now. And like Alex had found out when he tried, it would have been under fiction."

That does make sense. It would seem to be a waste of time and money for those bastards to pursue him any longer. He can't live the rest of his life under a rock. I guess only time will tell.

"Good for you, Adam. And what about Ed?"

"Ed is a distant memory," says Tor. "I surveyed the area last week and there are some wildflowers, brush, and a couple of tree shoots sprouting up there."

"That's good, but I was referring to our episode at Dakota's with the FBI."

"I guess looking back, getting rid of Ed wasn't something I should have done. It was more a reaction from my previous life back home. When you felt cornered, you eliminated the problem. I wish there was a way to get them off my back."

"I may have a solution."

"What is it?" says Tor.

"I don't know right now, but I do know where to find it."

—

I leave Bridgeburg and know that my only hope of getting the FBI out of the way is to talk to the man from manna land—Alex.

I'll meet Grace for lunch and talk it over with her since it's her father we have to deal with. I wish she would just call him Alex. I don't know why, but the word *dad* seems awkward to me. I guess it's just something I have to get used to.

—

"Well, you're a little early today," says Grace as I make myself comfortable by our favorite spot by the window.

"Everything all right at Ben's?"

"Splendid. The breakfast crowd is down a little."

"I'm sure that will pick up in the fall when the weather changes."

"That's true. And that's just around the corner—again. Everyone wants to get those outdoor Ds right now."

"I should be with you in about ten. Would you like to look at the big city paper while you wait, sir?"

"I think I may be brave enough to take a peek at the world today."

"I'll have Joyce bring it to you."

"By the way, how are the lovebirds doing?"

Grace smiles. "I'll let her tell you."

A moment later Joyce arrives with a smile a mile wide. "Good morning, Paul."

"And good morning to you. Is it Joyce or Joy?"

"One and the same," she says with a grin while placing the coffee and newspaper on the table. "Life couldn't be sweeter."

"I know exactly how you feel. No matter what goes on in my life, Grace is my world, and it's always sweet."

"Exactly. Dakota's going to take me to meet his family on the reservation—I mean the REZ."

"And how do you feel about that?"

"Excited and nervous."

"You just keep smiling the way you do and you'll be fine."

"Thanks, Paul."

She leaves me with a faint trail of rose perfume in the air. Yes sir, she'll be just fine. I take a sip of coffee then glance through the paper that seems to be so repetitive each and every day. The violence and corruption is first and foremost, with only the locations and characters shifting. I move to the fourth page and notice a small and seemingly unassuming article, *UWC hires retired former CIA agent.* That doesn't sound like a big deal, but then I read the copy.

Retired CIA agent William Bass to head investigation into former agent-turned spy, Alex Miller, who had perished in a car accident twenty years ago. According to reports, Bass thinks that the death of Miller was a cover-up and that he is still alive and continues to plot against the UWC. Insiders have mentioned a vendetta that Bass has always had against the disgraced agent, but Bass denies the accusation, stating, "In my opinion this has always been a case with holes that need to be filled and put to rest once and for all."

Oh no! This is bad—really bad. Since this just came out to the public, that means Alex has known about it for some time. Then it hits me. This may be why he kept saying he may need my help. Now that this is out in the open, he may be ready to call up the troops at anytime. I suddenly feel lightheaded. I'll have to put Tor on the back burner for now.

My throat is dry and my palms are wet, and I don't know what the hell my face is doing, and here comes Grace. Think good thoughts—good thoughts.

"There, finally. Have you ordered yet?"

"Now that wouldn't be polite." I try to smile and hope that the one acting class in high school resurfaces.

"Such a gentleman. So what are you having?"

After reading that news I'm not sure if I can eat a thing. "Once again, ladies first."

"All right, cheeseburger and fries, nice and simple."

I do enjoy a good cheeseburger. It will be easier to swallow under the circumstances. "I'll have the same."

She eyes the newspaper. "Any new developments in the world today?"

Good, she hasn't seen it. However, if I don't tell her, Alex will, and I can't have her thinking I held that back from her. This would be the perfect intro, but if I tell her it may be quite some time before either one of us has an appetite. I think it would be better after we ate first.

I take my time getting down my burger. I need to figure out how I will approach Grace with this bombshell.

Grace is down to her last two fries. "Well, that's a switch."

"What is?"

"It's usually me that's the slow one."

"This one tastes so good, I'm savoring it." Good answer.

Our conversation is more like a ping-pong game—Grace serves and I answer. "You don't seem very talkative today, honey. You sure everything is all right?"

I leave the last few of fries on my plate. "Grace."

She knows right away from my tone that all is not right. "I knew there was something bothering you."

I pick up the newspaper, fold it over to the article, and hand it to her. "It's best you get the full story."

She keeps her eyes on me, but turns her head to the side, then looks down at the paper like she's about to open Pandora's box, which is pretty close.

"Has someone we know passed away?"

I want to say, *not yet,* but that would add fuel before she even sees the fire. "Read it." I know that sounds blunt, but I tried to say it in the softest tone.

As she begins to read it to herself I can see the tension building in her face with her eyes, her eyebrows, her lips. I feel my face mimicking hers. Her fists tighten their grip on the paper. She lowers the paper. "I have to call him right now."

This is a different Grace than I'm used to. I expected her to immediately turn into an emotional wreck. I hand her my cell.

"At least it's ringing."

"Can you put it on speaker and lower the volume."

"Grace, I assume you're calling in regards to the article."

"Oh Dad, this is scary. What's going to happen?"

"I've been in tighter spots than this. That guy Bass does more talking than anything else. He may tell everyone he's focusing on me, but has no more evidence than he had when I died. He's one of those characters who enjoys the spotlight."

"But this is the UWC, aren't they very dangerous?"

"They can be if you don't keep at least one step ahead of them. Remember, I was there and I know what they know and how they think. He's already made the mistake of alerting me to the fact that he's after my ghost. So while he's doing that I'm now watching every move he makes."

"I know you're right, but it's still upsetting."

"Don't you worry, leave it to me. I'll keep in touch."

Any other time I would jump right in to ask him about Tor and the FBI, but this is not the time. I'll have to handle that on my own, and it's something once again, I'm afraid I'll have to hide from Grace. Alex has done a lot for us both. I really owe him. I must be loyal, if nothing else, a friend. I have to be ready for action—whatever that may be.

—

After lunch I leave Grace to her work and hope it burns off some of her anxiety and allows me to freely think about Tor. I decide that the first thing to do is to get rid of his vehicle. I could go to a used car lot and pick up something that wouldn't fit his profile, like some older-model car that would be unassuming, perhaps even something with a few scratches and a dent or two. Second, once again, change his phone; and third, a short-term move to another residence. Offering him a room at Rebecca's would be out of the question—we still have all the rooms pre-booked. I'll leave that open for now.

—

Driving home I'm glad we didn't take Alex up on hiding the house. I think it was over the top. Seeing the house always gives me a great feeling in my heart and reliving those wonderful memories from the moment I stepped foot in Willow's End.

I grab a cold one and sit out back to get a little sun and mental therapy before I call Tor. I think about the back patio, another reminder of the great firesides with Grace and friends. Then the bad memories creep in—the barbecuing of Wagner, the deadly confrontation at Rebecca's with that poor agent that was shot by his own for standing up for us. The explosion under Rebecca's that killed a pile of agents, and the swamp burial of Agent Ed and the...okay, this has gone from mental therapy to mental madness—I'll call Tor.

At that my cell rings. It's Tor, how convenient. "I was just about to call you."

"Good thing you didn't. I just purchased a new phone and number."

"That's one of the reasons I was calling."

"If it's any help, my next move was another car rental."

"Boy, you're right on top of things. Here's one you might not have thought of. Instead of another rental, what about an older model from a used car lot? They would never expect that."

"Sounds like you're right on the money yourself. That's a great idea. I'll get right on it."

"The last thing is your living quarters."

"Hmm. I'll talk to Adam about staying with him for a while. I don't think they have a clue where he is, and as we discussed, I don't think he's on their list anymore."

"Then I think we've covered all the bases as far as you're concerned at the moment."

—

Now that's cooperation—I can breathe again, and that means time for a long overdue candlelight dinner at home. Maybe something Italian, that's romantic. I'll try to replicate our time in Tuscany. Now, what to make?

"Grace, could you get them to bake a take-home lasagna for tonight?"

I think I can do the uncorking myself.

—

The dinner was perfect, and even though Grace brought it home, she really appreciated the thought and effort it took to open the wine—both bottles.

"Paul, we still have an hour of daylight. Why don't we start a fire out back and watch the day come to a nice sunset end?"

"I'm all for that." I hear my cell in the kitchen and decide to ignore it.

"Shouldn't you see who that is?"

"Grace, right now I just want to be one with you and nature."

It sounds out a few more times then stops. "I'm sure if it's important they'll call back."

And there's the encore. "All right, I'm coming."

I see it's Alex. "Alex, everything all right?" Please, say yes.

"Not quite. I need a small favor."

Here it comes. "Sure, nothing too physical I hope. I am getting on." A little levity never hurts.

"I don't think it will be anything you can't handle, even at your age. I have a hunch about Bass. I wouldn't put it past him to want to dig up my grave at the old church to see if anyone's home."

"So—what would you like me to do?" I hope he doesn't say to dig up Ed and throw him in there.

"Just take a walk up there with a garden trowel and gently lift the stone marker and switch it with another one. If he decides to go through the trouble of digging it up, all he has to know is that there is a body there and that will be enough."

"That's certainly doable. Is there a timeline on that?"

"Now."

"The sun is going down, but I think if I hurry I can get there in time."

"Paul?"

"Yes."

"If you don't make it in time, perhaps that great little invention they call a flashlight may help."

"Right." Smart-ass. He seems to have picked up one of my finer qualities.

"Grace!" I holler from the patio doors. "That was Alex. I have to go up to the cemetery."

I knew that would get her up. "The cemetery? What's that all about?"

"He thinks Bass might dig up the grave to see if he's there."

"And what are you supposed to do?"

"Switch stones in case he does. Once he sees a body in there that should be the end of it."

"You need help?"

"No, sweetheart, just a garden shovel and a flashlight. I figure fifteen minutes to get there, fifteen back and another ten to change them around."

—

I should have added some extra time on that. It's a steeper hill than I remember from the time Ben and I climbed it. The only light is where the sun is hitting the top half of the church. Let's see, where was that stone marker?

Ah, here it is. I place the flashlight on the ground facing the stone. I work the trowel all around the edge of the stone then try to dig a spot underneath to lift it—there, got it. Okay, now the one beside it.

I switch them and carefully put them back into place. That was easy enough. It's a small task, but the implications are huge. If Alex has any more favors like this, I'm game.

—

"Grace, you can call Alex and tell him, job completed."

"He'll be happy to hear that.'

She throws her arms around me. "That was so nice of you."

"It's all in the family, right?"

"Right," she says with a smile and kisses me.

"Now, since I exerted myself climbing that mountain—"

"Mountain?"

"Grace, do you know how steep that is? Anyway, it took some effort, and I was wondering if any of that lasagna is still available?"

"I think I can manage that."

"And possibly some red to wash it down?"

"I'll have to open up a new one."

"Gee, I hate to see you do that for one glass."

"One glass? Dream on."

CHAPTER 28

Three days have gone by since the cemetery shuffle. All is quiet on the northern front. Tor is doing well at Adam's place—no incidents with the FBI, and even Dakota seems to have his life back in order—more so now with Joyce.

Yes, everything is as it should be, which makes me a little on edge. I don't know if I would call myself a pessimist, but I've always had one saying rise to the surface since my first marriage —*the calm before the storm.* Speaking of weather, I've lessened my trips to Ben's Place. The season is rapidly coming to a close, which means tourists are almost nonexistent—only the weekend autumn nature lovers with cameras and binoculars to capture the brilliance of the forest and foliage, and, of course, the localse.

Now that I have more time on my hands, not that I did much when I was supposedly working (which I would only admit to myself), I am able to spend more time with Grace. Though she is working, I now have most of my meals at Rebecca's. She told me she likes having me close in case she needs me to run errands, but she also said it makes her feel safe and warm inside to see my face—likewise. And, it's nice to be waited on by the staff.

I sit at my table by the window entertaining these thoughts while waiting for my first cup of coffee and the newspaper. Being Saturday, I especially look forward to the Saturday edition—more articles, and a rarity these days are the comics, which are usually in the political columns. I also enjoy the fact that the staff has memorized my routine, with only slight variations from weekday to weekends. Like clockwork they both arrive within two minutes of my ass in the chair.

I usually glance at the front page, but today is different. A small rectangular box of type at the bottom spikes my adrenaline like two pots of coffee. The headline reads—BASS UNEARTHS GHOST.

Alex was right about Bass. He did get to the cemetery and he did dig it up. He of course found a coffin at the bottom, so that should be it. If I hadn't followed through, Alex might be the NOT walking dead.

The article continues on page six...

One reporter said that Bass doesn't seem bothered by the find and feels that Miller is still alive and will continue his investigation.

—

This guy scares me for two reasons. He has a personal vendetta, free rein, and it's been on his Christmas wish list since Santa was in diapers.

Here comes Grace, she must have been in the office. I can't tell from her expression what she knows. She glances at the newspaper.

"Well, I guess that's that."

"You haven't heard the update," she says as she seats herself.

"What do you mean?"

"I just got off the phone with Dad. It looks like Bass is going to have the body exhumed."

"So he'll see that it's not Alex."

"No, he won't. Dad said the grave is almost twenty years old. Between fifteen and twenty years and the body has completely decomposed and only the bones would remain."

"What if it was embalmed?"

"I asked him that. He said it wouldn't matter. Embalming hardly slows the process. A waste of money."

"So that's it. He doesn't have any proof that it wouldn't be Alex," I said.

"That's right." She smiles. "The only way for sure would be a DNA test, of which he has no sample of my dad."

"Perfect. I guess that should be case closed."

"I know it would be for me, if I were Bass."

"I'm sure Alex is relieved."

"He doesn't express too much, but I know he is."

"Grace, let's celebrate. Care to join me for a glass of wine?"

"You're asking?"

—

It's been awhile since we have been able to relax by the fire, taking in a movie without something festering in the background. No loose strings—everyone's shoes neatly tied with perfect bows. We make it to the end of the movie and they announce the eleven o'clock news is on its way.

"I didn't realize it was that late," says Grace.

"Did you want to catch any of it?"

"Not me. I'm going to bed."

"I'll watch the headline stories and I'll join you in ten."

"I'm sure I'll be out in five, so tiptoe."

"I promise."

First stop—politics. Something I think should air last, since you're going to sleep through it anyway. I've always considered the White House and whitewash interchangeable.

I suck back the token gesture Grace left in the bottle, and being true to myself, I feel the blinds pulling down over my eyes. I reach for the remote and the anchor mentions something about the UWC, and my eyes blink open. I hear the name Bass and immediately sit up. I listen though it seems to process at a slower rate than usual. Replaying it in my subconscious state the one word that stands out is *female.* The anchor reiterates the sentence. *"You heard it right. The skeletal remains have now been identified as female."*

I feel like I just got smacked in the face with a cold dishrag.

In lightning speed my memory leaps back to the event of switching the stones and realize I switched them without even thinking of checking the other stone.

I'm sure Alex already knows about this. I wonder why he hasn't called to give me a verbal beating? I'm sure I'm out of favor—again. He's probably going to wait until morning and call Grace, and between the two, drag whatever self-confidence I have established over the last two years through the muck and mire of some street-like, rain-soaked, medieval village, and have my head, feet and hands through those wooden holes—and now I'm supposed to sleep.

Hey, where the hell are you going with this? Get a grip. After all, you were only following his instructions. If he was on the ball he would have told you to check the stone first to make sure it was a man.

That's true, and I was only working with a flashlight that was dim at best—that's a good point. At least I have some form of defense in place. It's not Perry Mason, but—

Glad I had that talk with myself. I'm feeling better now, and I'll be off to join Grace.

—

I still had a hard time settling in but here it is, almost eight in the morning and feeling pretty good. Ready for whatever comes my way. Like they say, wake up and smell the coffee.

My cup is beside the coffee pot, but where's Grace? Looking out the patio door I see her sitting comfortably in the Adirondack, sipping coffee, taking in that sun. I open an untouched box of muffins and put two on a plate and with my coffee cup in hand, I join her.

"You're finally up. You must have slept well."

"I guess I did. Brought muffins to share."

"That's nice of you. It looked so inviting out here that I didn't even turn on the radio. Just made the coffee and came right out to enjoy this lovely morning."

So she doesn't know the final outcome of the dig.

"I can't fault that. It is warm and inviting. We won't be seeing too many of these days ahead."

"I dread the thought."

"I thought you enjoy the winter, Grace."

"I do, until New Year's, then it's downhill from there."

I notice she has her cell phone resting on the arm of the chair. "You expecting a call?"

"No, in case I did get one, I didn't want it to wake you."

"That's thoughtful, thank you."

I think it would be wise for me to tell her what I know before she has to hear it from Alex—don't want her to think I was hiding it from her.

"Grace—I caught the news last night."

"And—"

Her phone emits a LOUD BUZZ.

"There, you see, this might have happened if I left it in the house."

I hope I'm wrong about this call.

"Joyce. Everything all right?...sleep in. Not me...what's up?...The order didn't come in. I've had that happen before. They usually show up in the afternoon if they've had other large orders to fill first...No, you were right to call...Bye."

Back in my court. "Grace—"

"Oh, sorry sweetheart, you were talking about the news."

"Yes, I found out that—"

BUZZ!

"This is crazy. Go ahead, Paul. I'm going to ignore it."

"You might want to at least see who it is?"

"True." She picks it up and glances at the screen. "Oh, it's Dad. Good morning. I guess it's nice to have that guy Bass out of the way... what! Oh no. So what's going to happen now?...So what does that involve?...All right, I'll try...Yes, love you, too."

"Paul, Dad just told me—"

"I know."

"You know? Why didn't you tell me?"

"Because I was interrupted by two phone calls."

"Oh, that's right. I'm sorry, Paul."

"So what did Alex have to say?"

"He keeps telling me not to worry, but—he said, don't pay any attention to any media coverage about it. They really have no idea what's going on. They're following Bass, but so am I. He said that Bass will be coming to the end of his rope shortly, whatever that means."

"Sounds like he's turned the tables and has Bass in the crosshairs."

"Crosshairs, that sounds like guns and violence to me. I'm going to call Joyce back and tell her I'm going to take some time off until this gets resolved. I'm just too upset."

At this point I have to agree with Grace. I think deep inside she is feeling what I am, the water in the pot is slowly rising from simmer to boil, and we decide to stay close to home—to be more precise, we don't go anywhere, limiting ourselves to the patio.

—

Two days have passed. There have been no news reports and no further communication with Alex. I could say, no news is good news, but not in our case. We walk around the house as though we were on tiptoes, anticipating a visit or a phone call.

BUZZ!—and there it is, the silence has been broken. I can see that it's Sam, our backhoe, alias gravedigger who placed a record number of bodies under that cement pad at Ben's house. I put the phone on speaker so I won't have to repeat it to Grace, and to show her I'm completely up-front.

"Hi, Sam. It's been awhile, how have you been?"

"It has. Listen. I may be off base with this but thought you should know. About forty-five minutes ago I had a visit from some fella claiming to be a news reporter. Said he was doing a story about Willow's End and the advantages of living in a rural community. He started off with simple questions then quickly jumped to asking me if I knew Ben, and had I done any work for him at anytime. That's when I got the red flag. I told him that Ben died a ways back, and I couldn't remember doing any work for him. Then I raised my bristles and said I've been retired for some time and just want to be left alone—I think the rifle I had over my shoulder helped it along."

"Thanks, Sam. Appreciate that. If anything else pops up that seems out of the norm, I'd appreciate hearing about it."

"Will do."

"Paul, this is getting scary now," says Grace.

I'm way ahead of you on the scary. "I would say concerning." Not the best response, but I had to tone it down for her.

Another call comes and my mouth turns dry. "It's Charlie."

Anticipating a similar call I answer with, "What is it, Charlie?"

"Well, that's what I'd like to know."

"You're the second call I've had about it."

"The reporter? Who was the first?"

"Sam."

"Sounds like it's time for a good Supreme. If he comes back I'll entice him with a free one, then I'll call you to pick him up."

"Good enough, Charlie."

"Sounds like this guy is getting a little too close, Paul. I really could use a—"

Another call. This time it's Mike. Normally the only time I would hear from him these days would be for an overdue tire rotation or oil change.

"Hi, Mike, what's up?" Not like I don't know. What I received in response brought back a chill up my spine I haven't felt in some time.

Mike said the reporter's questions were too close to home. They went all the way back to Wagner and his sudden disappearance, and the community confrontation outside of Rebecca's with the UWC agents.

That's more than close, that's on our doorstep.

Mike played his dumb card, which at times is in his wheelhouse. He told him he didn't have much to do with stories and gossip, and his work kept him too busy for much else.

"That's perfect, Mike, thanks."

"If you need any help—"

"I will. Thanks."

"That means he's in earshot of Rebecca's!"

"I need a minute to think."

I focus my attention on the reporter and come to a conclusion regarding which of the two groups he is representing—UWC or FBI?

The FBI is looking to find and solve the disappearance of Agent Ed, so asking about incidents that went back to the UWC would eliminate them.

Now, I'm not Holmes or Columbo, but the UWC with Bass at the helm is looking for Alex, and I think he suspects that Alex has gone full circle and resides somewhere in the area, and that's why this so-called reporter is all over the map, hoping for a connection that might give Bass a bead on Alex.

My other fear is that this may not only expose Alex, but open up a can of worms for the rest of us. I think his next stop will be Rebecca's, which means he could be there right now. They all gave me the same description of this character: He's thin with a goatee and about five-ten, with one easy giveaway—they were fascinated with his footwear of two-tone, oxblood and white-colored shoes.

"Grace."

"I'll get it," she says, then walks over to the cupboard to grab a bottle.

"Just one double. That's not something we need right now. Clear heads prevail. I'd like you to call Rebecca's and give Joyce a description of that reporter, and to call you right away if he shows up."

Now, what the hell do I do if he does? Any questions he would ask, the staff would be oblivious to them. Not one was around when everything tanked.

"Paul, I've got Joyce on the line. She says he's there now. He sat down and ordered lunch."

"Good. Tell her I'll be there in five and just treat me as regular customer."

"What are you planning on doing?" asks Grace.

"Right now? I'm going to have a cheeseburger and keep an eye on him. When he leaves, I'll follow him."

"This does not sound like a good plan, and that concerns me."

"Don't worry, Grace. As soon as he gets to his destination, I'll call Alex and let him handle it from there."

"Promise?"

"I promise."

"Call me right after you call Dad."

"I will."

—

Joyce greets me at the front door of Rebecca's.

"Where is he sitting?"

"I'm afraid he's taken your table."

"How did that happen?"

"At first the waitress offered him another table, but he zoomed right in on yours."

"That's very strange."

"I thought so, too."

"Joyce, act like this is my first time here and escort me to the farthest table from him."

On our way into the dining room Joyce grabs a menu and seats me a good distance away. "Menu, sir?"

"No thank you, I'll just have a cheeseburger and fries."

The reporter glances up at me then settles back into the local newspaper.

"Anything to drink?"

"Yes, I'll have a Labatt's Blue, please."

"And would you like a copy of our local paper as well?"

Great idea. "Yes, thank you."

He has his rock to hide behind and I have mine. I peer over the newspaper and he seems to peer back. This is reminiscent of that old cartoon, "Spy vs Spy." But I think I'm feeling more like Clouseau. I, too, noticed his Oxfords jutting out under the table like Jimmy Durante's nose from under his hat.

For the next twenty-odd minutes I was the lone wolf in this peek-a-boo game—he just sat quietly finishing his lunch.

The waitress drops off his bill, and within seconds he's placed an amount on the table and quickly heads out through the archway.

Sadly, I leave a half order of fries on my plate.

Too far away to know what type of car he's driving, but it's a two-door and light gray or metallic-looking. He drives down the main street heading up the hill that leads to the highway. The Magnum's in the glove box and TED is where he should be, according to Alex—in my pants pocket.

Approaching the highway he has a choice. Right will take him to the city and left would be on the way to Bridgeburg. Interesting —he's pulled over and talking on his cell phone. Now what do I do? Being the only other vehicle on the road I can't pull over, that would be a giveaway.

I'll have to go past him and make my decision. I'll take Bridgeburg. The whole area is forest. I turn down the next country road which is about fifty yards on the right. I make the turn and then a U-turn. Pulling over I walk up to the road, and looking through the trees I can see the corner and wait for him to make his turn.

I see the gray nose edging to the intersection. His signal to turn left comes on. I quickly get back into the car and wait for him to pass. Before I arrive at the corner another car passes. Perfect, I can follow without being noticed. I loosen my grip on the steering wheel and feel relaxed enough to start asking questions like, why Bridgeburg and who was he talking to?

Okay—let me at least try to come up with something here. Our restaurant's in Bridgeburg. I met Alex in Bridgeburg. UWC agents were killed by Alex's people on a farm just outside of town. Alex's invisible hideaway is about ten miles out from the town. Tor killed FBI Agent Ed at our house. A basement full of dead agents at Rebecca's, and the list goes on. Too many things pointing in my and Grace's direction.

The car that was between us is no longer there, and I can see the gray car about a quarter-mile up the road. His brake lights glow red. He makes a right turn down a country road. I push my speed to catch up.

Turning at the country road the dust from his car is still in the air from the gravel road. I continue over a small hill, and to my amazement he's nowhere to be seen. Looking around, there are no farmhouses, just empty fields—no place for him to turn or hide—vanished. I guess I should call Grace. At least she'll be happy to hear it was uneventful.

Strange, she's not answering. I leave her a message.

These country roads aren't meant for U-turns, so it will have to be a three-pointer and back over the hill. On the other side are two black Hummers parked sideways with no way around. This is not something I anticipated. I feel the outside of my pants pocket for the TED. I stop about a hundred feet away. At that moment, what look to be UWC agents step out. Next, the big surprise—out steps the ego-driven Mr. Bass. He's a big man with slick, thinning grey hair and wearing a light blue suit with slightly longer sleeves that gives him that *Mommy dressed me funny* look.

"Paul, isn't it?"

I don't respond.

"I believe you're the piece of the puzzle that's missing."

I feel like a deer in the headlights. "Puzzle?"

"Let's not play the dumb game. You will find that your time is much more a concern to you than you think. Where's Miller?"

"As far as I know, he's been dead and buried for years."

"I'm afraid the stone has been rolled away. The myth has been exposed. I know he's your wife's father."

Shit! I think I'm going to pass out. How does he know—

"I'll bet you're wondering how I know this. Well, you told me. You and your lovely wife, Grace."

"Me? I've never laid eyes on you before. And I still don't know what you're talking about."

"The reporter you were following from Rebecca's. You think he was there about gathering information about Willow's End? In a way he was, but he was also there for a more specific reason."

He advances a few steps. "Your favorite spot to sit by the window—so many wonderful conversations with Grace." He raises his right hand to reveal a small object. "The reporter was there to pick up this small device from under the table."

"You bugged the table!"

"Now, where's Miller?"

Can't think straight. What do I do? Not TED. There is no way I could use it under these circumstances. I don't even have it set for this. I'd be dead before another breath.

"Perhaps this will help you. Have you contacted your wife lately? She didn't answer, did she?"

"What are you saying? You've kidnapped her? Where is she, you bastard?"

"She's fine, and a very nice-looking woman to be sure. All I'm asking for is Miller's location. I have no doubt he's in the area."

"I want you to let Grace go."

"That would be out of the question, Mr. Fenton. Like I said, she's in good hands. I don't believe in putting physical pressure on a woman for answers—that's not my style. I'm counting on you to choose between your wife and a man you hardly know."

The only thing I can come up with is frivolous talk. "Kidnapping is against the law."

"Don't talk stupid, Paul—I am the law. You're hiding a criminal. I have all the rights and you have none."

I have to try to make some concession here to get Grace back. "All I know is, I'm picked up and dropped off at some secluded place and have no memory as to how I got there."

"Interesting—" He looks at his wristwatch. "I'll give you until six o'clock to find that place."

"That's only five hours."

"—which is plenty of time for someone who is desperate to have his wife back. You've got your cell, I presume? Take this number down."

I'm tempted to go for the TED, but quickly switch to the other pocket and pull out the cell.

He calls out the number and adds, "I want the location as soon as possible. Any bullshit and you'll have no one else to blame if things go badly."

They depart and leave a trail of dust that blows into my eyes. I squint and hold my breath until it clears and wish this nightmare would clear as quickly.

The only function I seem to be able to handle is driving home. Usually driving gives me the solitude I need to calm down and rearrange my thoughts into some recognizable order that make palatable sense. But not this time—my mind feels like a bell jar that's had all the air sucked out of it. The only picture I envision is Grace trying to keep it all together—this whole event could take a toll on her—and I have no idea what it may do to me.

The anguish I'm feeling is overwhelming. I have to pull over. For the first time in my life I really want to kill—commit murder —grab that asshole Bass by the throat and squeeze. Watch with glee as his eyeballs bulge from their sockets and hear the last gasp of air leave his body.

What the hell is happening? That's not me! I'm a nice guy at heart—peace loving. I still listen to '60s music.

My hands are shaking and my thoughts are all over the map. I really need to calm down. Wait a minute. The one person that started this whole thing is a phone call away! Alex has to fix this.

"Alex!"

"I'm on it."

"You're on it? You know that bastard has given me" I look at the dash clock "less than five hours to hand you over."

"I'm surprised he's given you that long."

"This is the UWC we're talking about! This is life or death for all of us!"

"Paul, I want you to listen carefully to what I am about to say. First, this is not the UWC. They have no knowledge of any of this, and they don't care one way or the other what goes on with the FBI. This is a small branch in that organization headed by an idiot who couldn't find his own stool in a toilet."

"Okay, that sounds a little calming. So what are you going to do?"

"Right now it's what you're going to do."

"Me?"

"I grew up in Willow's End. I know how these communities work—they are as united as the United Nations. Okay, not the best example, but you know what I mean. From what I have witnessed from you as a leader in this community, you should have no trouble getting all the locals together. I want you to get on the phone and have some of your friends spread the word that Grace is in trouble and needs their help. Tell them all to show up at the park in Bridgeburg at five o'clock with any weapons at their disposal."

"All right."

"And Paul, make sure you bring TED and your gun this time."

Still a smart-ass. I have to admire that.

I call Charlie, and there is no love lost between him and any government agency. He's so pissed off that they've got Grace involved by kidnapping her that I haven't seen him this fired up since our standoff at Rebecca's.

Next, I call Mike at the garage, and he's right on it.

Then I call Joyce to let her know so that she can keep things going at Rebecca's.

Now, I'm off to Bridgeburg. I have one more person to call on.

CHAPTER 29

My best bet is to drop in to see Gus. He should be able to round up a few supporters, especially knowing that Ben's Place could be in jeopardy.

I park in front of Gus's little shop. I feel a slight sense of guilt that I haven't dropped in to reciprocate the business he has given to our establishment, but like they say, there's no time like the present.

It's the quaint little place that I imagined it to be—from clothing to an old wringer washer. In a small way it has the feel and look of the Emporium, but not much of anything antique, more of items that can be used on a daily basis.

There he is at the counter. It looks like he's making up some price tags.

Gus looks up. "Paul, nice to see you on this side of the street for a change. Need a nice older-model suit?"

"Not at the moment, Gus, but I do need your help." I explain the situation and what's at stake.

"So, a few good men with some firepower." He squints his left eye along with raising his mouth on the same side. "We've got four hunters in the area and three scary lookin' Vietnam vets that I'm sure would be up to the task."

"That's great. All we want to do is have a show of force."

"Okay, I think I can throw in a few farmers as well."

Before walking out the door I notice a Western belt and holster from the Old West.

"Say, Gus, would that holster fit a Magnum?"

Gus smiles. "It'll accommodate whatever size you have."

Hmm. "Okay, I'll take it."

I head back across the street and throw my purchase into the truck, then up the stairs into Ben's.

I check the time and it's just coming up to four-thirty. I decide to slow the pace with a beer, and then I'll head over to the park to see where we stand.

As I raise my glass I can see the front door open. I can't believe it! I'm in shock! It's Alex dressed as the old blind man.

He sits across from me.

"How did you make out?"

"I think I was very successful in pulling the alarm, but I guess the only way of knowing will be when I get to the park."

"How are you going to contact Bass?"

"I have his number on my cell."

"I want you to call him at five forty-five and give him these instructions to my place."

He hands me a slip of paper. I glance at it and realize that's not the same location.

"But this isn't—"

"It will be, for him. Have all your troops drive out to Forge Road. There's a large hill there. I want everyone to move quietly to the top of that hill, create a long line across the crest, and lay down out of sight."

"So what's on the other side?"

"Our trap—Anas will be there to instruct you further."

"And where will you be?"

"Close by."

The paper in my hand begins to shake.

"Paul, I suggest you order yourself a drink or two. Looks like you could use it."

That tells me that I'm worse off than I thought.

He stands, and before walking out places a hand on my shoulder and gives it a gentle squeeze. It sounds bizarre, but that little gesture, on some level, gave me a feeling of security; and it's strange to say it, but a sense of bonding like a deep friendship.

—

It's five to five as I walk down the street to the park, not knowing what I will find when I get there. To my amazement, I can't see the park for the people. I spot Charlie and he rushes over.

"Beautiful sight, isn't it?"

"It sure is."

"So, what's the plan?"

"Follow me."

I don't feel it's the alcohol, but more like Alex's gesture that has given me a boost of confidence that I have never come across before. It was like a transference of energy. I hop up on a park bench and shout out for their attention.

"First, I would like to thank you all for coming out. The reason I have asked you all here is two-fold. First is—"

This feels like an out-of-body experience. I'm watching and listening to myself as though it were Noam Chomsky or Jordan Peterson up there. The words just flow like water. By the end there is a rousing cheer. They get it all—from saving Grace to the underlying theme of community versus corporation.

We're all pumped as we roll out the *Bridgeburg Brigade*. I ride shotgun with Charlie in his truck. Me with my Magnum and Roy Roger's giddy-up belt and holster—and TED, of course, while Charlie cuddles up to his 12-gauge.

Our convoy, as the truckers used to call it, veers off the main road before Forge Road. We maneuver through the obstacle course of potholes and debris along an old cow path then reach our destination, the back of a substantial-sized hill.

I remind everyone the importance of silence and lying low when we reach the top. Then I reiterate the fact that this is a show of force and hopefully not a force to be reckoned with.

—

I feel like Moses climbing the mountain with all his followers in tow. Reaching the top everyone spreads out as planned. So far so good. There's a cool breeze rustling the leaves on the trees that feels invigorating after the strenuous climb.

Down below sits the trap. A building the size of Alex's headquarters if you were able to see it from the outside instead of the illusion with the shack.

I receive a tap on the shoulder. Turning, it's Anas. For the first time since we met, he slaps on a look of concern.

"How we doing?"

"Fine," but I think that question should be mine.

"Good. You've done a superb job of rounding up the locals. That should show Bass we mean business, as well. There's a big difference in motivation when it's ego against survival. Since we have everything in place, I think now would be the perfect time to call Bass."

Just before I call, I look down the line of volunteers once more and I'm glad I did. At the far end is Dakota and six of his tribe. He looks at me with a smile, and puts a fist to his chest. I follow suit.

Feeling more confident, I call Bass. It only took one ring, which tells me he may be more nervous about this than I am.

"What's the location?" says Bass.

"What, no greeting? No, 'How are you this evening?'"

"Not a good time to be a smart-ass with your wife on the line. Just give me the location—and one more thing, if I don't find him there, you won't find your wife either."

"I'll just be happy to have my wife back."

"Good. You just keep that thought. Now, what's the location?"

Knowing what he will be faced with when he arrives, I'm not afraid anymore. I can't wait for this trap to spring.

"Wherever Bass is coming from in the area it shouldn't take him more than twenty minutes. By the way, what's in that building?" I ask.

"A big surprise," says Anas. "A quarter-mile of mazes. It should keep them busy for quite some time."

"Perfect. Where's Alex?"

"He's here, but I don't know where," says Anas.

"Well, that's just great."

—

It's been close to a half an hour and no Bass. I start to wonder if somehow he's outsmarted us with some other scheme.

The men are beginning to talk amongst themselves, and right now silence is crucial.

"Anas, tell the men to pass along to put a cork in it. And they're not to fire a shot or even throw a stone. I just want them to follow me down the hill when I decide the time is right."

It only took a minute to hear the birds and leaves rustling again. But there's another sound that we've been waiting for.

Three extended vans roar in from the main road and screech to a halt. Agents pile out like they were after Bin Laden. That is excessive, but if that's what Bass is expecting, we can certainly entertain that train of thought.

Wearing bulletproof vests they encircle the building like a swarm of bees while brandishing the AK-47s. At least fifteen in all, enough to take over a small country—say Coney Island.

One starts hollering orders. Bashing through the front door they all file in, yelling—*Nobody move! Everyone against the wall!*

And now for the main attraction. It must be Bass in a limo. He exits slowly and raises his chin to the sky with the arrogance of Mussolini. He better have Grace in there.

All goes quiet. I look down the row of my heroic volunteers and feel the tension. Some fidget while others are trying to keep a bead on the building with their rifles.

Bass sees me and then my men amongst the trees. We both stand firm until Bass says, "As soon as my men bring him out, you can have your wife."

Now what? From what Anas said, they won't be coming out for some time. How long will Bass wait without making a desperate move? Worst of all, would that move include Grace?

Suddenly, I see some of the lower brush at the base of the trees moving. Out comes Alex in his blind man getup. He casually walks between Bass and the building.

"That you, Miller?" says Bass.

Alex doesn't move or say a word, but quickly lifts his arm that shows a Q4 in his hand and points it at the building. Before Bass can react, he clicks it. In an instant the building with all its occupants disappears. Bass stands there looking desolate.

All the volunteers are completely in awe. Mouths locked open and eyes like saucers.

"Well," says Bass, "I guess you've turned the tables on me, Alex." He looks at me. "I'll get your wife now."

He turns to walk to the Hummer, and after three or four steps he turns on a dime with a gun in his hand. He quickly takes aim at Alex.

A single shot rings out! It echoes through the forest. I look at the volunteers who are looking amongst themselves to see if it came from one of them. I turn back to see Bass on the ground with no movement. I quickly scan the forest. There, behind a fading cloud of smoke is an older fella standing with a rifle. I zoom in on his face.

He waves to me and smiles and as I look closer—

Oh my god! It can't be—it's...it's Ben! I wave back. "Ben!"

He turns and fades with the smoke into the trees.

I race over to the Hummer and open the back door to see Grace with tape over her mouth and her hands tied behind her back. I help her out of the Hummer and gingerly pull the tape from her mouth.

"Oh, Paul. I was so afraid you were going to get hurt!"

"Me? I was thinking the same about you."

I untie her and we hold each other so tight you couldn't slip dental floss between us. "Grace! Did you see who that was?"

"I didn't see anyone. I just heard a shot."

I look back at Bass on the ground and then up to see that Alex has vanished.

—

We finally make it up and down the hill to the other side with everyone spoken for and without one shot fired, at least not by us.

Charlie walks up to me with a question mark looming over his head. "What the hell happened back there? None of us pulled a trigger."

"I wish I could answer that for you, Charlie."

"I think I'll go home and make a large Supreme for myself."

"Sounds like a good idea."

Before we hop into Charlie's truck, Anas arrives. The back door opens and there sits Alex inside without his masquerade.

"Looks like we'll be going in another direction, Charlie."

"You know, Paul, it's times like this when I miss that old bugger, Ben. He was always ready to do battle for the community, and he wouldn't have missed this one for all the Supremes in the world."

"Charlie, I have no doubt he was here."

www.ingramcontent.com/pod-product-compliance
Lightning Source LLC
Chambersburg PA
CBHW051247260626
47162CB00002B/652